MAKING CRAZY
LOVE, SANTA FE STYLE

Also by Michael Scofield from Sunstone Press

Acting Badly

Whirling Backward into the World

They're not making whoopee, they're...

MAKING CRAZY

LOVE, SANTA FE STYLE

Second Novel in a Trilogy by

MICHAEL SCOFIELD

SUNSTONE
PRESS

SANTA FE

This book is a work of fiction.
Names, characters, places, and incidents are either the product
of the author's imagination or are used fictitiously.

Cover photograph by Michael Scofield,
with thanks to Darlene Parker, Feathered Friends of Santa Fe.

Author photograph by Noreen Norris Scofield

Sunstone books may be purchased for educational, business, or sales promotional use.
For information please write: Special Markets Department, Sunstone Press,
P.O. Box 2321, Santa Fe, New Mexico 87504-2321.

Book and cover design ✳ Vicki Ahl
Body typeface ✳ Palatino Linotype
Printed on acid free paper

Library of Congress Cataloging-in-Publication Data

Scofield, Michael.
  Making crazy : love, Santa Fe style / by Michael Scofield.
    p. cm.
  "Second novel in a trilogy."
  ISBN 978-0-86534-667-3 (softcover : alk. paper)
  1. Married people--Fiction. 2. Santa Fe (N.M)--Fiction. 3. Domestic fiction.
I. Title.
  PS3619.C63M35 2009
  813'.6--dc22

                        2009001334

WWW.SUNSTONEPRESS.COM
SUNSTONE PRESS / POST OFFICE BOX 2321 / SANTA FE, NM 87504-2321 /USA
(505) 988-4418 / ORDERS ONLY (800) 243-5644 / FAX (505) 988-1025

ACKNOWLEDGMENTS

Special thanks to my wife, Noreen, my initial editor. She continues to make of our home an ideal writer's retreat.

Thanks also to Dr. Paul B. Donovan, mentor in how to rebalance my life. Thanks to Santa Feans Peter McCarthy and Rob Wilder for their back-cover comments.

I am grateful to the following individuals who served as fact checkers: Cheryl Brown, David Caldwell, Lisa Caldwell, Jane Chermayeff, Jane Clarke, Laura Cooley, Robert Denison, Kathleen Elsey, Mary Joy Ford, James Galanis, Juliana Henderson, Chip Lilienthal, Alston Lundgren, Clint Marshall, Carl Miller, Shane Miller, Elaine Nelson, Jan Nelson, Phil Norton, Darlene Parker, Jennifer Sprague, Sandra Thomas, and William Weldon.

Added thanks to Sunstone's Jim Smith and Carl Condit for their support and friendship, and to Vicki Ahl for book design.

CAST OF CHARACTERS

Christopher Ryan—counterterrorism specialist

Heather Ryan—biotech writer, Christopher's wife

Bill Ryan—high-tech patent attorney, Christopher's father

Sissy Ryan—Christopher's mother

Derek Johansen—college-text indexer, poet

Natalie Johansen—painter, Derek's wife

Chad Hopp—woodworker

Abigail Hopp—nature photographer, Chad's wife

Jan Gray—co-owner of gym

Gerry Gray—co-owner of gym, Jan's son

Armando Trujillo—Bill's and Sissy's contractor

Tony Trujillo—Kullman College freshman, Armando's son

Greer Eddy—Library Director, Kullman College

Meredith Dewsbury—life coach

Yuri Livnat—acupuncturist

EPIGRAPH

I have discovered that all human evil comes from this,
man's inability to sit quietly in a room.

—Blaise Pascal (1623-1662), *Pensées*, 139

MAKING NICE
SATURDAY 7 MAY 2005

Heather's lopsided ponytail whipped as she jerked around at the sound of crashing outside. Inside, squeals from the pair of red-throated lovebirds she'd brought to her in-laws' new house split her ears.

She was carrying a tray holding lemonade, a decanter of sherry, and four goblets from the kitchen. Through the front window she glimpsed the pile of gravel a truck was dumping beside her husband's sedan—just as a toe hit the rolled-up Navajo rug Sissy had bought yesterday on the Plaza.

"Oh, hell!" she cried out. Plunging, throwing the tray forward, she shut her eyes and spread her hands for the fall. Tumbler, decanter, and goblets smashed against the living room's Mexican tiles. The lovebirds flapped their green wings at the end of the kitchen counter. Their squeals turned to screams.

Heather hit the rolled-up rug as if to embrace it. The ends of the boa she'd flung around her neck flew straight out. Her wrists stung and her breastbone felt broken. Thank God I'm not pregnant! she thought.

"Little Sweet Pea!" Sissy—her mother-in-law—yelped from the chair near the sliding door. She rose and clacked across the tiles, crunching bits of glass.

"Good Lord," Heather's husband, Christopher, barked. Furious, Heather opened her eyes.

He loomed under the ponderosa ceiling vigas. One had split, cracking the new plaster. The creases she had given his charcoal jeans that morning—how she hated ironing—shone like the edges of knives. She'd love to rip a button off his collar so he didn't look so damned plastic. Arms akimbo, he glared at her under brows combed before breakfast after gelling his crew cut.

"Are you badly hurt?" Heather's mother-in-law asked, kneeling to lift Heather's chin.

"Your perfume's so strong," Heather murmured.

"Bill's preference, dear."

The helmet-like wave of Sissy Ryan's hair jiggled like jello. She'd had it done in Palo Alto for this mid-May, two-week visit to Santa Fe.

"What a klutz!" Sissy's peach-colored sweater and pleated skirt seemed so tasteful compared to her own nasturtium-splattered dress.

"Me, Sweet Pea?"

"Of course not you, Mother, Jesus Christ. Heather, come on, get up, you can do it. Mother, you, too." Christopher bent to take Sissy's wrinkled elbow. Though Trujillo & Son had sealed his parents' new retirement home—and low heat radiated from tubing encased in the slab—the coldness of his mother's flesh made him shiver.

Heather felt tears smart as she rose by herself. She swiped them away and stared down at one of the rug's whirling-log motifs, shaped like swastikas.

"Can't someone quiet those birds?" Christopher's father, Bill Ryan, called out. He got up from a pueblo armchair beside the kiva fireplace, marched over in tasseled loafers, and paused in the living room halfway between its tiled borders of donkey carts.

In the kitchen Pity and Merciful fluttered from perch to perch like giant, neon-colored moths as their screeches lessened.

"Kiddo, you gonna be okay?" Bill asked.

Heather shrugged.

"Chris, did you bring some kind of cloth?"

"What for?"

Bill Ryan's sole religion was ensuring patent rights for Silidyne Corporation in Silicon Valley, yet the back of his Mexican-cotton shirt displayed Our Lady of Guadalupe clasping her hands. His khakis wrapped a home-exerciser-hardened belly.

Though his mustache was white, brows black as Christopher's dropped as Bill Ryan threw out his hand. "Anything to shut the damn things up. I gotta go see what damage that bozo is doing outside. Go on and get one of your mother's dish towels, Chris."

Fuck you, Dad, Christopher thought. He strode past the dining table into the kitchen in the black-leather boots he loved to wear on days off. He ducked under pots dangling from an iron frame suspended between two rafters. A chicken ready for roasting sat on the granite next to the double sink. In the cabinet under the counter, he yanked open drawer after hand-tooled drawer.

While Sissy helped Heather to stand, Bill depressed the latch of the door he'd commissioned a santero to incise with Saint Peter waving a key to the Kingdom. He hauled the heavy oak inward and clicked onto the flags of the portal, sweeping fingers through his thick, white mane.

A cement truck fifty yards away, barrel revolving, chugged out of sight toward Atalaya Mountain. The three mesas of Los Alamos peeked through cumulus clouds thirty-five miles to the northwest. To the southwest, housing developments glimmered in the five o'clock haze that had spread up from Albuquerque.

Armando Trujillo of Trujillo & Son, Contractors of Perfection, hunched beside his pickup, billed cap jammed on backward. He shoveled gravel onto the Ryans' drive from the pile unloaded a few minutes ago.

Not gray gravel, you fool! Bill shouted inside his head. He searched for what caused the crash that had set off the birds, and gasped. Surrounded by fragments, the top of a shoulder-high pillar of sandstone lay in the dirt near his son's silver-gray BMW. A hole gaped where something had sheared the stone away. The front of the mailbox, embedded to save it from drive-by bashings, now puckered like aluminum lips. Even two of the house numbers that Armando's son, Tony, had chiseled into the pillar showed cracks.

Yet such a beautiful Saturday evening! Bill thought. The green tank that supplied water to Kullman College just over the hill rose between Sun and Moon mountains like a round casita. Closer by, a gust mixed the turpentine of chamisa with the honey wafting from lupine and yellow groundsel. Sunlight silvered the Ryans' split-rail fence and the bottoms of cloudlets drifting overhead.

"Armando!" Bill bellowed, hopping down the porch-wide steps onto the red earth. "What's what, here?" He retreated back onto the portal as the contractor came trotting, gripping his shovel across his Levis like a lance. A cottontail dashed between the two men into a tangle of juniper-piñon.

The old man yanked an unfiltered Lucky Strike from cracked lips that were nearly black. "Not a problem, Señor Bill. The driver with the gravel forgot to shift out of reverse. He will of course pay. I will talk to the mason tonight and in four days you will see perfection once again."

"But we don't want gray, Armando! When I phoned you from California, I asked for rose. To match the sandstone, to complement the stucco. Rose-colored gravel. Not gray."

"I was thinking you might want it to match the street."

Bill's chest muscles knotted while Armando leaned on the rim of a ceramic urn holding geraniums. He struck a wooden match on his boot sole, sucked, and blew out smoke. The wind took it as his tongue flicked the cigarette to a corner of his mouth. Letting it droop across his lip, he twisted his cap so that the words Brighter Days perched above his eyes.

"Okay, Señor. Rose gravel for you. My cell phone's in the Dodge. I'll phone Enrique. You may see his truck before your guests leave."

"Don't you let him hit my son's new car." Bill felt thankful he'd tucked his own rented Lexus SUV into the garage. "You watch him."

"Not your son, you mean."

"What?"

"You don't mean watch your son."

"I mean watch your friend Baca!"

"Of course he won't let the driver hurt your son's car. That would be foolish."

"It would be foolish all right." Bill clenched teeth he'd had cleaned and foamed at the dentist's three days ago. "Armando!"

He turned. "Yes, Bill?"

"Pick up that piece of insulation that just blew against the fence, will you?"

"It will be taken care of before I leave."

"Where's your son Tony, anyway?"

"At the college with the librarian who's helping him study for finals."

"But Sissy and I expected the two of you to be working today."

"All will be taken care of, Bill. Tony is on scholarship. He must pass."

A Townsend's Solitaire warbled in the fluttering top of one of the aspens clumped outside the master suite, as Armando began to scrape the gravel back toward the pile.

Bill frowned at the graffiti that blackened the adobe perimeter wall of the hacienda across the street. He pushed at the front door and arced his left arm back to scratch. His hives raged like fire ants.

A bath towel imprinted with roses now hooded Pity's and Merciful's willow cage. Bill's stomach growled as he spotted his family. They sat in high-backed chairs under the umbrella beyond the sliding door at the living room's far end. He strode past the coffee table on tiles now swept free of glass and heaved open the slider.

"She's been on edge a lot," he heard Christopher say. His son poured a couple of fingers of sherry from the pitcher he'd half filled.

"I have not," Heather retorted. She flung an end of her boa over her shoulder. It landed on a branch of the plum that Tony had planted beside the row of Apache plume.

"Maybe she's pregnant, Chris." Bill poured himself some sherry and took the remaining chair. He scratched his shoulders against the white wicker, knowing full well that the motion would only inflame the hives.

"Wouldn't pregnancy be a relief!" Sissy leaned forward to grip Heather's wrist.

"Ouch, Sissy!"

"Oh, Sweet Pea, you see? I already forgot your fall—but what if there's new life forming?"

"Not a prayer."

"Well, may we celebrate the possibility tomorrow at your house?"

"Celebrate at their house?" The sores under the back of Bill's guayabera felt damp.

"It's Mother's Day. Surely you can remember that. Heather and Chrisy are having us for lunch."

Heather grabbed one of the crackers Sissy had spread with Camembert. "Will you all quit talking about me in the third person? I'm sitting right here. Me." She raised her glass in a Statue-of-Liberty salute, finished her lemonade, and clunked the tumbler against the umbrella-table's top.

"Rotter," Bill mumbled.

"Rotter, Dad? You don't want to come?"

"I promised myself to do something selfish—pick up half-a-dozen floribundas for the garden outside our bedroom. This Trujillo-and-Son can of worms is stressing me big-time. They were supposed to be finished before we showed up. The driveway's the wrong color, the mailbox pillar's busted, the powder room isn't tiled yet, the canales don't have their copper shields, and I bet we have thirty windows with stickers still on them. Kiddo, sure, I'll help you and Chris celebrate." He plopped his hand on her knee, making her flinch. "What great news. Finally, hey? What's the due date?"

Heather shoved her chair back, rose, and clamped her palms to her hips. "Is anybody home? I'm not pregnant! Christopher lives down in Albuquerque at the Labs. You get it?" She yanked at her ponytail, glared at her father-in-law, mother-in-law, and husband—then sat and hopped her chair close to the table again.

"Embarrassing me feels good, does it? Got any more dirty laundry to spread?" The belly muscles that Christopher worked hard to sculpt at Jan & Gerry's Gym clenched.

No one spoke until finally Christopher said, "Looks like I'm up for promotion."

"Oh, Chrisy!" Sissy closed her glossed lips, opened them, and closed them as her hand flew to one of her small breasts.

"Good for you, Chris," Bill said. "What's the assignment? Years ago I helped Silidyne draw up an agreement with your Cholla Labs to develop a computer ten times faster than anything our country had."

Christopher raked fingertips through his crew cut. "I'm moving out of radioactive-dispersal-device identification—"

"Out of what, Chrisy?"

"Dirty bombs, Mother. I've told you before. Mixing conventional explosives with nuclear wastes can poison a whole neighborhood. The only cleanup possible is to bulldoze everything in sight. Those babies fit in a suitcase."

"You know I try to forget whatever you tell me about terrorism as fast as I can, Chrisy. My heart won't take it."

"You better thank God for people like me, Mother. At the end of the month the Labs are moving me to the International Advisory Center half a mile away. Section Two Manager running a team of eight."

"Doing what, son? God blast it, I'm hungry. Sis! Can't you and Heather get that chicken going?"

"In a moment. I want to hear the news."

Christopher snorted.

"You and my parents want grandchildren," Heather blurted, "and now your son may end up in Iraq."

Christopher twisted to face her. "What I said was that the IAC—"

"The what, Chrisy?"

"The International Advisory Center launched a branch in Lebanon in the late nineties. Now we're thinking we can rebuild elements of Iraq's science infrastructure from there. It doesn't mean I'll have to go over—we can do a lot by satellite."

"Such as what, Chris?"

"Nonproliferation technology training, beefing up our monitoring capabilities. Look, I've already said too much."

"We're grateful you're doing what you can to keep the nukes from spreading, son. Though I doubt this conference coming up at the UN is going to see much happen except whoring and drinking. And who gives a rat's ass? If contamination from Los Alamos doesn't do us in, something's going to. How about global warming? Bioterrorism. Cyberterrorism. Collision with an asteroid. An accelerator-generated shower of quarks that turns all the atoms in the universe into strange matter."

"Billy, please, not again, not just before Mother's Day."

"I can't wait until retiring at the end of the year to move out here, focus on roses."

"We know, Bill. Chrisy, you come help me, come along." Grasping his hand, Sissy pushed down on the chair's wicker arm, stood, and wavered. "This altitude unsteadies me."

"Are you all right?" asked Heather.

"If I stand still a moment. You stay with Bill. I need to speak to Christopher alone. With the new convection oven my thoughtful husband gave me, we'll be able to ring the dinner bell by six. Chrisy, wipe the dust off the dining table first, will you?"

Taller by half a head, Christopher followed his mother inside.

Bill rose to shut the slider, then walked back over the sandstone flags. He leaned down beside a columbine's fireworks to take Heather's shoulders and look into her eyes. "It's Chris who's more on edge than you, isn't it, kiddo?" His manicured fingertips dimpled her boa.

Get away from me, she cried in silence. She inhaled the fetid sweetness of the petit corona he must have smoked before she and Christopher arrived at four. His razored cheeks with their capillary maps jiggled a foot from her.

"Don't let him get to you. The poor sap doesn't know how lucky he is to share your bed. But we gotta figure how to get him into it more." His smile raised the hairs at the end of his mustache. He straightened, thrust his elbows behind him hoping to shake the ants from between his shoulder blades, and sat facing her.

She shuddered.

"Cold, are you? Brief me on what you're up to careerwise before we join them. Chris says last year Genesure paid you close to eighty grand; he's proud of you, kiddo. Me, too."

Hearing footsteps on the path, Bill turned to see Armando planting his forearms on the back-patio's faux-adobe wall. Its joints were whitening because Tony had neglected to veil its cement blocks in wire before stuccoing.

The distant windows of Kullman College's tower and dorms glittered like mirrors behind Armando's face. He twisted his cap around and down over his forehead, and plucked the cigarette from his lips. "Very good news, Señor Bill. Enrique Baca was on his way to a job nearby. He has come here instead. With rose-colored gravel. He and I will load some of the gray into my truck now. A backhoe will come up Monday to load the rest. No extra charge. Okay by you?"

Around the corner, gravel began to clang against the Dodge Ram's metal bed.

"You watch my son's car."

"Yes, sure."

"Thank you."

"De nada, Señor." He pinched his cap's bill and lifted it from the wavy white hair.

"That man will put me in the hospital," Bill said when the contractor had disappeared.

Heather pressed her boa to her chest. "We've told you and Sissy over and over that everything built here is botched."

"And you've told me that you love this place regardless. As I intend to love it."

"I do love Santa Fe. It's our lifestyle that sucks. Genesure's launching an antibody to knock out nerve-growth pain. So I'll be on overload updating the Web site and writing backgrounders. Christopher's always in Albuquerque and I'll be flying to San Francisco at least once a month. We left the west coast to soak up Santa Fe's magic—the art, dance, music, all the literature. I want to write poetry, damn it, not biotech bullshit to cheer all the nonagenarians tottering around a one-size-fits-all world."

Heather brought a leg over her knee. Noticing Bill's eyes shift, she pulled her dress taut.

"One size fits all?"

"Empire—American style. Chinese style in fifteen years. Though it's true that having a separate income does build my self-esteem. Christopher wishes I'd spend some of the money to hire a house cleaner and go work out at his gym. No way. I'm saving up to retire long before I reach your age. Christopher and I live in a dreamworld. So what? Damn it, I'm crying again."

She dropped her head into her hands and started shaking. The end of the long ponytail flopped against her elbow.

Just then, a clamor of metal smashing metal came from the direction of the front yard.

"I knew it!" Bill leapt toward the gate that Armando had fashioned from grilles ripped off the old Truchas jail. Outside the patio wall he high-stepped through dirt clods Sissy had left. She'd been troweling the ground for wildflower seeds brought from Palo Alto.

He ran along the path past the guest suite and up the side steps of the portal. Christopher and his mother already stood there gawking. Bill could hear the covered lovebirds screeching in the kitchen.

Chris's BMW parked beside Baca's battered dump truck looked unharmed. Armando brandished his fist at a straw-hatted woman who had stumbled out of a Lincoln Navigator. He cursed in Spanish in the middle of the road while Enrique Baca waved a forefinger at her from near the pillar that encased the Ryans' battered mailbox.

Her SUV—as black as the graffiti filigreeing the woman's perimeter wall—sat almost out of her red-dirt drive. She and Armando had backed into each other. Her bumper pressed the crumpled rear of his truck. Their vehicles formed a dam across the street.

"End Time!" Bill cried as the goggled driver of a Miata convertible rounded the curve just east of the Ryans' fence.

The woman gripped the brim of her hat and scurried back along the irises and beetle-browned piñons lining her drive. The fringed doeskin jacket flapped.

The Miata flew up off the yellow-striped speed hump, tire walls bulging when it hit the asphalt again. Christopher grabbed his mother's upper arm. The brakes' squeals coalesced into a screech that changed to a head-splitting clang and tinkling of glass. Its top furled, the convertible skittered sideways into Armando's truck and the Lincoln. The driver's head jerked forward as his outside mirror flew off the door.

"Bat guano," exclaimed Heather, hurrying up the portal's three steps. "What's going on? Oh, shit." She jerked the hem of her dress off the nail head that jutted from one of the portal's posts.

"What's it look like's going on?" Christopher asked, ignoring the ripped chintz. He hauled his camera phone from its holster, flipped its cover, and jabbed the numbers 911.

A pair of ravens veered low over a polypropylene bag marked Whole Foods. It bellied along the path bordering the asphalt.

"The way out of here's blocked," Christopher moaned. "I hope the cops can untangle that mess soon."

"An hour should do it," Bill said.

"Good luck! This is Santa Fe, Dad. I need to be in bed by eight. I'm hitting the freeway before dawn."

"Did anything I said in the kitchen sink in, Chrisy? Tomorrow is Mother's Day."

Armando stood talking to the Miata's driver, whose forehead pressed the steering wheel.

"Mother's Day, Father's Day, Easter, Thanksgiving, Labor Day, I told you he's never home," Heather said.

Glaring at his wife, Christopher squeezed Sissy's shoulder. "I'll be back for your party in plenty of time, Mother."

"That has nothing to do with it."

MOTHER'S DAY
SUNDAY 8 MAY 2005

"Punk!" Christopher shouted to the skateboarder in shorts and a bowl haircut who careened in front of Christopher's BMW. Buckteeth flashing, the kid erected a middle finger as he pushed his board across the parking lot toward the Camel Rock Apartments.

A tagger had spray-painted a scarlet Fuckin A on the two-story stucco building opposite that held Jan & Gerry's gym, just above the bike rack.

Christopher swung in next to a blue Dodge Neon. A bullet or rock had created a spiderweb of cracked glass on the windshield's passenger side. From under its bumper an empty potato-chip bag skipped toward a New Mexican locust planted near the gym's entrance.

Christopher grabbed his camera phone from the cup holder near the gearshift, jammed it into the holster on his belt, and pushed open the car's leather-and-wood-trimmed door. He approached the gym in jersey shorts and a red-and-white-striped camp shirt, left sneaker squeaking. The wind that propelled dark-bellied clouds overhead cooled his calves and forearms. His knee ached from a twist given it climbing out of bed.

He stooped to pinch up the empty bag of chips and pulled open one of the gym's glass entry doors.

An old man—fingers locked against his few curls—grunted out sit-ups beside the drinking fountain in the cavernous, fluorescent-lit space. The gym's co-owner stood nearby in a sweatshirt emblazoned Work It Out With Jan & Gerry. He was talking to a couple Christopher didn't know. The Sons of the Pioneers crooned "Tumbling Tumbleweed" from loudspeakers bolted to the ceiling.

"Hey, Chris, c'mon over here." Gerry Gray, Jan's son, fingered a blond curl high up on his neck and flipped a toothpick free.

Christopher threaded his way between a woman hefting a dumbbell to her forehead and a goateed man tramping one of the isokinetic steppers. The smell of bleach, though it irritated Christopher's throat, reassured him that the gym stayed clean. Wiggling his nose, he tossed the crumpled chip bag into a wastebasket.

"Hey, buddy, you know Derek Johansen?" Gerry's voice squeaked like Christopher's shoe. An evaporative cooler whirring on the floor's cushioned vinyl rippled a leg of Gerry's sweatpants.

Christopher shook his head.

"Derek, meet Chris. Chris, Derek." Gerry's eyes closed to slits.

Derek's hand felt cold. Shorter than Christopher, he faced him in white shorts and a yellow muscle shirt. Derek's ringlets on the left side and tangled tufts on the right—the same brown as Heather's—seemed a perfect match to her lopsided ponytail.

"This here's Derek's wife. He's brought Natalie in to give anaerobics a try so she can cut down on her supplements. You oughta bring in your own ball-and-chain, Chris."

"I've tried to persuade her."

"I been telling Natalie that anaerobics burns five hundred percent more fat than aerobics does. Not that weight's exactly her problem."

"Hello." Natalie stood on high-heeled sandals, a string of ceramic bells circling her left ankle. Her right fingers grasped a hip draped in ragged-hemmed cotton. A wisp of hair straggled past the edge of an eye. Like a doe chewing its cud, she worked a bit of gum behind rouged lips.

Natalie's breasts swung outward, her nipples poking taut the dress's bodice. How different from Heather's breasts, small as a girl's just past puberty.

Christopher lifted his eyes to the bags under Natalie's. "A pleasure."

"Chris, you got kids? I gotta talk Mom into starting a youth program here."

"We're trying for children but my wife's pets keep getting in the way." He forced a laugh and glanced at Derek's blank stare.

Natalie crossed one sandal behind the other, anklet jingling. "What kind of pets does she have?"

"A couple of lovebirds, a goldfish, two horned toads, and a tailless cat with an eye gone." Christopher spotted a paper towel on the vinyl below the drinking fountain. He moved close, stooped, and lobbed it into the wastebasket.

"No time for baby-making," Natalie smiled as the "woo-woo-woo" exhalations of the man on the stepper grew more insistent. Christopher smelled mint before Natalie closed her mouth and began to chew again.

"Flirt with Gerry if you have to flirt," Derek muttered. "At least he'll know how to make you feel better without all that osha root and boneset leaf."

"That was mean." Bare arms dangling, Natalie glanced at Christopher and then at the floor. She bit her lower lip.

"My wife's ticked I didn't help clean up after the lunch for Mother, but I had to clear out to keep my sanity. I better get started exercising. Good to meet you both," Christopher said to Natalie, who had raised dull eyes to his.

Gerry stuck the toothpick back in his mouth, then pulled it out to point at Derek. "Better go easy on the sit-ups a while longer. We want to firm up that lower back before tackling one of the two pinnacles of conditioning, the snatch or the clean and jerk. You been spending maybe too much time at the old desk grinding out those poems?"

"Poetry anchors me." Jerk is right, he added in silence.

Gerry faced Natalie. "He shows me up as always. Let's go create you a routine."

"That scent is giving me a headache."

"What scent?"

"Like Clorox or something."

"All right, gotcha, the disinfectant. At Jan and Gerry's we try to keep everything spic and spotless." He led her into an office with windows that looked out on the exercise floor. The office's back wall displayed Gerry's four-color rogues' gallery of TV wrestlers.

Derek lowered his buttocks to a padded board and secured his ankles under the bar. An end chain of one of the fluorescent fixtures had snapped, leaving the fixture dangling toward him. He stared at it a moment, locked his fingers behind his head, and—gasping—muscled his torso up as the Sons of the Pioneers launched into "Cool Water."

Stay out of that asshole's way, thought Christopher. He limped toward the horizontal-leg-press machine, passing a woman groaning under a barbell weighted with orange-colored disks.

Christopher sat on the bench about to lie back when a door in the concrete-block wall near the racks of barbells flew open.

Gerry's mother Jan scurried along the wall in blue-and-red running shoes, denim skirt riveted at the pockets, and a shirt patterned with locomotives. When she spotted Christopher, the sinews in her neck bulged under UV-tanned skin. She stopped and saluted him.

She strode over, gray-blonde ringlets plastered to her scalp. He couldn't recall seeing her lips glossed before—pink this afternoon. The flesh tone of a sports bra that flattened her breasts peeped above the shirt's undone button.

"Nice?" She raised a gravelly voice above the hum of a cooler and pointed to a cotton locomotive on her stomach, gripping Christopher's upper arm with her other hand. "Gerry says I'm his engine. Come see what he's bought me besides this shirt."

"Jeez, Jan, can we make it quick? My wife is pretty upset I'm not home."

"You left her alone with the kids? On her day?"

"No kids yet."

"So what's her prob? Doesn't like you makin' yourself lean and mean at Jan and Gerry's? Hey, she's a lucky girl to be hooked up with an exterminator."

"Exterminator?"

"You protect us from terrorists, don't you?"

"Well, I'm trying. Been slaving at finding better ways to sniff out dirty bombs for three years. But the front page of this morning's *Times* claims much of the four and a half billion this country's spent on counterterrorism equipment since invading Iraq has been wasted."

At that moment, "We Wish You a Merry Christmas" tinkled from his camera-phone.

"Crap, why'd I bring that thing in?"

"The wife?"

"Wouldn't surprise me."

"Lemme talk to her."

"You want to kill my marriage?" He punched his phone off, forced a grin, and jumped from the bench.

She patted one of his buttocks, scuttled ahead, and hauled open the steel door. It clanked shut as she marched along a ten-foot hall and opened the door to her office. He followed her in.

Near the cedar-paneled wall, a six-foot polyvinyl skeleton slouched on a stand. Numbers inked on its bones marked muscle attachments. The lower jaw thrust forward. Its skull looked past a shoulder as if in alarm. The three-cushioned sofa where Jan napped rested opposite.

Filling his lungs, Christopher took the chair that faced her glass-topped desk and two filing cabinets. He spotted Gerry's Mother's Day gift among the photos of female track stars framed in birch.

"Like it?" Jan glanced up at the wall, then faced Christopher. "Those tulips are real. Gerry noticed the guy's flier at the elementary school where Gerry runs his weight-trainin' program."

Christopher studied the shadow box that framed a color print of Gerry squatting, about to start a clean and jerk. Braided sunflowers circled his neck above an Army-camouflage T-shirt. The sign on the dais read New Mexico State Champ, 300 lbs, 2004. A lined, wooden vase holding a couple of candy-striped tulips flared from each side of the frame.

"Somethin', huh? If you want to get your wife framed, Chad Hopp's the guy's name."

"Okay, so where did you bury it?" Christopher asked Heather after dinner. He continued staring out the great-room's picture window.

Their Rancho Viejo home sat five miles southwest of the gym and ten miles southwest of his parents' hacienda. Across the community's flatness, the almost-constant wind shook the white blossoms of three pear trees Heather had asked the developer's permission to plant. The day's last light ignited the contrails of crisscrossing fighter jets, turning the clouds that lined the horizon to magenta.

"In the cactus garden outside my office." Heather faced him in a silk bathrobe that covered a bra she didn't need and a string bikini. Her dark-brown hair hung loose. She'd stripped the plum from her toenails and painted them pink before Christopher got back from the gym.

He brought his eyes to the foot he'd set on his knee, pleased with the beads he'd strung along the moccasin's rim. Don't tell me I have no artistic gift, he said to himself. "One horned toad less because you couldn't find enough ants to feed it is no big deal," he said aloud.

"Will you look at me when you talk? Algonquin was my baby. They all are."

Finally he shifted his gaze to his wife. "Not funny, Heather."

Though he still wore his gym shorts, he had changed to a forest-green knit top. A yellow duck—mascot of the basketball team at the

University of Oregon where he'd taught chemistry—stared open-billed from the breast pocket. "That makes the terrarium in the child's room and fishbowl in the kitchen your babies' cradles? You're planning to diaper a half-blind cat—here she is! Sic 'em, Trixie."

The marbled Manx came hopping like a jackrabbit out of the kitchen across one of the throws. She settled in front of Pity and Merciful's at-home cage that perched on the credenza beside the dining table. Merciful, the female lovebird, shot off her perch above the litter of corncob granules and arced onto the swing. Blue-breasted Pity fluttered to the vacated perch and began to squeak. Guffawing, Christopher lifted his other foot to his thigh and kneaded his still-sore knee.

Heather jumped out of one of the ladder-back chairs. She grabbed the cat and closed her in Christopher's office.

"Not in there. C'mon! She'll shit for sure."

"Which'll serve you right. You scare her. I'm going to shut your mother's present in there, too."

"She calls this art?" Heather lifted a sheet of fiberboard from the mantel. On it Sissy had glued a photo of a swimming pool and adobe-style home pulled from *Sunset Magazine*. Above these she'd glued a sunrise fashioned of pressed rose petals.

"Oh, no, you don't!" Christopher abandoned the sofa bed, limped close, and gripped Heather's wrists. He glowered at her above the photomontage framed in twists of pink and blue yarn. "Mother said her gift's to bring our firstborn peace. It stays put or goes in the child's room. Got it?"

"How dare you address me like that?" Heather shook free of his fingers and backed up. "Ouch!" Her thigh had bumped the edge of the dining table. She set Sissy's picture down and reached to snap on the floor lamp. "Why do you keep bringing up a child? There's never going to be a child if you keep working eighty hours a week and your father has his way."

"Fuck him, what about tonight?" Christopher felt his cock stir.

"What about it?"

"Look out the window, the pear blossoms blowing, the windmill near the Indian college turning against the haze. Romantic! We have some time. Let's try. I like that perfume."

Heather watched the remaining sun highlight a red-tailed hawk through the double-glazed glass they'd left free of curtains. It banked across one of the trails that laced the greenbelt bordering their backyard.

She turned and threw open her robe. "Why do you think I'm wearing black lace? Why do you think I ran out to buy Cartier's Kiss of the Dragon while you were at the gym? Sorry, babe, after your father's call I'm no longer in the mood. And I can't shake my mind free of the pileup at your parents' place, those paramedics forcing that fool into the ambulance. I bet your folks won't see their home finished until fall. The rear end of that contractor's truck looked like an accordion. And how can you want to make love after that phone call?"

"Yesterday you blamed me for not being available," Christopher said.

"You never are!"

"I am right now, goddamn it!"

She sidled over to the cage. "It's all right, babies. Shhhh. He doesn't mean to frighten you. He's an old clumsy."

Squealing, Pity clambered up and down the ladder as Merciful's green wings splashed water from the dish.

"Did you talk to your father live?"

"I pulled his bullying off my cell when I got home. What a lousy workout. One of the owners had me meet some asshole poet type. The tits of his sicko wife kept flopping around."

"At least they flopped, you're saying? It's not working, Christopher."

"What's not working?"

"Us—plus your father's hogwash." Heather mimicked Bill Ryan's baritone. "'Sissy would be furious but I must urge you and

Chris not to have children.' What bat guano."

Christopher wrapped his chest in his arms and stared at the Zuni rug. They'd bought it in February to celebrate four years of marriage. He bent to pinch up a bit of foil from one of Heather's energy bars, thrust the foil into his shirt pocket, and hugged himself again. "He thinks you're too old. That's what I made out of the message on my cell. He thinks pregnancy's a risk."

"My gynecologist and I don't know more than your whacked-out father does? I'm only forty-one."

"You should start coming to the gym, Heather."

"And you should keep your mouth shut! And tell your father to stop touching me."

"What?" Christopher jerked his chin up.

"Shhh, shhh, little ones." Heather made kissing sounds while she stroked the cage's wires, then faced her husband. "All this talk is getting us nowhere. I've got to feed Primrose and Ruby and give Trixie some milk. You hear her crying? And don't be surprised when I bring a male horned toad home for Ruby."

"Goddamn animals. What do you mean my father's touching you, the son of a bitch?"

"On the knee. And he always smells of those little cigars. You know what? His problem is not me growing old. He's projecting his own exit from the world."

"Maybe he's looking forward to it—the world's in big trouble."

"Frig the world. You want to know how I feel?"

Heather snatched up a see-through hut she'd woven from red willow that perched on a table against the low partition separating their kitchen from the great room. She shook it. Inside, a rag doll with clown-like cheeks toppled onto its belly. "Like her! You left Eugene and I left San Francisco to make a new life. Yes, there's mayhem in the streets here and bad-news construction—look at these floor tiles!" She stomped on one beside the nearest table leg. It made a clicking sound against the slab. The mastic had powdered.

"But I love this town and I was in love with you. If we don't go see a marriage counselor fast, it's splitsville, buster. I hate your eyeballing women who can flop their tits. I hate it."

Heather flung the doll's hut against the credenza. She sank to the coffee-table's top, clutched her cheekbones, and started sobbing. The robe's lapels parted. Her string bikini glimmered below the sash.

An unexpected tenderness propelled Christopher off the sofa bed. He reached to embrace her, wincing at the pain that knifed through his knee. Suddenly the kitchen fluorescents and the bulb in the floor lamp winked out. The refrigerator stopped humming. In the gloom Merciful and Pity turned silent.

"This happens too often, Heather! Where are the candles?"

"Where they always are."

"Where's that?"

She thrust a forefinger past him.

"The kitchen? Where?"

"Stop it! I don't know exactly. Do I have to do everything for you? Don't move, I'll find them."

She straight-armed herself off the table and butted his shoulder.

"Hey!"

"Sorry, I'm blind. I'm sorry." She rushed forward and yanked out a drawer under the counter supporting the fishbowl.

He grabbed the top of one of the ladder-back chairs for support. Why couldn't he follow her and cry, "I love you, darling Heather!" Instead he caught himself wondering how much tit Jan's sports bra confined.

Heather emerged with a lighted taper fragrant with bayberry. Its flicker caused the tears on her cheeks to shine.

"Perfect for romance," he managed without loosening his grip on the chair.

"I'll bring you off later, how's that?"

At least he needn't waste energy on foreplay. "Better than nothing. I'm facing a long Monday."

"Me, too. No different from any other—we haven't had time to stroll Canyon Road for over a year. Ouch, that candle wax hurts!"

He managed to push himself free of the chair's back, though his moccasined feet seemed bricks. "Heather? Let's stop bickering, okay?"

In Christopher's office Trixie's meows grew strident. Pity and Merciful renewed their squeaking in the unsteady light.

Heather yanked three tissues from the box on the partition and wrapped the candle's base. "Go brush your teeth and close the door so I don't hear you floss, it drives me nuts. And figure on sleeping in here with your mother's whatever-it-is; your snoring's getting worse. Oh, Christopher!"

Gobs of wax scattered onto a throw rug as she ran to him. She circled his neck; the taper's flame soared at right angles to its shaft. "How can you stand me?"

VOWS
MONDAY 9 MAY 2005

Derek sat at one of the tables in Riece Library at Kullman College, a quarter mile down the hill from Christopher's parents' new home. He craned his neck toward the study lamp, though plenty of morning sun filtered through the skylight running the length of the sixty-five-thousand-book facility.

Students lounged, or slept on couches to his left, or bent over books at tables along the windowed wall. One of the doors to a normally-locked study room, its glass gone, stood open against the jamb. Last week a drunken student had hurled a Literary Classic through it.

Derek's *Roget's International* and a *Webster's Collegiate* rested beside the lamp. He crumpled up a yellow sheet and threw it under the table, where his backpack lay. The wad pinged against the metal wastebasket and fell to the carpet among others.

Blue Mind, he scribbled in pencil on a fresh sheet. *This canvas blown from the resonance/ of gale, clouds of the soul-drenched—/ hunger of storm—my middle age/ tattered.*

"Balls," he muttered, stamped a rubber-soled flip-flop, and slapped his left palm to the opposite armpit. His shirt felt damp, though on this day the library needed no air-conditioning. He wondered if Library Director Greer Eddy—the woman he pictured when Natalie and he attempted their occasional lovemaking—was sitting in her corner office.

A sepulcral voice sounded behind him. "Hi there. I saw you come in and I have a question."

As usual, Greer's scent seemed that of mown clover. Why did she always kneel beside him while he was writing, the bitch?

"Hello," he whispered, looking down at her coral blouse and blue slacks. Had she any breasts at all?

"You look pale. Are you sick? How progresses the work?"

So close, her lithe body seemed a radiator. "May I answer sequentially?"

"Of course!" She leaned back.

"I'm sick at heart and the work progresses toward the wastebasket."

Her glacier-blue eyes locked on his and flicked away. She bent to glance at the discarded drafts under the table. "I walked over here to see if you'd index a new book by one of our professors."

"A book about what?"

She opened her hand to study a scrap torn from an envelope. *The Way In and Way Out: Reconnecting to Reality through The Republic and the Bhagavad-Gita.* What would you charge for five hundred and forty pages in manuscript?"

"The way in and way out? Sounds pornographic."

"Pornographic?" She lifted a knee, stood, and in broad-heeled shoes marched sternly back over the carpeting, passing a girl on a sofa. The girl's pigtail drooped along the leg of a boy who sat stroking her wrist. His other hand lay on a dog-eared paperback of Blaise Pascal's *Pensées.*

Derek's lower back began to ache. He arched his spine, ducked to grab the yellow wads, and tossed them into the wastebasket. He clenched his teeth as his head knocked the table's underside. The Dress-for-Less khakis that Natalie had bought him swished as he left his chair, followed Greer to her office, and paused in her doorway.

One of her papier-mâché sculptures he'd not seen sat beside

her window, which looked out on daylilies blossoming below the cafeteria.

The lacquered, two-foot-long tarantula on whose back she had painted an American flag shared a tabletop laden with issues of *Library Journal*. On the carpet rested a corrugated box smelling of baby powder. A small dog rose from a bath towel, stretched, and poked its head out, sniffing. Hair fine as silk, the same blue-gray as the towel, fell to its paws from both sides of its body. Greer had tied a neckerchief under the dog's chin. The royal-blue-and-off-white tartan formed a sort of shawl.

"Hello, Jules," Derek said.

"That's Rupert. Here today because the dean won't know. He's in Boston again. What do you want?" She returned to signing letters. The dog heads of half a dozen breeds on her charm bracelet tinkled against the blotter.

"How many have you?" he asked, staring at the tarantula.

"Rupert the Yorkie, Jules the poodle, Carlos the hairless, and Marilyn the Afghan. Your memory stinks. You've already met the three boys."

"Not them. Spiders."

She looked up. "Mostly I do insects. There's a whole studio full at home—guardian spirits for my dogs."

"Invite me to come see them once I get their names right?"

She squinted at him. "Why are you pestering me?"

"I'd like to see that manuscript. Not true. I came to apologize."

At that moment Armando Trujillo's son Tony, wearing paint-spattered boots, pushed past Derek.

"Dad's cell's gone dead."

"What's he doing here? It's your Work-Study job," Greer said.

"His truck's in the shop. He's been moping around about Mom being sent up to Brighter Days for dealing crack." Tony pushed out his already-protruding lip. "I didn't think you'd mind giving him something to do. But right now he's breathing into Jason William's mouth."

"What?"

"You better call nine-one-one, Miss Eddy."

Derek withdrew to the case displaying nineteenth-century editions of Wolfgang von Goethe's *Faust* outside her office. He braced himself against her glass doors, glowering in at Tony.

"We were painting out graffiti on the pillars when this old SUV swerved to make the turn. Jason flew off the hood. Before he hit the curb he yelled, 'Absent while present!' Heraclitus, no?"

"Why ask me? I graduated from here ten years ago. The only books I read are the ones you're assigned. Easy, sugar. It's okay." Rupert stopped shaking, pivoted, lay down in his box, and sighed. Greer yanked the receiver from her phone, punched in 911, and handed the receiver to Tony.

He hurried details to the operator, passed the receiver back, turned, and clomped past Derek. "Sorry," he muttered. "Emergency."

Derek's back hurt worse. Last week the doctor had suggested emotional stress. After waiting for the reek of Tony's sweat to ebb, he limped into Greer's office.

"Oh, God, Derek, what?"

"Who was that guy?"

"Really none of your business. He's a partial-scholarship student I'm mentoring."

"That's all?"

"Of course that's all, good Lord."

Derek's hands became fists. His fingertips felt cold against his palms. "Greer, I need to say I spoke stupidly to you out there. Why was that? I'm crazy about you. How you kneel when you come over. How you look up at me while I write. Sure I'll index the manuscript. I'll do whatever you ask."

He swung away from her openmouthed stare. The heels of his flip-flops flapped against the carpet as he hobbled toward the table where his pad and reference books lay. He grabbed them and reached down for his pack. He headed toward the brick apron beyond the vestibule's double-glazed doors—then veered right toward the public telephone hanging on the wall, trying to remember the code needed to call outside the campus.

Derek wheeled right onto San Antonio at the elementary school, a block off Canyon Road. He spotted New Mexico's tallest redwood through the spiderweb of cracked glass on the passenger side of his Neon. The tree loomed opposite Chad and Abigail Hopps' fifty-year-old home.

Chinese elms, their catkins dangling like strings of pearls, lined the red-dirt, dead-end road. A breeze fluttered the needlelike leaves of soft-cone cedars under a cloudless sky. Poppies and grape hyacinths lined the foot of the wall fronting the neighboring adobe's yard.

Derek's friends the Hopps lived at the corner of a lane. Flakes of stucco curled from under their adobe's ponderosa sills. Outside the splintery fence, their Subaru's front bumper boasted the sticker, When Women Vote, Democrats Win.

Derek turned left over a pothole and stopped under the flowering cherry. Honeysuckle grew along wires past the kitchen and guest bedroom to the rye that lined the lane, camouflaging the scabbed wall that extended from the garage. Near the lane Chad had posted a wooden sign, Bowls and Frames.

In this neighborhood Derek felt he could leave his car unlocked. Blossoms sweetened the odor of tung oil that wafted from the garage. His gloved, masked, and goggled friend bent over a lathe, under the unlit bulb strung from a rafter. The bill of Chad's cap, emblazoned Get a Life! bobbed inches from the whirling wheel.

As Derek approached the roar, shavings spewed in long arcs from the chisel Chad held against the lathe's tool bar. A green canvas jacket zipped to his collarbone protected all but his dungarees from the flying chips.

Derek slapped his palms to his ears. "Chad! Ho, Chad!"

His friend's grizzled beard jerked up and he switched off the power. Derek covered the sneeze brought on by the sawdust that drifted around him.

Chad waved and set goggles and painter's mask on the table holding the grinder. He positioned the rounded block of manzanita next to a row of bowls sitting on a sheet of fiberboard supported by sawhorses. Each bowl showed his trademark, a hole or two drilled—or notch sawn—through the side, transforming a functional bowl into an art piece. Light showed through a cluster of natural holes in a twelve-inch bowl turned from a clot of mangrove roots. Chad clamped tongs to the lip of a hand-sized bowl streaked with fungus, dipped it into a fifty-gallon drum of oil, shook the excess off, and placed it on a grate that capped a second drum.

He peeled off his nylon gloves, stuffed them in the pockets Abigail had stitched to the back of his jacket, removed it, batted the shavings off, and draped it over his mask and goggles. "Abbie's fixing lunch. On my cell . . . I've never heard your voice shake like that."

Chad's own voice resembled a rasp. He whisked sawdust from the frayed cuffs of a dress shirt and sidestepped past the photo frames that rested against his band saw. "Talk here?" He pushed a beach chair toward Derek and pulled close a stool whose cushion sighed when he hoisted himself onto it.

"I don't deserve to sit," Derek said. Standing, he gazed at the three furrows that carved a permanent triangle between Chad's nose and salt-and-pepper eyebrows. "Jesus!" Derek clenched his left hand and thumped the madras draping his chest. "Twenty minutes ago I made an unforgivable ass of myself."

"We do that sometimes, pal."

"I implied to Greer that I wanted to sleep with her."

Chad whistled through his teeth. "You and Natalie not getting along?" The bald man's brows rose as he picked a speck of manzanita from his lip.

"The thing is, Natalie paints, she has no feeling for words. Last night I asked for feedback on an ode I'm composing to a ridge of eucalyptus I remember from my Berkeley childhood. Her comment? 'What are you saying here, Derek? I can't follow it.'

"I've told you my dad left my mom for a black mechanic who worked in a Harley-Davidson shop in Oakland. My own marriage—eight years!—gives me stability and I'm sticking it out. But in the library Greer comes over and gets down on her knees next to me. My heart's turned tail, Chad."

"Hold on, I forgot to cover those frames." Chad jumped down and swiped sawdust from their tops with a dry brush. Two of the frames sprouted wooden vases, like Gerry Gray's gift to his mother. Chad grabbed a folded sheet of polyethylene from the table holding his drill press, shook it flat, and spread it over them.

"Abbie and I are having our own troubles," he said, returning. "She wants to leave the US for some place like New Brunswick or Nova Scotia."

Derek stared at him, filling his lungs and wrapping his arms around his ribs, thankful his back pain had eased.

"Canada's too cold for me. We've started seeing a life coach."

"Life coach?" Derek dropped his arms. "She couldn't be a fat neocon named Dewsbury?"

"You got it, pal. She drives over here once a week to learn the basics of woodworking. Says she wants to create religious folk art. Bultos and retablos."

"Natalie's started seeing the woman, too—why, I can't fathom. She's a Rapturist, Chad."

"So I'm gathering. Her lesbianism's not a problem so long as she doesn't hit on Abbie. But her religion? Getting in the way for me big-time. Abbie admires her strong-mindedness. I'd rather spend the hours with my broken sentinels of emptiness."

"Your what?"

"The bowls. I'd stay closed in here working twelve hours a day if Ab'd let me. She and Greer walk Greer's dogs up on Atalaya Trail, though she claims she wishes Greer were me. I don't know. They seem pretty close. But I guess I'm like you. Creating other worlds consoles me for having to fend off surprise attacks in this one—like Abbie yesterday announcing she wished I'd wear a hairpiece. Let's go get some soup."

The cushion whistled as he sprang free of it. He strode to the front of the garage, pulled its warped doors shut and slid the inside bolt, then reached to twist a knob on the dangling bulb's socket, transforming the gloom to a yellow haze. Derek followed him through a fire door that led into the laundry.

From there, Chad snapped off the light in the shop and pulled at the door to the kitchen, admitting the sweet, biting scent of vegetables simmering.

Two of the walls displayed Abigail's outsized Kodachromes framed in birch that Chad had varnished: two ravens flapping north from D.H. Lawrence's ranch house south of Questa; and Abbie, Chad, and Greer self-timed from a tripod along the Rio Grande at Embudo Station. A six-burner range faced a center island topped by a mahogany cutting board. Chad had long ago replaced the floor's linoleum with random-planked oak.

Abigail stood up from her chair at the dining table near the open kitchen. A blue-denim skirt that stretched across her tummy hid the top halves of beefy thighs. Gold hoops the size of dog collars swung under a pixie cut of black hair that concealed right-angled ears. The scooped neck of a knit top revealed freckles on each side of her cleavage.

"Derek, welcome," she said in a baritone. "Please. Sit."

After he left the library, had Greer phoned Abbie to share what he'd blurted out there, Derek wondered.

A minute later, leather sandals slapping the planks, Abigail served him a steaming bowl and returned with two more. "Dig in, you two. Soybean minestrone made from scratch, super low on cholesterol."

Derek and Chad spread tasseled napkins over their laps as she came back with a corkboard holding slices of bread cut from a hot loaf.

"Raisin pumpernickel, ditto on the cholesterol. Oh, ChaCha? Would you mind bringing us some water?"

He glanced at her. "Sure." He scraped his chair back and rose.

"This is gorgeous. Natalie needs to see this." Derek picked up a casserole-sized bowl turned from an oak burl, one side a lacework of light, the other solid except for the silver-dollar-size hole Chad had drilled near its top.

"Gorgeous? I guess. Will the man make me four I can fill with soup? Nope. You see *The Courier* this morning, Derek?"

Her voice seemed friendly enough. Perhaps Greer had not phoned.

"Page one tells how our military softens up prisoners in Afghanistan before flying them to Guantánamo. Trained German shepherds rape them in the ass. Then our soldiers fill a water tank to just above their nostrils, forcing them to stand on tiptoe for an hour. The article says it's an Egyptian technique.

"We learn torture from Muslims and they learn torture from us. A fair trade? Our country's as vicious as the rest of the world and Santa Fe's become a lead dog. This morning on Paseo a guy in a pickup whipped over the double line, opened his window, and flipped me the bird."

"Hardly the same thing, Ab." Ice clinked in the handblown glasses Chad brought close. After setting them down, he bent to kiss her cheek.

She pulled away and tousled her hair. "ChaCha says something upset you this morning, Derek?"

"Spring makes me anxious is all." He pursed his thick lips, watching her.

"Let's hope the meal helps. Bon appétit."

The front chimes tinkled as Chad was lowering himself again to the table. He straightened and strode toward the door he'd found at a church sale, which he'd sanded, painted scarlet, and shellacked. He pulled it wide.

A woman faced him, dappled in sunlight, backgrounded by the elms dripping catkins and the Hopps' Subaru. She wore a reverse print of ferns. The sandals' big-toe straps glowed the same pink as her toenails. A floppy straw hat slanted across her forehead.

"Are you Chad Hopp?"

"Yes?"

"I've been looking at the bowls you have at Shannan-Orrin on Canyon."

"Sorry but we're just starting lunch."

"Shoot," she pouted.

"Come on in for a moment. That's my wife Abigail back there and our friend Derek."

"Hello! I'm Heather. Oh, look at that one on your table! Your bowls are all poems in wood. They stir me like—I don't know—Wallace Stevens's poem titled, I think, 'Tea at the Palaz of Hoon.' Right now I'm writing for a couple of high-techs in Silicon Valley, but I want to write poetry. And I did write it this morning! About the bowl with the two holes your gallery calls Winter Suns. I sat right there beside the receptionist and scribbled the poem out. I had to come find you and tell you."

"Well, I'm flattered. How about coming back in an hour? I'll show you the shop. Derek here's a poet. Perhaps he'd like to hang around."

DO IT NOW
TUESDAY 10 MAY 2005

"You promised not to wear perfume again," Natalie blurted from the couch, snapping her eyes open when the timer dinged.

Natalie and her life coach had just completed their preliminary five-minute meditation.

"I should have brought it up when I came in," Natalie added, taking a stick of gum from the beaded purse at her feet.

"I forgot, dear heart."

"It gives me headaches."

"I forgot. I'll wipe it off."

Dressed in slacks and a loose, crimson shirt, life-coach Meredith Dewsbury heaved her hundred and seventy pounds from the armchair. The faux-pine planks laid on the slab in her former garage squeaked as she lumbered toward the water heater, washer, and drier that lined the far wall. She unbuttoned the shirt under a lit ceiling fixture of multicolored acrylics beside the sink, scrubbed the pumpkin-pie scent from her neck and between the bra's cups, and buttoned herself up. A branch of the cottonwood looming over the house scraped the grilled window she'd not washed since fall.

"Hey, where's Shadow?" Natalie asked. She began to work the spearmint as Meredith plumped down close by.

As the life coach scratched her nose, the bracelet's wooden crosses clinked—a Valentine's Day gift from her most recent partner. Meredith's huge breasts heaved. "The memory's too ugly. I was leashing Shadow for our walk when the German shepherd across the street ran over and snapped my doggie's spine. I buried her under the cottonwood last night and, before you arrived, called my lawyer."

"Oh, my God!" Natalie covered her mouth. A dull pain began over one eye. "Derek wants a dog. Not me. Kids neither."

"No kids ? Why not?"

"Last week I told you my brother set himself on fire when he was three. Anyway, my pelvis is too narrow."

"Children aren't that important. The world's already overloaded. Shall we begin? I've got a full day." Parted in the middle, Meredith's blonde hair trembled as she touched the back of Natalie's hand. Her nostrils flared. "Where on the Wheel are we?"

Natalie used her foot to shift away from Meredith's bulk, imaging the life coach as a soft, potbellied stove. She grasped the Wheel chart that lay atop her skirt. "We're pathetic, I'm afraid."

"We're?" Meredith asked. "But I'm proud of the me that self-discipline has made real. Proud to know that Jesus Christ will soon descend to Temple Mount to jump-start His new reign. Proud of America's iron will overseas. Though beginning life as a Quaker, I shall never condone torture—never. I'm proud of my gender preference and proud that under an Anglo master I've carved my first bulto. Finally living a life I relish. As will you, dear heart. Go ahead, face our Maker."

Natalie winced. She'd bit her lip instead of the gum. The tip of the blue jay's feather dangling from an ear tickled her neck as she followed the life coach's forefinger. Atop a chest beside the window stood an eighteen-inch wooden figure raising his arm. Like a Nazi salute, Natalie thought. The winged bulto, nude and painted brown, wore a sombrero of golden felt.

"Gabriel," Meredith said, "expelling our first parents. With my santero's help I've just started to shape the brutalized Eve. But now we need to find authentic Natalie, not her mother, not Eve, not even Meredith. But Natalie. This week's positions on the Wheel?"

The flesh under her upper arms wobbled as she lifted both hands to press the sawed-off hair against her temples.

Natalie sighed. "Money first, I guess. I'm at position two. This month the only sale I've had off the Web is a sketch of three aspens planted upside down. The buyer said they symbolize where her children are heading. Career? I'm at one on the Wheel. I can't find a gallery. My abstracts are piling up in the studio.

"Forget Fun and Recreation. All Derek wants to do is sit in the Kullman College library or go to Lannan lectures. They bore me, Meredith. Physical Environment is at eight. We rent close to the Plaza and I like the space though Derek says I—"

"Derek, Derek, forget Derek! The word reminds me of an oil rig."

"Well, anyway, he says I'm crap as a housekeeper."

"Good for you! Look at this office." Meredith waved her hand. "Mess is the sign of a powerful mind. Ratso, I forgot my delicates in the washer."

Pain pulsed in Natalie's eye. She shuddered, wondering if the sudden barking outside was the German shepherd that had killed Shadow.

Meredith's right buttock, then her left, stretched her slacks as she shambled past the boxes spilling file folders onto the floor. The life coach lifted the washer's lid, grabbed soap from a shelf sagging from the books stashed on it, poured in the scented liquid, clanged the lid down, and punched a knob. The whoosh of water began.

"I've met another coach on the Internet. She's driving up from Albuquerque for dinner tonight and I had nothing clean to wear." Meredith lowered herself to the couch. "Next?"

Natalie stopped chewing. "Okay, Friends and Family. I like a couple who Derek—sorry. I like two of my husband's friends and I like my acupuncturist. I have no close friends in Santa Fe. Maybe my health's the problem. I have a friend from grammar school who lives in Schenectady where my mom's in a sanatorium. We phone each other some. My dad and I don't talk. You already know that.

"Personal Growth? Zip. For Health I'm starting at a gym. Romance—are you kidding?"

Meredith stood. She swiped a fingertip of dust from the glass-topped table that held the timer. "Madeline never did her chores. Look, you have an emotionally abusive husband? Threaten to sue the sucker. I sued mine and won. Sick of failure? Become a life coach; everyone's crazy-nuts to learn to do life right. Which means embracing conflict. Because pacifism always and forever loses out."

Under ceiling-high shelves of books the washer began to chug.

"Did you write out your resolves?"

"Yes."

Meredith folded her arms. "And they are?"

The washer seemed to be shaking more than Natalie's did. In fancy she penciled a grin on the water heater towering beside it, then gazed at the top sheet of her pad. "I came up with two goals other than what to do about my husband."

Meredith stepped to what she called her Confrontational Chair. The carved heads of cougars formed the ends of its teak arms. Lapis lazuli filled their eye sockets. She eased herself into it and waited.

"I thought my first goal would be to abandon abstracts."

"Not thought! Not would be."

"My first goal is to abandon painting abstracts."

"Explain please."

"They picture my mother's dementia. The squares I do in orange are my father's arrogance—he made millions selling garbage-collection franchises. If you can believe that."

"I can, indeed. Keep going."

"I think I'll—"

"Not think!"

"Sorry. I will start painting tropical flowers because I love them. I will lay on the acrylic thick and juicy to see what happens."

Meredith thrust out her right fist. "Excellent!"

"Meredith? Your washing machine is vibrating a lot. Do you think it's all right?"

She twisted her head to look. "Old Merry Steadfast? Not to worry. Next goal?"

"I can't say exactly. I want to teach again but doing workshops seems too exhausting. One-on-one maybe?"

"No maybies, woman! It's resolve that builds confidence. This week write down the pros and cons of returning to teaching. Now about that husband."

"You don't want to hear his name."

"Forget his name. Read me how you're going to confront him."

"Meredith!"

Both leaped up at a squawk and the sudden grinding. The washer's lid had lifted to a tsunami of gray suds, panties, and bras. A couple of floor-plank ends not glued down acted as jackhammers against the wall's plasterboard, toppling books and the open bottle of soap. The wave fanned under the appliances but stopped short of the cardboard boxes spilling folders.

"Meredith, the water heater's leaking, too."

"I just bought that!" Meredith hustled across the room, ripped the washer's plug from its socket, and crouched at the water heater's base. Her right shoulder heaved as she wrenched the knob of the heater's flush-out valve clockwise. The stream turned to drips.

Though most of the water had seeped down between the planks to the slab, the sweetish stink of soap started Natalie's head throbbing again. "I'd better go," she breathed.

"Not a prayer. In this room we learn the power of self-discipline." Meredith stood and filled her lungs. She skirted the sopping lingerie to reach the desk near the outside door, flipped through an address book, picked up the phone's receiver, and punched seven buttons. "Meredith Dewsbury. A disaster with my washer and that water heater you unloaded on me. Best call back fast, you son of a bitch."

She fitted herself into the Confrontational Chair and gestured

Natalie to the couch. "As before. What you'll be telling your husband."

Natalie stared into Meredith's eyes, then blinked at her pad. "I wrote out three requests."

"Demands."

"Demands. The first is, 'You mustn't say mean things to me anymore.'"

"Right!"

"Okay, the second is, 'I want to go dancing.'"

"You mean let it all hang out."

"I guess. Sure. There's one more."

"Well?"

Her voice softened. "I need you to touch me."

"Me, dear heart?"

"Not you. What I say to my husband."

"All you want him to do is touch you?"

"No," she whispered, her eye throbbing.

"Details please?"

"It's embarrassing."

"Good Christ, woman, I'm your coach, you pay me for this!"

"Okay, but you have to hear his name. 'Derek, I need lots of foreplay before we make love or I get terrible headaches.'"

Meredith pushed herself from the armchair, swung close to the three appliances, stooped to grab up a handful of lingerie, and set it on the drier. "How much foreplay?"

"He won't even kiss my breasts now though he used to love to. He knows the moles on them are benign. I like other places kissed, too. I'd kiss him wherever he wanted but he doesn't ask. He'd rather bring himself off. I'm supposed to straddle his knees and pinch my nipples and lick my lips and watch."

Natalie hung her head like a waterlogged mop.

"Oh, the bastard, oh, no, he doesn't get away with this." Meredith paced back and forth across the damp faux oak until she wheeled close. "We women excel at foreplay." She bent and clamped Natalie's temples. "Choose your gender."

Natalie stiffened. The big woman's palms were hot. "I don't think I'm interested that way, Meredith." Looking up, she attempted to laugh but it came out a cough. Goose bumps prickled her forearms.

"Some of us still can't prefer women. Two weeks ago I threw Madeline out for bawling that she'd fallen in love with the Mexican illegal who trims my forsythia."

From the front yard came a rumbling. Meredith glanced at her steel-banded watch and looked past Natalie out the window. "That's my santero and his wife pulling in for their half hour. Next Tuesday same time for you and me?"

"Are we getting anywhere, do you think?"

"A long ways once you tell that husband what you just told me. No more pitypats for Natalie Johansen. World, meet superwoman."

"I can't come Tuesday, Meredith. I'm starting a xeriscaping class at the Tropic of Capricorn. Can we change to Mondays?"

The heavy blonde brows dropped. "You better call me later."

"Sure." Natalie tucked her pad under her elbow. The ceramic bells on her ankle jingled as she started to leave.

"Fee?"

"Oh!" From her purse Natalie extracted two twenties and a ten. She yanked at the door's glass knob, left temple pounding.

That looked like Abbie's When Women Vote, Democrats Win plastered to the Outback's front bumper. Was Meredith's santero Chad Hopp? Natalie squinted into the morning's cloudless sky.

As the door opened on the driver's side, sudden barking broke the neighborhood's quiet. Across the dirt road a German shepherd rushed past the opened gate next to pyracantha bushes that bristled beside a high wall. It galloped over the gravel, ears flattened. Rahr, rahr—rahr, rahr, rahr, rahr.

Natalie shrank against the jamb and chomped on her gum. Chad stooped to grab one of the river rocks surrounding a soaring cholla. The dog leaped over the hedge of forsythia that fronted Meredith's lot and closed in through a patch of dandelions, its legs a blur. Chad cocked his arm and hurled the rock. It hit the shepherd's muzzle head-on.

Yelping once, the dog thrust its head to the side, shuddered, and walked back toward the road, tail arcing between its legs, head jerking as if jabbed by a cattle prod.

"What the fuck?" cried a man in a white-feathered fedora running past the gate.

Chad's chin jerked up. "There's a city leash law!"

"Porg gets lonely all cramped up. Poor pussycat. Are you hurt?" The man knelt at the lip of the drainage ditch skirting the road and grasped the dog's jaw. He raised his own head to shout to Chad, "I'll need your name and phone!"

"Take down the license plate, pal, if you like, but you're in legal doo-doo."

Chad turned from the road and in a softer voice said, "Hello there, Natalie. Your other half said we might see you here."

The passenger door opened and Abigail leaned out. Her pixie cut looked uncombed.

Their dirt-streaked Subaru glistened in the sun. Chad snapped at his wife across its top, "You go in. I'm through wasting my time with this. If she still wants to pay for carving lessons, fine. I'll pick you up at noon."

———————————

The mid-May sky remained without a cloud as Natalie waited for a path to open on St. Francis Drive through the traffic that bullied its way south. Since leaving Meredith's, she'd picked out three pots of begonias at the Tropic of Capricorn, lunched on salmon tacos at Harry's Roadhouse—where she'd added to her resolves—and bought two pre-gessoed canvasses at Artisan.

She gunned her old Chevy left into the parking lot and stopped under a cherry tree. Its blossoms drifted onto her van. The drumming in her temple had spread to the base of her skull.

She clacked across the asphalt until she reached the first in a row of offices where a carved sign listed Dr. Yuri Livnat among other professionals. A gust swung the blue jay's feather up under her jaw as she stood aside to let a humpbacked man in a wool vest hobble out.

Jolly, the roly-poly nurse, looked up from her desk, glossed lips glistening. "Hi, Natalie, right on time—oh, jeez, have we been busy. We're looking for a receptionist. You know anyone?" She yanked the string of her apron free from where it had caught in the desk's middle drawer and set the sign Be Right Back on a stand. "Let's go on in."

Natalie followed under the arch and down the hallway, munching a fresh stick of spearmint. Jolly opened the door to a room dominated by a glass-fronted cabinet even taller than Yuri Livnat.

"Let's get you weighed. Shoes off and purse on the chair."

The room smelled of Yuri's licorice twists. Natalie smiled. Just their sweet aroma turned her on. She grasped the edge of the examination table that Jolly had draped in a white sheet, shook off one high-heeled sandal, then the other, and stepped onto the scale. Jolly wrote down her weight and wrapped a blood-pressure cuff around her upper arm.

"High," the nurse murmured and left the room.

Natalie was mounting the footstool to clamber onto the table, breasts swinging under her yellow blouse, when the hall door pushed inward.

Yuri Livnat appeared in oatmeal-colored boots. Over his lab coat, a necklace of braided silver looped across hairs that blackened the hollow of his collarbone.

His cleft chin jutted out. "What may I do for you today, Mrs. Natalie Johansen?" He pulled a couple of red-licorice twists from a pocket. Cheeks burning, she gulped down her gum, took one of the twists, and nibbled its tip. The released saliva made her nipples harden. She wished his eyes would move toward her breasts but they stayed fixed on her face.

"Last week's treatment worked?" Already his dimpled cheeks showed a five o'clock shadow.

"It worked until Friday, Yuri." Her legs dangled off the table. She swiped a strand of hair off her forehead. "I've a terrible headache this afternoon."

He bit off the end of his twist, took the empty chair, set a clipboard across his thighs, and looked up. "In a minute we'll shoot more studs into your ear. You've been waving the little magnet I gave you across them three times a day?"

"Yes."

"Punched in the wrist tacks for anxiety?"

"Yes, Yuri."

"Each week the salutary effects will linger longer." His lips stretched into a grin.

May I have a massage afterward? Natalie asked in imagination. Embarrassed, she lowered her eyes. If you wish, she fantacized him replying. The bells clinked as she crossed her ankles.

He thumbed through her history clipped to his board. "Ongoing treatments should ameliorate cranial discomfort and prevent lumbar pain. Depression and any menstrual difficulties should decrease. In Santa Fe we also benefit from an overall therapeutic ambiance."

"It used to be a lot stronger," Natalie groaned, her left eyelid twitching.

"For you perhaps, but pretend you're me. You grow up in Gush Katif, earn your MD at Hebrew University, fight in sixty-seven's Arab-Israeli War, become minister with the Likud party, and last year Sharon announces that all nine thousand settlers must leave Gaza. Our homes will be bulldozed, our million Palestinian neighbors will divide up every good we leave behind. What would you do? Since it's about to happen."

"I don't know."

"My cousin in real estate here says, 'Learn acupuncture in Santa Fe, relieve suffering that other doctors cannot.' So now I do that and march for peace in a place where toddlers don't hurl rocks and snipers in flak vests don't shoot at me."

Yuri set the clipboard on the vinyl tiles, jumped up, and washed his hands. He took a black box and chromed instrument resembling a staple gun, called a Pinna Prompt, from the cabinet against the wall. Its half-moon dial measured the strength of nerve impulses coursing through the outer ear.

"This will hurt a little—sharp breath out." Natalie gasped as he shot a gold-plated stud into her right ear, below the two he'd placed last week.

"Again. Deep breath, and out."

She flinched.

"One more."

The jab felt like the stinger of a bee.

He returned the box and Pinna Prompt to the cabinet, and carried back a tray of throw-away gloves, stainless-steel needles wrapped in polypropylene, and a cigar-box-size, battery-operated console sprouting red and green wires.

"On your back, please, and use the neck and knee pillows."

Before marrying five years ago, Natalie had worn a thong but Derek thought it immodest. After last Tuesday's appointment with Yuri, she'd bought red G-strings and hid them in the drawer under the hi-cut panties Derek preferred. Now, beneath her skirt and new G-string, she felt a delicious prickling as she watched Yuri unroll the gloves. The fine hair under her arms had dampened.

"Today we insert four needles in the scalp and four to electrify the tummy and after two days I want you to phone me how you're feeling."

"All right."

"Hiccup. Damned pastrami. I should have ordered chicken broth."

She laughed but he warned, "No, please, laughter loosens the needles."

Yuri tore the wrap off one. "Breathe slowly and make believe those arms along your sides are limp rags."

She twitched when the steel slipped under her scalp.

"Relax. And—hiccup—no laughing."

She concentrated on the hum of the twin fluorescent panels while he clustered the other three needles above her ear.

"I need to see the tummy, please."

She rolled her blouse up to the bottom of her nipples. When his palm pressed her skirt's waistband and a tip pricked the skin below her navel, she cried out.

"Three more only."

"I know."

A moment passed.

"Now breathe evenly while I attach the stimulator wires. There; there. There. And there. Say when the taps in the tummy become painful. Hiccup."

She watched his dark pupils flick. Had he been admiring how her breasts lifted the blouse? Why did Derek no longer want to fondle them? Engorging, her nipples tingled.

"It hurts yet?"

She shook her head. Soon the needles, become electrodes in her belly, throbbed nearly once a second. "Now!" she blurted.

"Good. We'll keep current at four milliamps, but I leave the control beside you and the remote, too, if you need to call. Ocean waves or birdsong?"

"Birdsong, Yuri."

"Ah, at last the pastrami settles. Jolly will return in half an hour to free you."

"All right." She fingered the licorice twist that had rolled against her thigh.

"Try to doze, speed neurotransmission. The healing will speed as well. Is the music too soft? Are you warm enough?"

"The music is perfect and I'm happy." Did his tone contain

personal concern? Though she pretended that the electric pulses were Derek's fingertips drumming her flesh, she longed to reach up and pull Yuri to her. How much chest hair had he? Derek's own chest was smooth.

Yuri threw away his gloves and turned the ceiling panels off. Recorded chirrs, trills, warbles, and twitters filled the room from a black speaker on the floor. He shut the door carefully behind him.

Sunlight through the curtains kept the room a grayish yellow. Was that a meadowlark soloing? Adjusting her neck on the pillow, Natalie breathed deeply as the tap-tapping sent healing current into her belly.

She wet her lips and smiled. In her mind, the cornucopia of birdsong turned the room into an orchard of blossoms. She moved deep into the singing, imaging petals falling on her and Yuri, each naked and sun-warmed. From one end of this meadow-room to the other came the voice of Yuri murmuring, "My love, my love." He stroked her in ways Derek had never done. A rush of pleasure engulfed her.

Suddenly she flung her head to the side, jamming a needle all the way into her scalp. Hair whipped across her face.

"Help!" she screamed. "Help me!" She goggled at the ceiling and clutched panties that had grown wet. "Help me!" All at once she remembered the remote's call button and jabbed it. But her forearm thrust the control box to the floor, yanking the wired needles from her belly.

The door burst open. Yuri, then Jolly, ran close amid the caroling birds. "You're all right—lie still," he commanded. She inhaled the sweetness of his breath, glancing at his lowered brows. An eyeball ached and the base of her skull pounded.

"This will hurt—you're in no danger. Every needle is sterile." Jolly's hands clamped Natalie's cheeks as Yuri yanked out the bent steel. He extracted the other three and tossed all into a tin wastebasket where they clinked against the bottom.

He straightened. His necklace swung over the hairs curling out of his T-shirt between the lab coat's lapels.

"What happened?" Jolly whispered, stepping back.

Natalie watched Yuri's olive eyes flick over her breasts and pulsing belly. He looked back at her flushed face. His chin thrust forward.

Unable to hold his gaze, she felt her left temple explode. "My husband and I aren't getting along. I had a nightmare about him."

BAD VIBES
WEDNESDAY 11 MAY 2005

The following evening Christopher parked outside the gym, beside the Neon with the shattered windshield, under a buttermilk sky turned scarlet. This time he'd decided to leave his camera phone at home. He noticed a scene spray-canned in red and black next to the Fuckin A scrawled on the stucco: one stick figure, whose hair fell to its waist, raised a knife above its head. It pointed the knife at a second figure in a billed cap set backward who aimed a pistol at a third figure.

That's new since Sunday, Christopher thought, beep-locking the BMW. Captures Santa Fe's secret, big-time.

A gust shook the blooms of lilacs planted near the bike rack. Drawing in their fragrance, he saw two bats hanging from a crossbeam in the entryway. Their leaf-like wings lay against tiny bodies that snuggled each other. "Like Heather and me once, dreaming of moving here," he muttered, and pulled the glass entrance door wide.

"Couldn't get the wife off her fanny?" Gerry grinned at Christopher next to a young man who struggled to lift a dumbbell. Gerry pulled a toothpick from the pocket of his camouflage T-shirt, ripped the cellophane from it, and shoved the pick between his teeth.

"I've given up trying," Christopher said.

"Tough Wednesday?"

"It's the goddamned sixty-mile commute back from Albuquerque."

"You've come to the right place, Chris. Go easy with yourself tonight." From the loudspeakers bolted to the ceiling grid, Merle Haggard growled out, "Workin' Man Blues." "You hear that?" Gerry asked. "Appropriate, hey?"

After a day of workouts, the air smelled of salt in addition to the bleach. Christopher moved in camp shirt and knit shorts to the fountain for a drink. He squeaked past Gerry's windowed office to a stationary bike, climbed up, punched a couple of buttons, and began to peddle. Two women chattered while straining at the handles of rowing machines next to him. Christopher's gaze across the gym blurred as the bike's flywheel cooled his calves.

While Gerry steadied the shoulders of a man with white muttonchops trying to balance on a wobble board, Gerry's mother leaned against a desk, in her office off the hidden hallway. She faced Derek in capris and a fuchsia blouse, the top two buttons undone.

Derek sat in the middle of the couch, staring as she talked. His lower lip wrapped his upper one.

"It's somethin', huh? Real tulips in the vases!" She nodded at the wood-framed photo of her son on the wall. "I don't know how much Gerry paid for it, and I'm not askin'."

"The woodworker is my best friend," Derek said.

"Yeah? Would you look at how the glue under these panels is disintegratin'?" She edged past the polyvinyl skeleton and gripped the wall panel closest to Chad's frame, vases attached. At the sound of a drawn-out caw, the cedar ripped from the plasterboard, scattering dust like gnats. She let the panel fall against the filing cabinet. "You know how much this is goin' to set us back?"

"Not a clue. And who made that?"

"Made what?"

He pointed to an assemblage that perched on the cabinet's top. Half a dozen shellacked strips of muslin painted orange and maroon twisted toward the ceiling. In the tip of each nested a pink marble. Jan had knotted the strips around a river rock the size of a volleyball.

"I made it! You like? I brought it in to cheer me up."

"Looks like a bouquet of phalluses."

Chuckling, she strode two paces to him, bent, and patted the cheeks he'd not shaved since yesterday morning. "I call it Anasazi Flames, honeybunch."

Against his stubble her palms felt hot. He vised her wrists, pulled them away, and stood.

"We're dancin'," she laughed.

"No, we're not." Her breath smelled like peppermint. The phrase for a new poem, ". . . spiked beds of wintergreen and peppermint . . .," lodged like darts in his mind. He sidestepped toward the door. "I like you, Jan. A lot. But I don't like your touching me—I'm a committed man. Gerry may have shared that my wife is starting workouts soon. She's not here now because she threw up last night."

As he was about to leave, Jan grabbed his bare forearm. "You're strange, Derek."

The knob, cool in his palm, twisted on its own.

"Hey, hey, what's all this?" Gerry blurted, pushing inside as the doorknob clunked the wall. He glared at his mother, then at Derek. "What are you two up to, anyways?"

Derek waited to speak until his heart stopped pummeling his breastbone. "Your mother wanted me to come to see the photo you gave her."

"What happened to that cedar?" Gerry paused. "What's going on here, Mom? You're not making up for lost time, are you there? Are you? Didn't we have enough of Dad fooling around? How do you think I feel coming in like this, seeing you . . ."

"Stop it, Gerry! I invited Derek in for why he said. I showed him your beautiful Mother's Day gift and my artwork, and I showed him the crummy job that Sheetrock shyster you hired did on my office. Charged me double what he should of. I want you to get him back here tomorrow mornin'."

She pressed her palms to her thighs. "And what in hell are you doin' burstin' in when my door's shut? You want to knock. It's just polite."

Gerry coughed. "The air's bad in here." He slapped his shirt. "Mom, Chris Ryan's knee buckled and his head hit the rim of the trampoline. I can't find the liability release I hope he signed. Could be you have it?"

"Don't you keep those?"

"Yeah, sure, but his isn't with them."

"I'll look. Is he hurt bad?"

"Don't know. Do know he's damned upset."

"Go soak a couple of towels in water cold as you can make it. Wrap his knee and his face, too. In a sec I'll run across to the coffee shop for ice. And son, you hear me? You knock next time. Your father used to burst in like that when I was in the tub or on the johnny. He thought he owned me, but I'm not ownable. You got it?"

Fingering a blond curl, Gerry nodded hard, whipped around, and marched into the hallway. Derek turned to follow.

"Leave the door open, will ya?" Jan said.

The gym closed at eight. Only a few clients were finishing their routines. An evaporative cooler whirred beside a pregnant woman attempting push-ups off a rubber mat. Near her a man with a cleft lip, who'd just finished exercising with a physioball, lay on his back on the cushioned vinyl, waiting to catch his breath. From the loudspeakers Merle was belting out, "The Fightin' Side of Me."

As Gerry started toward the men's room for towels, Derek approached Christopher. The taller man sat woebegone on a padded bench, palms clutching his temples.

"Say, friend?"

Christopher looked up. His thick brows rose.

"That cheekbone looks painful."

Christopher said nothing.

"You know what? You and I and my wife may be seeing a lot of each other here. I want to share that I don't want you and her to get too chummy. You don't need more trouble."

"Oh, brother," Christopher moaned, turning his gaze from Derek's shadowed jaw to the cleft-lipped man who had once again draped himself prone over the physioball. He arched his back, fingers locked behind his head.

Derek leaned forward and jiggled Christopher's shoulders. "Understand?"

"Take your fucking hands off me, asshole."

Derek flung his arms behind him, brought the left one back, and with the tips of his fingers lifted Christopher's chin. "People don't talk to me like that. Ever."

"Go hide somewhere," Christopher snarled.

"What's all this going on?" Gerry carried four wet towels across his forearms. The end of his toothpick bobbed.

"This yo-yo is threatening me. This isn't south Santa Fe. Get him off my case. Goddamn this knee."

"Can you stand?"

Christopher planted his palms against the bench's pad and, breathing hard, pushed himself halfway up. "Sort of," he said.

"Go ahead and sit, we'll take care of it. Derek, what is this now?"

"I don't like the way he eyed my wife."

"When's that, Derek?"

"You saw them flirting Sunday afternoon."

"I did? Listen, don't you worry none. He's not going to bother her while I'm around. Go write a poem about it. All right? Go on home. Hopefully that wife of yours is wondering what's keeping you."

"What's that crack supposed to mean?"

"Oh, man, don't you ever back off? Chris here's hurt. Go home. We'll see you next time."

Derek glared at him, pivoted, and headed for the entrance. He squinted across the parking lot at the words Camel Rock Apartments that flashed off and on through a window.

"Maybe best to lie down, Chris."

Christopher lifted his thighs and stretched out on the bench.

Gerry wrapped two of the towels around the swelling knee. "Go on and lie your arms against your sides." He folded the remaining towels lengthwise and draped them across Christopher's forehead.

Meanwhile, near the entrance, Derek thought he saw the woman he'd met at Chad's arrive. She unwound a rust-colored boa from her neck, though to him the night air blowing in felt balmy. She'd bundled in a turtleneck, yet wore only clogs. They clacked as she entered.

Heather threw her palm to her lips, lowering it then to her shoulder bag. "You work out here?" Her lopsided ponytail swished as she peeled off a knit Tam o' Shanter.

Derek discovered himself smiling. She and he had talked poetry for an hour in Chad's garage two days ago after lunch. All at once the skimpiness of his muscle shirt and short-shorts bothered him.

"I'm glad you work out here."

"This gym was located at Villa Linda Mall until last February, when the owners found expanded space." That sounded stiff. He'd forgotten that she had green eyes. All he could think to do was blink.

"Is this the office?" She pointed at Gerry's space, cap in hand and boa swinging.

"It's the main one."

"My husband's been nagging me to start a program."

Heather's clogs flopped off bare heels as she headed toward the windowed enclosure where wrestlers in postures of attack garnished two of Gerry's walls. She was staring at a blond hunk whose tattooed biceps loomed larger than his cheeks, when she stumbled against a dumbbell left near a stepper. "Bat guano!" Heather pitched forward.

Derek sprang close and grabbed her upper arms from behind. Under the bulky cotton they felt as slender as Natalie's. He found himself hoping she didn't have Natalie's udders. As he pulled Heather upright, her shoulder bag knocked his hip and he noticed a short white scar that curved across her neck under the ponytail. Jesus. His sister, before she killed herself, had carried the same kind of scar under her ear where, as a toddler, she'd fallen on the raised lid of a soup can.

Heather stepped from his grasp and looked back, frowning. "I'm such a klutz."

The muscles in his hands felt as if he were still holding her. "That had no business being left there." He turned and lifted the dumbbell to its iron rack.

"Christopher!" she shouted suddenly. "You're hurt!"

He watched her run toward Gerry and the big man with the crew cut who was easing his white sneakers to the floor.

GETTING REAL
THURSDAY 12 MAY 2005

I'm sick, too, Natalie, Derek complained in his mind the following morning. Sick to death of your ailments.

He jammed the sole of his slip-on to the brake pedal, to keep from slamming into the back of a Cadillac Escalade. Its upper taillights burned as the signal's yellow changed to red. Derek forced his lungs to stretch and—determined to relax—focused on the grace with which old cottonwoods shaded the courthouse lawn.

When a horn blared behind him, he tramped on the accelerator and spun up Washington past the Scottish Temple's arches. The sack of medicinals for Natalie skittered off the seat, smacking his paper cup from Starbucks Coffee that rolled across the floor. The sun shot sparks through the passenger window cracked by a flying stone six months ago.

He wheeled right at Callecita and right again into the driveway behind his wife's Chevy van. It faced the studio she'd fashioned from the rental home's garage. That weeping birch whose trunk rose from the lawn she insisted on watering—why not anthropomorphize it in a poem, weeping for the misfortune of being human?

But a din assaulted Derek as he stepped from the car. So instead of heading for the house to write the idea down, he ran to the corner. There a backhoe was loading chunks of old adobe into a dump truck whose cab blocked half the street.

Unpruned rosebushes and their browned blossoms spread

along the original stone wall that had surrounded the demolished home. The wall waited to give a false sense of history to a five-unit, two-story condominium. Derek skirted the truck's grille.

"Say, friend, are you going to be at this all day?" he called to the backhoe's operator.

From the perforated seat, the man in a T-shirt and cowboy boots shoved a lever forward to halt the steel bucket. He raised safety glasses to stare down at Derek. "Gotta be done, buddy."

"My wife is sick."

"My wife has hemorrhoids and my kid got beaten up at the Seven-Eleven."

"I bet yours is the backhoe that kicked a rock into my windshield," Derek blurted.

"Hey, Gil," called the truck driver, twisting his head out the window. "Someone harassing you?"

"This fella doesn't take to progress. By the way, buddy, you're standing on an anthill." He returned the safety glasses to his nose and jerked the lever into drive. The idling engine began to chug. Chunks of foundation clattered into the truck's bed.

The operator guffawed as Derek hopped off the anthill and glanced down at the pink grains mounded against the curb. Harvesters scurried into and out of the miniature volcano and over his feet. He grabbed one slip-on, then the other, brushed them free of ants, turned his back on the noise, and marched home in his trail shorts past the cable that clanged against the neighbor's flagpole. Why had he accused the backhoe guy of webbing his windshield? My mind's not right, he thought, recalling Robert Lowell's poem, "Skunk Hour."

As he crossed the street, he saw that the morning glories of the chandelier were blazing. So was the porch light above the birdbath. Light shown, too, through the fissure in the bedroom's Salvation Army curtains. He lifted the sack of herbs from his car.

His lower back had begun to ache. He stood beside the bench Natalie had painted purple, hauled out his keys, pulled open the screen, and unlocked the front door.

How he wished the panting of a Dalmatian or Irish setter were greeting him instead of Natalie's coughs. When they found this house five years ago, the landlord had said he wouldn't mind a dog, but Natalie—pleading susceptibility to asthma—so far had dissuaded Derek. He flipped off the porch light and chandelier over the dining table. He planned to use the table this morning for sorting out submissions to literary journals.

"I bought more boneset leaf for your stomach and the triple echinacea," he shouted into the bedroom.

Natalie had turned on the heat. He could hear the hum. In the hall he passed beside the chaos of her latest acrylic—an unframed canvas of black squares and triangles jumbled among swaths of lime-green, pink, and crimson.

He stepped over underwear needing washing that she'd piled on the kitchen's linoleum. He plopped her sack next to the bottle of osha root syrup and canister of cayenne-fruit powder sitting on the counter.

His forehead was dampening from the furnace's heat. At last he shut himself in the office he'd made of a second bedroom. He untucked the tails of the shirt festooned with leering mice that he'd found at Miller's Outpost and unbuttoned it to his navel, startling at Natalie's sneeze on the other side of the wall. He snatched a spiral notebook from shelves the landlord had let Chad build above Derek's daybed. What was that idea? A birch weeping for the human condition. Derek uncapped a ballpoint and wrote down the words to expand this afternoon in the library at Kullman.

On plywood across concrete blocks, he was squaring folders marked with the names of journals when Natalie rapped hard four times.

"What is it?"

"We need to have a conversation, Derek."

"Later."

"Now! Before my head bursts from the bedlam out there."

"I spoke with the backhoe guy. They'll be working all day."

"This is stupid, Derek. Open up!"

"Balls," he muttered, buttoned his shirt, and acceded to her demand.

The bags under the grey eyes she fastened on his seemed the color of stone-ground mustard. Her face glistened. She swiped a lank, auburn lock from the tip of her nose. "We need to talk."

"You said that."

The witch hazel she massaged into her body when she felt punk smelled like rubbing alcohol. Her open robe billowed as, hunching forward, she turned toward their bedroom.

She punched the pillow against the quilted headboard and climbed into bed in her robe. Another unframed acrylic loomed above, this one raining globules onto sand-dune shapes tufted green. Last year Derek had promised to learn framing from Chad but had never followed through. He admitted to feeling guilty every time Natalie finished another painting.

She tugged the blanket up above the pocket of her pajama tops. "Are you growing a beard?"

"I am." He wondered if Greer would comment on the two-day growth. He wanted to seem literary for her, Whitmanesque, much shaggier than Chad.

"I'm growing a beard and I'm going to get a dog," he said, stopping near the door and folding his arms.

She gazed at him as the rumble of the dump truck easing itself along Callecito came through the curtains. She coughed and slapped her palm to her chest. "I told Meredith how—"

"I can't hear you."

Natalie waited for the truck's noise to dwindle. "Last week I told Meredith how you and I met in the watercolor class I taught. The love match other students said we had. How fiery our sex was, how hungry we were."

His breath shortened. He remembered an exhausting afternoon he'd followed her from the community college to her casita where—after she'd turned on all the lights—they gave each other orgasm after orgasm.

"Now look at us compared to Abbie and Chad," she went on. "He's thoughtful, he keeps that marriage bedrock. Can't you learn from him? He's your best friend, Derek! You know, I wish you wouldn't wear that shirt. Those mouse designs demean you."

He took in air, blew it out, and moved to the upholstered chair draped in a throw. "Maybe I should spend a few days in the hermitage at Pecos Monastery. It did some good a couple of years ago."

"Sexually? That's a laugh. Now you're saying again you want a dog. I don't think you know what you want, but I'm pretty sure you don't want me."

She coughed and pushed her fist to her mouth, then drew a tissue from the box on the table that also held one of the begonias she'd bought Tuesday. She wiped her forehead and blew her nose.

"Do you?"

"Do I what, Derek?"

"Know what you want?"

"I'd like to stop seeing Yuri."

"Then do it. Those treatments are costing us a bunch. How are they helping, anyway? Look at you."

"That's what I want you to do."

"What?"

Natalie sneered and looked down. "Never mind. Yuri tries to be kind to me, but I think Meredith's helping more."

"Yeah? Chad tells me he's quitting her."

"He and Abbie pulled up Tuesday as I was leaving. I heard him say he wasn't going in."

"Meredith Dewsbury's a fat Christian neocon, Natalie! She's also a lesbian. You aren't by any chance attracted, are you?"

"Of course not."

As usual when he felt upset, his fingertips chilled. He raised his hands to blow on them. Into the silence came the clatter of the backhoe rummaging among the adobe home's ruins, the lip of its bucket clanging against concrete shards.

"I want you to touch me, Derek."

"Now?"

"Kiss my nipples, fondle my breasts. Most men would love to! Kiss me here like you used to." She pushed the heel of a freckled hand to the blanket covering the hollow below her belly.

"But you're sick, you're perspiring, you threw up two nights ago."

"I don't care."

"Your head—"

"I don't care!"

"Well, I do," he said, standing. "It's ten-thirty in the morning. I've got to get my poems in the mail and finish indexing *The Glory of American Democracy* for Houghton Mifflin."

A fly that had hidden in one of the begonia's purple blossoms rose to buzz slantwise across the bed, its wings sparkling under the cockleshell fixture that cupped the ceiling. They watched the fly spiral down to the floor lamp Natalie had turned on. Its shadow zigzagged up inside the shade.

"You know what I think?" Natalie blurted. "You can't get past junior high when you and your sister were experimenting with each other's bodies. You can't get past her overdose of uppers fifteen years ago. I think that's what happened after you and I married. You wished I was your sister!"

She began to weep. Damp hair fell across her hands. Suddenly her head snapped up and she sneezed. Ends of hair flicked her shoulders. She reached for a tissue and snorted.

Stung by her accusation, Derek hurried across the braided rug and stood with the back of his thighs pressing the edge of her table. He turned aside to avoid her breath and grasped her hands. The diamond of her ring bit his palm. "Look, Natalie, don't you think I feel rotten about what's happening? Sex between us used to be good. Maybe it can be again. You're still on the pill?"

"Yes, I'm the fool hoping her husband will tire of pumping himself off."

"But you've never wanted children."

"What's that have to do with anything? My gynecologist says my pelvis is too narrow. It might squeeze the baby's head." She shuddered, cleared her throat, and stared into the doorway.

"Caesarians are common." He released her hands. "You should get some sleep."

"I wish you'd come with me when I see Meredith next week. Or find another professional. To get clear, Derek."

He glanced down at the gold studs Yuri had implanted above the hole in her earlobe, grateful that the witch hazel cut her sickish odor. "Clear? I'm clear that these are last days."

"For you and me?" She snuffled, coughed, and grabbed another tissue.

"For everyone. Though most of us are hardwired to want to keep on populating, our main purpose is to destroy each other. What you and I do as artists doesn't matter anymore."

"What are you talking about?"

He moved toward the door, turned, and leered like one of the mice on his shirt. "Eat, drink, and be merry."

"I don't get it." Pleading like a child, she asked, "Will you take me dancing at La Fonda this Saturday? If I get lots of sleep? Meredith said Tuesday I had to ask you."

"We haven't danced since our honeymoon."

"I want to dance with you! Please don't go."

Filled with grief for her—for human beings—he hugged himself and stayed where he was.

"I'm going to start painting tropical flowers, Derek. Thick and juicy. Meredith says I need to tell you this."

"Okay by me."

"And I'm going to start teaching again. Not workshops. One-on-one to conserve energy."

"Fine." He began to shift from foot to foot as he watched the fly's shadow circle the shade's interior.

"Teach here, in my studio."

"I said fine! Just so you keep the noise down."

"I'll make as much noise as I like, you bastard!" She jerked the pillow from behind her back, flipped to her left side, drew up her knees, and brought it down across her face.

———————

While Derek parked up the hill a hundred yards from Riece Library, freshman Tony Trujillo was slouching in Greer's office. He stared at the sculpture she'd brought in this morning, a gigantic, papier-mâché grasshopper that perched on the table between stacks of magazines. Wings lay along its sides. The orange-banded femurs of its hopping legs jutted skyward. A sign hung from one of the wrapped-wire antennae, Bring Our Troops Home. On the other antenna hung Leave Our Troops There.

"You're against this war or for it?" Tony asked, twisting the cap that sat on one of his paint-spattered knees. The skin of the other knee showed through the torn denim.

"I'm indifferent, Tony. Whatever this government does makes the world a worse place for women." Her unrouged lips stretched into a smile. She grasped the ceramic head of a Mexican hairless that hung around her neck. "You came in to talk about your advisor."

"He has bad breath, Miss Eddy."

She threw her arms forward, palms up, and leaned forward. Her straight hair swung over her cheeks. "And what am I supposed to do? I can't tell him to go gargle. You need a shower, by the way."

He frowned. "The man interrupts me in class."

"Listen, I volunteered to help you through first-year math and chemistry because I know how tough it is to work and study. I did it the same way here. Plus we don't see many Hispanics at Kullman with your drive for an education. But I can do nada concerning your advisor. The semester's almost over. Let's see what he and the other professors say in your wrap-up meeting. If it goes well, you can ask for a different advisor next fall. Right now I want to read you something."

She pulled a sheet from her drawer. "'The Literary Classics at the heart of learning at Kullman have great relevance to the contemporary world.' Got it?" She raised her eyes. "It's true that except for Jane Austin, the classics assigned your first three years are all written by dead white men. Also true that developing your powers of reason by discussing these books won't solve most of humanity's problems. But I admire your wanting to take a stab at it, Tony."

He shook his head and extended his pendulous lower lip. "You make me want to when you talk like that, Miss Eddy. And afterwards, I'm getting my teaching credential to give something back to my people." He paused. "You're a good-looking chick, you know that?"

"Careful." Her glacier-blue eyes held his.

"No, I mean it, no disrespect, I wish you and me could get together on the outside, like maybe coffee downtown sometime? Or a couple of beers at Evangelo's?"

"Couldn't do that, Tony."

"Why not? Something wrong with me?"

"You're a healthy male."

"Right on!"

She stood and straight-armed her desk, spreading the fingers of both hands. "A specimen male—in danger of losing my help and a scholarship if he doesn't keep his mouth zipped."

A single furrow rose from his nose to his hairline. He stopped toying with his cap. "That's rude."

"Yep. Today upstairs at four we'll start at page one-twenty-two of Lavoisier's *Elements*. Now get back to your job."

She thrust her shoulder and right hand toward the window. "Is that your father pulling weeds?"

Tony hung his head. "It's him."

"It's he. Who hired him?"

"Nobody."

She jammed her palms to the waist of her khakis. "I told you not to bring him back here."

"He's suicidal over my mom, Miss Eddy."

"Oh, bullshit. Tell him to go find work that pays. He knows your financial-aid package doesn't cover every cost. The college will need some more money in a couple of months."

"He says he's got to sell off another piece of family land. He's got jobs but no wheels. Last Saturday he was finishing a house just up from here when a car—no, two cars—smashed into his truck."

"Good God! Can't he use yours?"

"It needs a new transmission. My cousin dropped us off."

She slammed her fist to the blotter. "Look! Don't let me see him again. You're pushing my buttons, Tony. I don't want to write a complaint."

He stood, jammed his billed cap on sideways, and stared down, knowing that against regulations, she often kept a dog in the cardboard box under the table when the dean traveled. "I don't want to write a complaint neither," he said. "But you're Anglo and you sure as hell do. You can't wait." He shuffled out scowling.

Meanwhile, Derek tramped down from the parking lot along the bark path, shoving aside piñon branches. He kicked a spring-water bottle toward a jumble of beer cans and box of Marlboro Lights that nested in some dandelions blossoming among the pine needles. Into his backpack he'd zippered a dictionary, thesaurus, and spiral notebook.

Green cottonwood and aspen leaves fluttered over the arroyo. The windows of the college's bell tower glimmered in the sun. He descended the steps, feeling queasy that following such a beautiful afternoon, he had to spend yet another night with the woman he feared he could no longer love. He wondered if he'd caught her cold yet. At least she didn't chew gum when she was sick.

Lost in the gloom of his heart, he felt something smack his hip as he rounded the corner of the cafeteria.

"What the hell!"

"Didn't mean to do that," Tony said, dangling a pair of clippers. In the arroyo Derek saw an older man, cap on backward and cigarette slanted between his lips, who gripped what looked like the handle of a rake.

"I remember you," Derek said. "Greer's pet."

"What are you talking about, man?"

"She likes you."

"You and I have met somewhere?" Tony asked.

"Three days ago in her office. You shoved your way past me and she let you do it."

The furrow between Tony's nose and hairline deepened. "Oh, yeah, I had to get to a phone. A guy outside was dying."

"Like me."

"Huh?"

"I'll see you." Derek plucked a whorl of needles from his hair that a gust had carried from a nearby piñon. He hurried away.

A hand-lettered sign, Think Before Bothering Me Right Now, hung on Greer's door but Derek knocked anyway.

"Who is it?"

He pushed the door open.

She turned from her computer screen and sighed. "Oh, God, not you."

"Thanks."

"For what?"

"For calling me a god and for that orange-and-black oddity dangling those signs off its feelers."

"Do you think your mice like it?"

He pulled one of the imprinted heads away from his belly and stretched its leer wider, then shrugged off his pack and leaned it against his calf. "I came to see if you've forgiven me."

"Probably, if I can recall why I should. Oh, right. The Way In and Way Out. The professor does want you to index it. I told him fifteen hundred bucks. Is that acceptable?"

"I said to name your price, Greer. You like the beard I'm growing?"

"Didn't notice." She dipped to open a bottom drawer and extracted the professor's manuscript she'd tied in yellow yarn. "How long will it take you? I need a call-up date."

"How about June fifteenth? I'm pretty backlogged." He wondered if she'd seen him sway when she stood. Her fragrance of mown clover filled his universe. She handed the bundle across her desk. Afraid he might topple, he bent to place the manuscript beside his backpack. "Where's Rupert?"

"He's home. The dean's back."

"Greer?"

"What? What?"

"When I see you I want to—would you have lunch with me, tomorrow maybe?"

She rolled her eyes and brought them back to his. "You, too?"

"Me, too?"

Sighing, she lowered herself to her chair. As he moved toward a wicker armchair, she waved her hands. "Forget sitting. You're about to leave. What is it about me that turns all you dudes on?"

"All you dudes? Probably that husky voice and young-girl's figure—"

"I practice Brazilian jujitsu at the campus gym four times a week, Derek."

"Brazilian?"

"Samurai combat, updated. I don't kick your head, I trip you up, jump on you, and force your arm back until you pass out."

"Do that with somebody else, okay? What gets to me is how you kneel when I'm out there working on poems."

"Oh, Lordy. Derek? Shut the door."

He closed it and turned. Through the window he glimpsed the student she mentored and the older man trudge past the daylily-colored slope below the cafeteria. Derek's bowels growled and he realized he'd eaten nothing since the morning muffin at Starbucks.

She crooked her forefinger. "C'mere, right up to the desk."

His pack toppled to the carpet as he came forward. Perspiration welled from his armpits and the backs of his knees.

"You want to know why I kneel? Which I do whenever I speak to a male sitting out there. Apparently you're not very observant. I want to confront each of you on your level. I do the same when I get serious with my dogs. That way everyone pays attention."

His head felt as if she had whacked it.

"I'm going to tell you something else."

"Like what?" The question came out a whisper.

"Men really turn me off. From Kim Jong Il authorizing the removal of fuel rods so he can extract more plutonium, to Bush announcing that our soldiers don't torture Muslims, to Sunni insurgents blowing up their Shia neighbors, to how my father got his jollies.

"And how was that, you ask? My father fucked Mother and he fucked me weekly. I'm partial to women and my pals, three boy-toy dogs and the Afghan hound, Marilyn. Okay? No more fantasies? I'd walk around this desk and wrench that writing arm from its socket if I dared. You still want that indexing assignment?"

ZOO
FRIDAY 13 MAY 2005

For Christopher this was indeed Friday the thirteenth. Since his fall at Jan & Gerry's two days ago, he'd been laid up at home with a swollen left knee.

His mother had already helped him into the bathroom to shave and gel his crew cut. Now she sat with him in the bedroom while he forked up the eggs and green chile she'd prepared in Heather's kitchen. The eggs, a plate of cinnamon toast, grapefruit juice, and coffee sat on the short-legged tray that straddled Christopher's thighs.

Outside, a couple of fighter jets chalked contrails overhead, while Heather poured shredded leaves from a bag of compost around one of her pear trees. Their white blooms trembled in the breeze. Trixie, the tailless, orange-and-white Manx, lay curled in a bed of strawberry plants. Heather had braided her leash from yarn and tied it to the trunk of the piñon—killed by bark beetles—that Christopher had promised two months ago to uproot and cart off.

A clatter of garbage cans followed by the rumble of an unseen truck came from the front yard. Heather wondered if this was also trash day at Derek's. She envisioned him and whomever he was married to leasing a falling-down adobe somewhere, surrounded by a mortarless wall of river rocks. Would he like the argyles that sprung from her garden clogs? Heather thought he would.

How she wished Christopher's father would hurry back to pick up Sissy. Today Heather needed to draft a backgrounder on Genesure's new injectable antibody for psoriasis and e-mail it to the company's San Francisco headquarters.

The one-eyed Trixie growled as Sissy came outside from the bedroom. The breeze that billowed her polo shirt rolled a tumbleweed against the desert side of the backyard's split-rail fence. White Bermudas half hid the veins mapping the backs of her knees.

"I do like these earrings you and Chrisy gave me for Mother's Day, Sweet Pea." In her yellow-billed cap, Sissy extended her arms and twirled. The hammered-silver coyotes sailed out from her wrinkled neck.

"Do you know when Bill plans to return?" Heather asked.

"An hour, maybe? I asked for some time for you and me to have a talk after I took care of Chrisy. The poor dear's dozing at last. How can I be helpful?"

Heather set down the bag of compost and stepped toward a spade that leaned against the bedroom wall. She handed it to her mother-in-law. "Dig around the sumac, will you? I'll mulch later. Ummm, what's that perfume? All morning I've been wanting to ask. It has a lilac kind of scent, doesn't it? But hot sauce, too." Heather sniffed close to Sissy's cheek, lopsided ponytail flopping.

"I'm a little sheepish about the name. It's Balanchy's newest. He calls it Letch."

"You're kidding!"

"Bill's been so depressed about the war. This morning he read an interview with the general nicknamed Mad Dog Something-Or-Other who led our troops to Baghdad. The fellow told reporters, 'It's a hell of a hoot to fight, you know? It's fun to shoot people.' Oh, Lord, Heather. And Bill's hives—"

"Hives?"

A gust pulled at the curls hanging below Sissy's cap. "Hives are plaguing his back, little red scabs all over. He says our new house is causing them. He had such dreams."

"But your place is gorgeous! I bet you end up entertaining even more than you do in Palo Alto." Heather hoisted a dish pan holding corncob granules she'd scraped from the bottom of the lovebirds' cage, and scattered them around a second pear tree.

"Yesterday the contractor's son broke the corner window above my desk. He'd pushed too hard trying to scrape the manufacturer's label off. That's when Bill discovered all the bedroom windows are single-pane. Armando claimed he couldn't find the right size in double panes. Then Bill caught him mixing clay and water to grout the tiles in the powder room. Clay and water — can you imagine? He'd forgotten his sack of grout and Tony had to take the borrowed truck to rush off to class."

"Sissy, I can't help laughing. But you're crying!" Heather stepped close to embrace the taller woman.

"I do cry, you know." Sissy wiped her tears away with the tip of a finger. "We only have a week left here. I want to ease my husband's burdens and so I'm trying this darned perfume. But I'm gaining weight again."

"You're slim, Sissy!" Heather knelt to pick up a trowel, and began to churn soil into the compost beneath the first pear.

"Bill says I'm flabby. I'm going to ask Chrisy to show me his gym."

"Christopher wants me to join. He thinks I'm getting too heavy."

"Sweet Pea?" The blood left her knuckles as Sissy gripped the spade. "Are you and Chrisy happy?"

Heather felt her eyes heat. Swallowing, she looked past the fence. The ant hill that served as her pet horned toads' larder rose under a branch of chamisa spreading from a circle of buffalo grass.

"Heather, dear? Last Saturday in our kitchen before all the commotion with Armando's truck and the cars, I told my son he needed to pay more attention to you. I asked him to recall how blest we all felt at your reception. Was it really four years ago?"

Heather's eyes brimmed. She managed to nod.

"Chrisy in that shepherd's shirt and rope shoes he'd found in Eugene and you up from San Francisco wearing your grandmother's pale-blue lace . . . you were barefoot, weren't you?"

Heather nodded again. The soil at her knees had blurred.

"I remember your mother's sheep nibbling the heads off those white daisies in the backyard grass and your father dressed in his proofreader's suspenders and green eyeshade passing canapés around. And the good merlot from their vineyards. You could really smell it! We had such hopes for you."

"We grew, up so differently, Christopher and I," Heather stammered.

"But this lovely home and such plum jobs. Your lives together would seem to be ideal."

Heather released the trowel, covered her eyes, and began to bawl. She tumbled from her knees to her side. Her arm cushioned the fall. How she wished it were Derek's chest that she shook against instead of the ground.

After a moment she grabbed the trowel and stood, flashing Sissy a quick smile. She pulled a tissue from her pocket, mopped her eyes, and blew, a little disgusted with herself. "Maybe if he stayed home more . . ."

Sissy took a step closer. "He's been home for two days, Sweet Pea."

"Sure—beached. I wish he'd never signed that form releasing the gym from liability. They owe us!"

"What's really the matter, Heather, dear?"

"Christopher's and my view of our future together is darkening," Heather snuffled, "and neither of us know what to do about it."

"You need to be pregnant." Sissy's palm cooled Heather's cheek. "You don't know how helpful that can be early in a marriage."

"I go back and forth, Sissy. Sure, my womb wants its fullness. And Christopher says we've got to have children, mostly for your sake, I suspect, though my folks would love grandkids, too. But you know what? I agree with Bill. The world's grown too chancy. *Planet Yearbook* says that our coal and oil and automotive moguls spent sixty million dollars last year to convince us that global warming is a myth. Last year, insurance companies forked over more than that for losses from weather disasters—three times what they forked out ten years ago. Caring for animals now seems to me the right thing to do." A gust made her shiver. "Come help me feed mine, will you?"

"Of course. And you listen to me. Bill knows nothing about children. Oh, I hope he's finding those rosebushes he needs."

"Needs for what?"

"His plans for a garden outside our bedroom have grown since you were over Saturday. Now he's set on filling it with roses trained to look like processors and printers and cell phones and CD players and anything else that uses Silidyne chips. Armando and his son have been constructing trellises from his drawings."

"Bill can't be serious, Sissy."

"I'm afraid so. The idea excites him, at least."

"Oh, jeez. Listen, I've got to go over the fence a second." Heather stooped for the mason jar she'd left under the canale.

She skirted the locust dripping fragrant clusters and scrambled over twin rails toward the patch of desert bearing the pink mound. She crouched amid the grasses circling the chamisa, scooped pebbles and ants into the jar, sealed it, and hurried back.

"Look at the harvesters! Ruby and Harold love them. I bet you didn't know that horned toads are the only reptiles that can neutralize these ants' venom." Heather set the trowel and jar down, untied Trixie from the piñon, swept her up to kiss the cat's moist lips fringed in black, and undid the leash from her collar.

Cradling yarn, cat, and jar, she passed the crabapple outside Christopher's office, then the upright slab of sandstone rising from the cactus garden that marked the horned-toad-Algonquin's grave.

Sissy preceded her inside the house. "My underwater grotto," Heather laughed. The screen of her iMAC G4 gave her office a blue glow. She placed the leash and Trixie in a basket set on a throw rug.

"Bat guano; that hurt!"

"What happened?"

"I knocked my shin against that box of biochemistry references."

From her office Heather hobbled into the baby's room where Christopher and she had repainted two of the walls pink and two of them blue.

"I love what you've done in here, Heather." Sissy lowered herself into the wicker rocker. "But it saddens me, what you said out there about children. I wanted scads of them but Bill told me no. So I asked if I could have dogs, little ones with bunches of silky hair to comb out. He said no."

"How mean of him!" Heather moved to the terrarium on a table under the window that looked out on the pebbled drive. Two fluorescent tubes wired into an aluminum top lit the hope-chest-size tank. Suction cups held heat lamps to its ends. She set down the jar frenzied with ants, lifted the tank's top, and scooped up one of the toads. "Food, Harold—you're getting fat, darlin'." She turned him over and kissed his belly.

Heather returned him to one of the granite rocks sitting next to Ruby, then unscrewed the jar's lid and shook the harvesters out. They and gravel rained down.

"I shouldn't be handling them, horned toads die easily in captivity, but I can't help it, Sissy." Heather watched Ruby wriggle into the sand until only her head spines and nostrils showed. Harold curled the tip of his black tongue around an ant. "C'mon," Heather said. "We need to feed the fish."

They heard water splashing from the bathroom off the master bedroom, as they clomped into the foyer toward the kitchen.

"Oh, listen, Chrisy's up. Perhaps I should . . ."

Heather took her mother-in-law's hand. "He's a grown man, Sissy, he can manage. Besides, I have a question. Why wouldn't Bill let you have a couple of cuddly dogs if he didn't want more kids?"

"I'd just as soon Chrisy didn't know about this."

"He can't hear us out here."

Sissy perched next to the willow cage that held Heather's rag doll. It sat on the table against the waist-high partition that separated the great room from the kitchen. She inhaled the lingering odor of eggs and said, "I suppose you've guessed by now that living with Bill has not been a bed of roses—maybe a lot like what living with Chrisy has been for you."

Heather gazed at her.

"I've lived a lonely life, Sweet Pea. Does that surprise you?"

"Not really." Heather widened her stance and jammed her hands to her hips. "I'd like to hear more about it."

"There were no storybooks for Bill while he was growing up. His father held him on his lap to read from the Constitution and Bill of Rights. According to Billy, his own mother kept her mouth shut except on Thursday nights at testimonial meetings. She'd become a Christian Scientist after her second baby was stillborn.

"When Billy boy entered high school, his father started him on weekend lessons in English common law. Ten years later, Silidyne was lucky to lure my husband away from tenure track at Columbia. His expertise in patent rights is a big reason the company stays near the top of the Fortune Five Hundred. You think Chrisy works hard? Child's play compared to Bill in his prime. Even during this, his last year before retirement, Bill's had to put in sixty-hour-plus weeks. But he never could abide distractions like pets or children. Dogs still give him sneezing fits. My conceiving Chrisy was a miracle."

Sissy's half smile dimpled a cheek. She decided not to tell Heather about Bill's women. "I never thought to ask for goldfish," she said. "Shall we go and take care of yours?"

The Manx had left her basket and hopped after them into the kitchen, where Heather handed Sissy a canister holding chopped mosquito larvae, oatmeal, and crustacean flakes. Primrose circled the fern and ceramic castle in her bowl on the counter, bulging eyes forever gazing skyward.

"Here you are, dear." Sissy made kissing sounds as the goldfish darted to the surface.

Heather grabbed a box of Cheerios from a cupboard and started for the great room. Trixie followed. "Bring that half banana on the counter, will you?" she called back to Sissy.

In their six-foot-by-three-foot-by-three-foot cage on the credenza, the lovebirds began to squeal, fluttering back and forth from ladder to perch when they saw the Manx.

Heather's neck had started to ache. She wrested the nail out that served as the cage's catch, shook food into the scalloped dish, and passed the cereal box to Sissy. "I bet Merciful is pregnant. I watched Pity mount her yesterday. Hand me the banana, please."

Heather placed the peeled fruit on top of the corncob granules. She caught Merciful with the net that hung in one of the cage's corners and gentled her against a collarbone. Pity's squeaks turned to screams. "Shhhh, Merciful's going to have a baby." Heather could feel her own energy draining away after all this talk about babies. Her shoulders sagged as Sissy's arm squeezed them.

"I just want to hold you, as much my daughter as the one I never got to try for and so much more a daughter than Chrisy's first wife. The world is not doomed, not with caring people like Heather McArthur Ryan in it."

"Mother! Heather!" came a shout from the master bath.

Heather dropped the net. Merciful wriggled free and flapped toward Sissy's photomontage hanging above the fireplace. Heather spun, but too late—Pity had also escaped the cage and was swooping up toward the ceiling vigas. Growling, Trixie started to track it in a series of hops.

"Where is everyone?" Christopher cried out.

They rushed into the bedroom. A brick-hued blanket patterned with images of Taos Pueblo lay crumpled against the bed's footboard.

In the bathroom Christopher huddled under a torrent of water, shivering on a folding stool he'd placed in the tub.

"Chrisy, please, cover up! What in the world are you doing?"

His appendix scar had reddened and the black hairs of his crew cut glistened. Water dripped from the thick black fuzz that edged his spine. Sissy's cap got wet as she bent to twist off the ice-cold spray. From a rack Heather pulled one of the big towels she'd just bought and tossed it. Sissy folded it around Christopher's shoulders. He hugged himself into the green terry cloth.

"Gerry at the gym told me the best cure for this knee is to alternate hot and cold water on it, to flush out the lactic acid."

"But why did you shout for us? Oh, dear, have you seen the corner up there above the toilet? It looks awfully damp."

"It is damp, Mother. It's rotting. Behind the baseboard, too. Same thing in the guest bath. Our contractor didn't seal the timber. We're going to have to pull off the wallboard—we're not, he is, but he isn't returning my phone calls. Goddamn it!"

A sudden whir filled the room as Merciful, like a gigantic, green-winged moth, whizzed around the ceiling and dived to the top of Christopher's head.

"Get it off, get it off!" One of his hands clamped the towel to his chest. The other hand fluttered like a prayer flag. The bird streaked into the bedroom. A crash followed.

"Oh, Christ," Christopher hissed.

Heather disappeared and came back with his robe embroidered with the University of Oregon's duck. "Trixie must have jumped on your table to go after Merciful," she said. "That ceramic lamp you beaded is history."

She left him to his mother.

He dropped the towel and grabbed the robe. "Fucking pets."

"Please watch your language, Chrisy."

"I'll behead them all. Let me have your arm. Why did I shout for you? I had to crawl in here and don't want to have to crawl out. I've got to do this hot-and-cold thing three times a day to get back down to the Labs by Sunday."

"Sunday?"

"At the latest. In two weeks I start managing a new team of eight, remember?" He eased himself up from the stool and fastened on Sissy's forearm to climb from the tub.

"Can't it wait until Monday?"

"No, it can't!" Breathing hard, he rested on the tub's marble-tiled edge, extended his right leg toward a moccasin, and teased it to him with his toe.

"What about the conversation in our kitchen last weekend, Christopher?"

"What conversation? Oh, that—don't bug me. Heather knows I'm giving her as much time as I can." He reached down to grasp the free moccasin and raised it. "I keep forgetting to show you this. You like?"

"You made this, you're saying, Chrisy?"

"No; c'mon! I beaded it. I'm also going to bead the collar and cuffs of a blouse I bought for Heather's birthday, but don't you breathe a word to her. You see? I'm not all work and no play. Play is why she and I moved here. Don't tell me I have no artistic gifts."

"I've never said that, Chrisy."

"You've thought it, though, you and Dad. I need your arm again. Can I have some hot chai? Or soup maybe? See what she's got."

From the great room came Heather's "Pity, come closer, I can't reach you with this net. Merciful, look! Yummy banana."

Christopher clutched his forehead. "What a mess everything is."

Sissy guided him to bed, unaware of the streaks her clogs were leaving on the carpet. As one crunched a lamp shard, the front chimes sounded.

"I'll get it," Heather called.

"Is that your father already?" Sissy wondered aloud. "Just a moment. I need to steady." Fisting the bed's iron foot rail, she closed her eyes.

"I'm worried about you, Mother."

"Heather says it's the elevation," she murmured.

She doubled up the pillows and helped him into bed, then bent to unfurl the sheet and blanket. He leaned forward to grab their hems and stretched them over his robe.

"I'll see what I can find for you to eat." But light-headed still, she decided she'd better sit and steered for the sofa bed in the great room beside the lovebirds' cage. Heather had managed to entice Pity inside it, where he pecked at the half banana.

Bill Ryan faced Heather in his white, Mexican-cotton shirt and alligator cowboy boots he'd purchased just this morning. Trixie hopped under the dining table as the blue-breasted Merciful flapped to the lip of one of the chandelier's blossoms.

"So what's going on with that cat and loose bird?" Bill grinned from the foyer's slate tiles. "Been having a little trouble, kiddo? Here, these are for you." He pushed yellow roses at her and waved to his wife across the room as if saying farewell to a friend receding on a train. "What a time I've been having. Lord, fun! Even the hives are behaving. I can't wait to show you and that poor-sap son of mine what I'm up to back at the ranch. Hey, Sis? The kids for lunch on Sunday?" His white mustache squirmed as he kissed Heather's cheek.

Flinching, she took the flowers by the tissue that wrapped their stems. "Ouch!" The bouquet dropped to her feet.

"That bozo at the nursery must have missed snipping off a thorn." Bill and she leaned down together and nudged shoulders.

"Sorry," she muttered, gripping the stems up near the blooms and straightening.

"That sexy dress looks good on you, kiddo. Hey, why the frown? I'm not the big bad wolf."

"I know that."

He stared at her. "So, how's our patient? Healing, you think?"

"Here's hoping."

His black brows rose. "You should see the Lexus. Bulging with floribundas mostly—Mister Lincolns and Hot Cocoas and Lavender Lace, that silver beaut. I want the kids over for lunch Sunday," he said to Sissy, who had stood to join them.

"Yes, I heard you." She stopped behind Heather.

"Say, that new perfume hangs on pretty good."

"I'm glad," Sissy smiled.

"Christopher may have to work Sunday," Heather said.

Sissy pushed her curls back under her cap. "I'm going to talk to him again."

"I think we'd better skedaddle, Sis, I've lots of stone-gathering to do. Armando and Tony should be there by now hammering up the trellises."

"I'm hungry!" came a yell from the bedroom.

"Oh, dear—Sweet Pea, would you mind? I've disrupted your morning long enough."

"Not true." Dangling the roses out from her hip, Heather pressed her mother-in-law against her.

"Got something like that for me?"

Releasing Sissy, Heather leaned forward to give Bill a halfhearted hug.

"Good enough. We'll see you in a couple of days. And you tell that son of mine that terrorist fighters need to take their ease. Oh, my, I'm in an excellent mood. And by the way, Sis, the pharmacist at the mall had my tranquilizers ready to go. Doc Crafton prescribed them from Palo Alto yesterday."

"Get some rest, Heather, dear," Sissy whispered.

After Heather shut the door, she noticed Merciful still perched on the chandelier. Trixie stared up, crouching next to a leg of the credenza, ready to spring. Heather set the bouquet down next to the cage and headed into the bedroom.

Christopher sat with one of the Lab's workbooks, *Depersonal-*

ization Techniques, spread across his thighs.

"How can you be hungry?" she asked. "You only finished breakfast an hour ago."

"Yes, and now I want something more."

"Like what?"

"I told Mother soup or chai but what's on the shelf?"

"Oh, Christopher, I don't know!" She startled at the brown stains on the rug. Her clogs? Sissy's? What did it matter? How she longed to lie down.

"That bird still loose?"

"Sadly, yes."

"Trix's big chance."

Heather clamped her lips and glanced out the window at the waving mass of pear blossoms. She felt trapped in this room that smelled like mold, and hurried out toward the kitchen.

Primrose was undulating around the bowl as Heather sank into a chair at the three-legged table. Neither breath nor heart's speed changed as she reached for the phone's receiver, punched the button for information, wrote the number down on a scrap, and stuffed it into her pocket. When the automated voice asked if she'd like to be connected, Heather pressed 1.

"Hello?"

"Is this Derek?"

"Yes?"

"This is Heather Ryan."

TOUCH ME
SATURDAY 14 MAY 2005

At the Hopps' this afternoon, Abbie's Nikon with its zoom lens, four leashes, and Greer's new sculpture—a greenish-blue scorpion—sat on the dining table next to Chad's oak bowl. Abbie had belted on canvas slacks with cargo pockets and zippered leg vents for the upcoming hike.

The sudden roar of Chad's lathe echoed through the wall of the open kitchen. The tail of Greer's Afghan hound, Marilyn, shot up from the old hooked rug Greer had laid over the floor's planks. She set the wire brush down, straightened the bandanna tied under Marilyn's collar, and rose from her knees.

Rupert, Greer's Yorkie, hopped off an armchair placed near the fireplace and began to yap. Jules the toy poodle and Carlos the Mexican hairless, themselves resplendent in bandannas Greer had bought at Hobby Lobby, stayed on ladder-back chairs near the door that opened to the master bedroom.

"Calm thyself, sugar," Greer murmured to Rupert, the alpha male. "You know the noise his machine makes." As she bent to stroke the Yorkie under his chin, the front of her jersey flapped open, revealing her tank top's fire-engine red.

"I need you here," Abigail breathed, standing and extending her arms.

Nails clicking on the planks, Rupert followed Greer toward the older woman.

The two embraced. Through the front window, the late sun beamed past mounting thunderheads to illumine one of Abigail's ear hoops. She smoothed Greer's straight, squirrel-colored hair and kissed her cheek. Trembling, Greer freed her head and pressed her lips to Abbie's.

Greer opened her eyes to smile at her newest guardian spirit rendered in papier-mâché. She had lacquered the scorpion's pincers the same orange as the segmented tail, painted its eight walking legs yellow, and its three pairs of eyes vermilion. Its stinger arced over its back.

Greer had bathed all four dogs before driving to the Hopps'. Jules, wagging his white pom-pom, watched the two women clasping each other. Greer kept him clipped like a lamb except for the tail. Carlos's black crest jiggled as he raised his tiny head beside Jules.

"Are we going to do this thing, Abbie, are we?" Greer freed her arms and moved backward. One of her boots hit Rupert's ribs. "Oh, sugar, I'm sorry." She shook her forefinger at her wide-hipped lover. "Say yes, Ab. You better!"

Abbie took a gulp of air and fingered the St. Christopher hanging over her T-shirt. She pushed her open palms toward Greer. Her baritone sounded assuring. "We leave as soon as I hear if Dora'll go for a six months' lease on the farmhouse."

"She's got to, Ab! You say she loves dogs. Just you and me and them. Her six acres are really only ten miles north of where you grew up?"

Carlos stretched and sighed. The hairless's gray skin glowed under the wrought-iron sconce that Abigail had flicked on outside the master bedroom. Rupert headed for the frankfurters that Greer had sliced and placed on a plate with a bowl of water. Jules jumped off his caned seat to follow, bandanna ends flopping.

Abigail leaned against the dining table and reached back to grip its edge. "Dad always said I'd return home. I told you he ran the Rockland post office, and Mother delivered the mail and washed and ironed for the lobstermen. I wish you could have met them, darling. We'll set up base camp in the farmhouse until we're ready to hightail it into Nova Scotia. Or maybe we'll love the art scene in Camden so much—can you believe two opera houses?—that we'll stay put in Maine."

"Until Greenland's melting ice forces us out."

"Don't be such a pessimist, that's twenty years off, at least! Anyway, the dealers that sell my photos don't care where I live. You're set as assistant at the Knox County Library, right?"

"On Monday I gave two-weeks' notice at Kullman and called my new east-coast boss again yesterday. I can start June first if I want. I'm so excited, Ab!" Greer ran to her and threw her arms around the stouter woman's neck. "Has Chad said anything about the flowers in your hair?"

Abbie laughed. The two Perky Sue daisies she'd fastened in her pixie cut jiggled. "I let him make love to me last night. He came twice. He thinks the flowers are for that."

"Damn it, I should be the one making love to you. Last night I lay in bed with a stomach cramp thinking our plan is working out too well."

"Guardian spirit, Greer, guardian spirit!" Abigail waved the scorpion at her. The pincers shook like fingers brandishing a V for victory. "Besides, Meredith Dewsbury has given me enough courage for us both, though I pretend to be partial to her."

Greer jerked her head around. "What does that mean?"

Marilyn had risen from her rug and paraded close. Greer shifted the Afghan's scarf so that the knot hung again at her neck. "The dog's jealous, too," Greer said.

Abigail stepped forward to nuzzle the Afghan's topknot. "Miss Jealousy smells like raspberries."

"It's her favorite shampoo. So what do you mean Meredith's partial to you?" The unbuttoned cuffs of Greer's jersey flapped as she crossed her arms.

"Don't be angry, Greer darling. Tuesday, after ChaCha refused to come in for couples counseling, Meredith kissed my ear. Believe it or not, she was married once. I'm using her to learn as many escape tricks as I can. I told her that I'm leaving my husband, that I want to travel solo. About you, my passion, she knows nothing."

"Abbie, have Chad go on a long errand tonight. I want you." Greer grabbed Abigail's upper arms and smacked kisses on her forehead, cheeks, and the tip of her button nose. Marilyn started to growl.

Suddenly Abbie stiffened.

"What?"

"Hear anything?"

"Besides thunder?"

"The garage has gone quiet. ChaCha may be coming in."

"Shit." Greer clutched the D ring on the smaller loop of Marilyn's collar. The other loop cinched tight as she hauled the Afghan back to the old rug strewn with the dog's long hairs. Greer pulled Marilyn down and began to brush out imaginary tangles on a foreleg.

At the next thunderclap, Abigail blurted, "I'd better get a bucket into our bedroom. He keeps putting off patching the roof." She ran to the kitchen sink, crouched to yank open the cupboard door, and hauled out a pail—then scurried past the wide-angle photo she'd taken of sheep grazing among coyote willows along the Chama River. It hung above two ladder-back chairs. The two daisies fell over her ear as she pushed the bedroom door open.

Back on the armchair, Rupert began to bark in a rapid-fire staccato. Jules followed suit. He jumped to the floor as Chad strode through the laundry into the kitchen.

Sawdust speckled his gray dungarees and scarred, crepe-soled walkers. The cell phone he kept close when at work hung holstered on his belt. He moved to the dining table and hefted the scorpion by its belly. "This your latest, Greer?"

"Yep." She shifted to a cross-legged position from her crouch on the living-room planks. The Afghan rose beside her. Greer reached to grip her collar.

"Frightening," Chad said.

"You think so?"

"But the beast overshadows my oak-burl sentinel of emptiness and that's no good. Let's have it defend the cutting board." He bore the foot-and-a-half-long sculpture to the island in the kitchen. "Can't you quiet those dogs down?" he asked, returning.

"Rupert, Jules, c'mere." Greer lifted a hip, extracted lumps of kibble from a pocket in her khakis, and held out her palm. The Yorkie padded close for a bite. Jules followed. The Mexican hairless stayed on his chair.

"Oh, ChaCha, darn it all, I've asked you to clean yourself off before coming in," Abbie said, emerging from the bedroom.

He flung out his arms. "You see? Clean shirt. That dirty old jacket stays in the garage. From the waist up I'm fresh as dawn."

"You stink of tung oil, Chad." Abigail sniffed and lowered herself into the chair he usually took at the dining table's closer end.

"Listen, Ab, Natalie Johansen just rang me up." The triangular furrow linking his nose and brows darkened. "Pretty distraught. She needs some advice about Derek. Last night he told her he no longer loves her."

Abigail's black brows soared. She combed fingers through her hair. As the daisies tumbled to the floor, the gold hoops dangling from her ears bobbed. "Did he say why?"

"I don't know yet. I suggested to Natalie that we meet at the gallery while you and Greer take your hike. We can use the owner's office. He's never there on Saturdays. I think it's safer than our place in case Derek decides to start looking for his wife." He paused. "You're not pissed off, are you?"

With her fist Greer muffled a guffaw and began to brush one of

Marilyn's ears. Light from the kitchen fluorescents glinted off Chad's scalp as he twisted his head to squint at Abbie's friend and turned back.

"Pissed off? Of course not, ChaCha. It's a loving thing for you to do. When would you like dinner?"

"Better delay it some. How about six?"

"Perfect. Tonight for a treat I'll fix pork enchiladas."

Thunder peeled again. To Marilyn's howl, Rupert and Jules added their yelps. The elms' strings of greenish pearls began to blow beside the front fence. A burst of rain spattered the glass.

"We ought to be going, Greer."

"Me, too," said Chad. "Ab, I'll see you in an hour. You two had better take umbrellas."

"Right." Abigail glanced at Greer, who rolled her eyes toward the ceiling.

"Line up, kids!" Greer stepped to the table to grab the dogs' leashes.

Chad opened the door to the cloak closet and reappeared in a poncho. He reached back to lift its hood and pulled the front door wide. Rain dripping from the lintel hit his head and shoulders. The drizzle smelled sour.

Rupert had left the armchair near the fireplace and positioned himself beside Greer. His gray hair brushed her khakis. Jules stood at Rupert's shoulder, pom-pom waving. Carlos stayed curled on his chair.

"Wait!" Abigail commanded, straight-arming the air as Greer extracted Marilyn's leash from those she'd picked off the table. Abbie strode to the door, hips swinging. On the porch she sucked up the fragrance of roses beginning to open from each side of the steps, and watched Chad march toward Canyon Road three blocks north, poncho billowing. A white cat trailed him.

Inside again, Abbie released a grin. She pulled the hem of her T-shirt out from her waistband in little jerks—from behind, then at each hip, then up from her navel. She crooked a finger at Greer, winked, and swayed toward the bedroom.

"Let's go, guys!" Greer shouted, flinging the leashes to the oak planks. She passed Abbie and ran through the doorway toward Abbie's and Chad's king-size bed and tore back the quilt.

Abigail hoisted her shirt over her head to reveal a fully-filled, front-hooked bra. Behind her paraded Rupert, Jules, and Marilyn. Carlos, his skin sleek with mango lotion, brought up the rear as rain from a crack in the ceiling's plaster pinged the bottom of the pail.

Chad had turned west at Delgado and Canyon Road and pulled his poncho tighter. Drops fell from its hem onto his shoes. He stopped to peer beyond the black Shannan-Orrin sign lettered in green that hung by chains from a crossbar reaching out from the post. A man and woman in a jacket red as a house finch's breast sidestepped into the street to hurry past. The umbrella she carried sheltered them both.

Plywood painted white covered one of the gallery's brick-silled windows, following an attemped break-in last month. Chad peered through the grille bolted to the other window's frame. He saw Natalie in a bucket-style hat talking with the receptionist, Marge.

Beneath the branches of a cedar, Chad followed the brick path bordered by lilacs and climbed up under the porch's awning. Aluminum butterflies circled on their pole in the wind. He peeled off his hood and pulled open the grilled glass door.

Heat streamed from the register under Marge's desk. "That feels better," he said after emptying his lungs with a short woo of breath. "Hi, Marge. Hello, Natalie."

A wisp of auburn hair straggled from Natalie's hat. An open umbrella sat beside her on the floor.

On her lap she held the largest bowl Chad had yet turned, crafted of fiddle myrtlewood. He'd drilled a hole toward the rim of one hemisphere and notched a V opposite. The two-holed Winter

Suns, about which Heather had written her poem Monday, sat nearby on a plastered pedestal.

Chad found his eyes searching for the edges of a bra beneath Natalie's sundress, but discovered none.

She stopped chewing her gum. Only one side of her rouged lips smiled. No blue jay's feather garnished her right ear. "This is a masterpiece, Chad." She lifted the bowl.

His clipped beard dipped. "Thanks," he said, struggling out of the poncho.

"Chad," said Marge, a bony woman in her early sixties, her hair professionally streaked. "After you phoned, Buddy called. I'm sorry, he needs to get to some files in his office for a trip to Los Angeles. He said the search might take him half an hour. I can put you and your friend in the storeroom if you like. There's a couch and good lighting—well, you know that."

Because of the pungency surrounding Natalie, Chad wondered if she'd been hitting the bottle. He shook water from his poncho and draped it across an arm.

Natalie rose as Marge opened a side drawer of her desk. She pulled out a hand towel, stooped next to Chad, wiped the bamboo flooring dry, and hung the towel over her chair. "Would either of you like coffee?"

"Black for me," Chad said. "Natalie?"

She wagged her head no. "Oh, look!" she exclaimed, returned the myrtlewood bowl to its pedestal, lifted her umbrella, cinched its pleats, and hurried toward an archway. The ceramic bells tinkling on her left ankle seemed to deny the joyless reason she had begged Chad to meet her. She stopped by a painting spotlighted from a ceiling track along with two other canvasses. A dark-pink Oriental poppy stretched up on its stem from the oil's bottom edge. To the right hung a man's button-down shirt on a clothesline. A bed headboarded in iron slanted toward the poppy, the whole backdropped in yellow.

"This is what I want to do! Mix the real and surreal, only I'm going to use tropicals, begonias and hibiscus and passionflowers, throw the paint on thick to show how the erotic batters us."

"I want to see it," Chad said behind her.

"And don't forget the gallery," Marge added, leading them past a pedestal that held another of Chad's bowls. Ants had tunneled this one when it was still part of a limb, creating fissures that now admitted light.

Marge unlocked an ironwork gate at the end of a short hall, pushed the door open, reached around the corner to thumb a lever up, and stood aside to let Chad and Natalie in. Light streamed from canisters aimed from crossed tracks. A three-cushioned couch sat back to back with an ancient rolltop desk in the middle of the room. Papers and a pile of T-shirts torn into rags littered the desk's blotter. Framed paintings and portfolios holding prints leaned against the far wall. Sculptures, a stack of Chad's customized frames, and several of Chad's bowls bulged under a Navajo blanket in a near corner.

From the main gallery came the sound of someone hammering the bell. "That's probably Buddy or a tourist. I'll bring your coffee in a minute, Chad." Marge pressed the wall lever halfway down to soften the room's brightness.

Natalie eased herself to a cushion, beaded purse swinging from her wrist. She put her umbrella on the floor and hat on her lap, and shook out her hair. Its ends bounced off her shoulders as she frowned up at Chad.

He had meant to take one of the chairs grouped near the blanket but changed his mind. Gesturing toward it, he said, "Too far from a friend who needs to talk."

"I'm just getting over a cold, Chad."

"Not a problem. That is," he laughed," if we can hold off from the heavy breathing." He moved toward the couch and spread the poncho over its back.

Her frown vanished as she gazed at him.

"I think I'd better ask, have you been drinking?"

"You're smelling my witch hazel. I rub it on for energy when I feel down."

He inhaled the scent and felt himself warming toward her. But he couldn't decide which of the two free cushions to take. So he sat astride the crevice between both. "These new paintings you're talking about—when can you show me something?"

"Was Marge serious about the gallery, do you think?"

"I do, yes."

"I started work two nights ago."

There were a couple of knocks. Steam wavered from the mug Marge brought in. Chad walked the few feet over to take it from her.

"Buddy says he won't be long. I'll let you know when he's gone." Marge pulled the door shut behind her.

Chad sipped the coffee, burning his tongue. "Derek once said he wanted me to teach him how to frame your work, Natalie, but nothing came of it. Those abstracts hanging at your place are powerful presences." The top of Chad's cell phone bit his belly as he bent to set the mug on the floor.

Her brows dropped. "Powerful? They're not selling."

"When can you bring over this new canvas?"

"Wednesday or Thursday, I guess. Though I always work in acrylics, Chad, not oils." She stared at him as she worked her gum.

"The medium you use isn't the key. Let's say Thursday. Now tell me what's up between you and Derek."

"Nothing's up, which is much of the problem." Perspiration dampened her cleavage.

They startled at the clap of thunder—a drumming began against the tarred roof.

"Ab will be soaked," he said. "She left for a walk." Should he mention Greer? Careful!

"I need you to tell me what to do, Chad." Natalie's breathing came in jerks. She began to twist her hat.

"I don't know the shape of the trouble yet."

"It's gotten very complicated and you're his best friend and I have no one else to tell it to."

"You're paying Meredith Dewsbury, aren't you?"

"I think she wants me physically, Chad."

"No doubt."

"I have to admit she helps me build self-confidence."

He shifted his eyes to the blanket covering the artworks and reached without looking to find one of Natalie's hands. Her flesh felt clammy. Imagining a small bird, he squeezed and let go, weighed by guilt. He picked up his coffee, blew, and took a sip.

"Derek never touches me, Chad," she whispered. "I need to be touched," she said in a louder voice. "Besides Meredith I'm seeing an acupuncturist. At least he's not a lesbian and at least his needles make contact. I pretend he caresses me."

Chad turned to watch a freckled hand slide up from her thigh to her belly to a breast, where it hesitated on the washed-out cotton.

"Derek has no interest anymore." Her hand fell to her lap. "Yet he stays jealous. Without cause!" She glanced at Chad's face, turned back, and began again to chew her gum.

He brushed away flecks of wood still caught in the hairs on his wrists. "I swore I'd never marry. The husbands of my two cousins beat them up pretty bad. But thirteen years ago on a Forest Guardians overnight, Ab fell into white water on the Rio Brazos and I leaped in and hauled her out. We fell head over heels for each other. Even now I can get jealous." He paused. "Do you think Derek might be seeing someone?"

"What? How should I know? That's not rain!" Natalie grabbed her hat, jumped up, and gazed at the ceiling's plaster. "Something's alive up there, Chad."

He chuckled. "Probably a pack rat. A leak'll start them scrabbling. Thank God the leak in our bedroom hasn't attracted one yet."

"A leak? I've never seen a house so cared for as yours."

"Mostly Abbie's doing. Me, I hide in the garage with my bowls and frames. We've got a broken rail on the side fence, a splintered canale above the guest room, and there's a sinkhole starting outside the fireplace. I've got to find a workman."

"At our place I'm the one who waters and calls the landlord."

Chad watched his friend's wife's breasts flop under her dress as she sat down. He shifted his buttocks, feeling desire rising. "I'm going to have a talk with Derek and find out what the trouble is."

"He scares me, Chad. For a long time he's been furious that I don't want children. Or even a dog."

"More and more of my women customers claim they don't want kids. Why you?"

She hugged herself. "Do you really care?"

"Why do you think I'm here?"

"Okay. Last week my acupuncturist told me about Baghdad's most popular TV show, Love and War—full of belly laughs about the brutality over there. Just being alive today makes me nervous. I have no energy to love children. All I want is to paint and be held. No wonder Derek said he feels nothing for me anymore. But it's more complicated than that."

Experiencing a tenderness he'd not felt, Chad wished he could press her to him.

She began twisting her dress where it covered a thigh. "In junior high Derek and his sister became lovers. He says that only lasted a couple of years. Yeah, maybe. But Monica never married. On her twenty-fourth birthday she downed half a bottle of the Elavil her shrink had been prescribing. Pumping her stomach couldn't save her."

"Derek never told me this!"

"He wants his sister, Chad, not me. I doubt he's seeing anyone behind my back except Monica. She was thin like me but wore slacks and combat jackets. Should I dress like her, do you think?"

"Of course not!"

"I don't know Derek anymore. He treats me like a stranger."

"The man's crazy. He no longer wants to touch you? Your face . . . your breasts . . . "

"I lift them in the shower," she whispered. "Even with their moles they're beautiful."

A full erection thrust at his dungarees as she grasped his left wrist and brought his hand to a breast. Her nipple felt like the catkin of a pussy-willow under the blue cotton. "Will you touch the other one?"

He stared into her eyes. His breath had turned into a wheeze. He pivoted, flung his right arm forward, and lunged at her.

Their shoulders collided and she fell back against the paisley cushions. He mashed his lips to hers, gripping her bare arms. He probed her mouth with his tongue, pulled away, straightened, and clapped his forehead. "What are we doing?" His heel capsized the half-full mug. He collapsed in the couch's corner. Coffee darkened the carpet. "I better get Marge," he managed, his chest lifting and falling.

She spit the gum into her palm and circled her breasts with her free hand. "Why, Chad?"

"Why?" He gestured toward the soaked carpet. "That's an expensive bungle."

"I mean why did you stop? I'm on the pill. Does my witch hazel smell that bad to you?"

"You're my best friend's wife!"

"And your own marriage has been a model for Derek and me. So what?"

He sprang up, hurried around the couch, and grabbed a few T-shirt scraps from the desk, knelt beside the stain, and pushed the rags into it, wicking up the brown liquid. "Abbie and I have been sleeping on opposite edges of the mattress for years. She wants us to leave for someplace more remote but I love Santa Fe! That's why we started seeing Meredith. When you heard me tell Abbie Tuesday that I wasn't coming in, it's because I'd begun to feel hopeless. Though for some reason she let me make love to her last night."

"So now, in spite of what's just happened, you're going to stay loyal to her and loyal to my husband? I'm wondering if you're not as nuts as the rest of us."

He looked up, hands and knees pressed to the carpet. "All I want is to lock myself in the garage and make art. Like you! No kiddies, no dogs. Much different than . . ."

"Than who?"

"Greer, a friend of Abbie's," he stumbled. "She owns four dogs. Most dogs scare the crap out of me. A pit bull nearly severed my hand in high school." He lifted his wrist. Scar tissue half circled it.

"Lots of things seem to scare you, Chad."

He clambered off his knees and stood gazing at her, arms dangling. He blinked. "I'm close to making a very bad decision."

Like the rain, the noise of claws scratching the ceiling's hidden side had ended. The only sounds came from his and her breathing.

She pinched up the gum and wadded it in a tissue from her pocket. "Will the door to this room lock?"

"I'll go find out."

Three knocks stopped him. The door pushed inward and Marge stood beside the gate she'd pulled back. Her eyes moved from him to Natalie, who sat huddled with her knees together and her hands clenched in her lap.

"It's after five, Chad. Buddy just left. The coffee spilled?"

"I've got most of it up."

"You can move into Buddy's office now if you like. I'm heading out to meet my fiancé." She stepped into the room. Her engagement ring's diamond flashed as she extracted a key chained to a steel miniature of the Shannan-Orrin sign from her slacks. "Toss this through the mail slot after you've locked up, will you?"

"Let's stay in here," Natalie whispered to him.

Yes! he longed to tell her but hissed, "I'm nuts, all right." He cleared his throat, faced the receptionist again, and growled, "We're through talking, Marge."

"To be sure about the stain, maybe I'd better go get that towel." She left the door open.

He reached for his poncho. Natalie's ceramic bells tinkled as, gripping her purse and blue hat and reaching for her umbrella, she stood and stepped toward him.

Chad backed away. "I told Abbie I'd be home for dinner by five-thirty," he lied.

FAMILY MATTERS
SUNDAY 15 MAY 2005

"These God-blasted hives! You keep that chow away. I don't need a sneezing fit, too."

Bill leaped from the chair in the living room of his new home, reached behind him to scratch, dug into the pocket of his khakis, and pulled out a vial. He unscrewed the cap, shook out a red pill, and swallowed it with a gulp of sherry.

"Bill, you took one of those at lunch." Sissy leaned forward in the elkskin armchair and, forehead crinkling, started massaging the back of her hand.

The late-afternoon rain had just stopped. A crackling tripod of logs filled the room with the scent of piñon. Christopher sat nearby, saying nothing.

"Hold that dog, I said. Away, you!" Bill pushed his palms at the mongrel chow who arced a bushy tail over its spine. Armando Trujillo stood behind Tony at the entrance to the hallway. The single furrow rising from his son's nose deepened as he grabbed the chow's collar and yanked him close.

"All right, Tony, what's the trouble now?"

"It's the wallpaper in the powder room, Mr. Ryan. All this rain must have seeped through the roof somewhere down into the plaster. The paste won't stick on the one wall. The others, not a problem."

"My boy's right, Señor Bill." Armando bit a chapped lip. He pulled the bill of the cap from Brighter Days Rehabilitation Center—

where his wife was convalescing—over the front wave of his hair.

"I know it's Sunday," Bill said, scratching, "and that you and Tony would rather be anywhere but here. And I wish with all the strength left in me that you hadn't needed to borrow your pal Baca's truck to come over. And that this canine of his weren't so neurotic that he, she, or it won't stay home alone without tearing up the upholstery. Nor stay in Baca's truck without going bonkers. And that Baca's mother refuses to have it in her house when Enrique visits her Sundays. So now we have to deal with the dog. My friends, before we return to California, you have seven days to replace those single-pane windows in our bedroom with double panes, and finish up my rose trellises, and do whatever else you need do to make this botch-of-a-retirement-place shipshape. So I can pay you before the little men in white coats cart me away."

He wagged a forefinger at them. "No, no, don't look to me to solve your problems. You're the predicament-solvers here. If I lose my marbles, you lose a lot of cash."

The reddish hairs of the chow's ruff shook and its head began to jerk. Saliva flowed over its lower lip. The blue-black tongue swiped gobs of the bubbly spit away. Its whimper became a growl.

Bill's white mustache twitched as he stared across the chow at the two workmen. Taller than Armando, Tony turned and, hauling the dog behind him, pushed at his father's back. They disappeared into the hall. In the wall it shared with the kitchen, Armando had recessed floor-to-ceiling bookshelves, so far holding only one volume, *Roses.*

Christopher held his tongue, trying to relax in the tooled black boots he loved to wear on weekends, creased charcoal jeans, and button-down. His left foot lay propped on the ottoman his mother had brought over from her armchair. He sipped his sherry and bent to massage his knee, olive eyes tracking his father's movements.

Bill swaggered back to the couch, which had arrived two days ago. He sank onto an embroidered cushion.

"Those colors are wrong, Billy. They're not what I ordered. Green and taupe don't go with the floor's borders of blue-and-yellow donkey carts. Who would think they do?" Sissy picked up one of the crackers circling the plate she'd set between her and Christopher. She'd spread them earlier with guacamole and topped each with a roasted pecan.

"Christ on the mountain, Sissy, I haven't a clue about colors. Chris, you started to air some domestic problems, and your mother and I want to hear you out, but isn't Heather—?"

"Bear claws for feet?" Sissy interrupted. "I never said anything about bear claws. They're for couches in log cabins, aren't they? The man from Mesa Furnishings saw our décor. Contemporary, for gosh sakes. And yes, I'll say it, sophisticated. Who would ever . . . ?"

"Call the store tomorrow, have them start over," Bill said, finishing his sherry and pouring the small goblet full from the decanter.

"No one pays the least attention to us women."

"Then I'll call, Sis! There's nothing we can do about it today—everything except the big-box stores closes on Sunday. I want to hear Chris before those two bozo Trujillos come tramping back with another complication. Didn't Heather say she'd be arriving by four? Chris can't open up with her here."

Sissy turned and blinked at her son. "You've a lot on your mind, we know that, Chrisy."

"And we sympathize, son."

"Jeez, shut up, just shut up you two, can't you? I need time to choose the words."

The only noises came from sparks snapping off the logs and an occasional plash into the bucket Sissy had placed on the counter to catch drops that had started oozing from the kitchen ceiling.

Christopher stroked one of the heavy brows he'd combed that morning. "I'm going to be straight with you. If Heather and I are to survive moneywise, we need to work weekends. Even my six hours at the Labs down in Albuquerque this morning weren't enough. No way I could get back for the lunch you wanted us to come to today. Look,

I'm pushing forty-five. Most of our managers are under forty. Heather won't have any work if she doesn't out-perform the Bay Area's hoards of power-crazed writers. They're twenty years younger than her. When you two fly back to Palo Alto, she and I'll be cranking up again to seventy-hour weeks. At least I will. Dad, you know what I mean."

"We're both poor saps in that regard." Bill eased a cracker into his mouth. The capillary maps on his cheeks glowed as he chewed.

"I know what you want to say, Mother, so stop squirming, okay? When you came over a couple of mornings ago, Heather bitched that I'm not around enough for her to get pregnant. Right? Well, you know what? She was lying."

"Chrisy!"

"Let me talk." He pushed his open palm at her. "It's now obvious to me—and probably Heather, too—that she and I are incompatible. She doesn't even care about staying physically fit. Though mostly it boils down to sides of the brain. She's right and I'm left. Okay? Once in a while she asks questions about my efforts to fight terrorism. Fine, left brain. But the truth is I gave up my love of teaching for this goddamn job in the New Mexico wastelands to indulge her right brain cravings. Heather cares nothing about my research, really, and she doesn't want children, at least with me."

"Let's tackle children in a moment," Bill said. "What I've always wondered is why, enjoying teaching as you say, you didn't apply for a job in the chemistry department at the University of New Mexico. No farther commute." Bill's brows dropped.

"I wanted you to be proud of me."

"What the hell. I am proud of you, Chris."

"I wanted to be a big shot, like you."

"Oh, Chrisy!" his mother exclaimed.

"Stupid, I know. But I also wanted to make more money than Heather, be the breadwinner when we started our family so she wouldn't have to work. It made sense then, anyway."

"You dead sure she's down on kids, Chris?"

Sissy looked across at her husband. "From what she told me Friday, it's a sticky issue. It's also evident that Chrisy is not paying her enough attention. I'll say it again and again."

"All bullshit, Mother."

"Chris, watch the mouth, please."

"Yeah? Watch your own mouth, Dad."

"Now what's what with you?" Scowling at him, Bill leaned from the couch's back to scratch between his shoulders. His manicured nails gleamed under the floor lamp.

"I'm saying keep your recommendations about us having children to yourself."

"You mustn't talk to your father like that." Sissy shook her head.

"I'm sorry, Mother, but it's necessary. Dad thinks he can fly twelve hundred miles east to build a retirement extravaganza in our space and that gives him the right to tell my wife what to do."

"Billy?" Sissy asked. "Explain?"

"I haven't the foggiest what the rotter means."

"Sure you do. A week ago, on Mother's Day for crap sake, you phoned our home and then you phoned this—" Christopher slapped the camera phone holstered to his belt— "with the pronouncement that we should in no way start a family."

"What?" Sissy smacked the sides of her pumps together. "Now you're doing it with Heather, Bill?"

"Huh?" The muscles in Christopher's belly clenched. He swept his gaze to his father across the reverse-swastika motifs on the Navajo rug.

"Enough, Sis." Bill stroked one side of his mustache with his fingertips. "Ancient history, son, before you were born."

Christopher faced his mother.

"The subject has kept me in silent tears for forty-four years," she murmured. "Your father wanted no children even before you—"

"I said enough! Didn't I just say that?" Bill waved his open hand in an arc. "Those were hard years financially for us, Chris. We needed to be prudent."

"What exactly did you tell Chrisy and Heather, Bill?"

"All right, who gives a rat's ass?" Bill leaned forward to scratch with all four fingers. "I merely shared my concern that Heather, being over forty, is at physical risk. As would be the fetus. We're talking birth defects, people. Someone needs to cut through the romantic mist. And what kind of world would the child come into? You know my concern."

"I'm in the counterterrorism game, Dad, remember?"

"He is an adult, Bill."

"I know that! Jesus H Christ." Bill drank down a finger of sherry.

"Please don't raise your voice at me. And I suppose I'd better suggest, before my daughter-by-affection arrives, that you not hurry across the street later to see if you can be of help to the woman there. She doesn't need your help, I'm quite sure."

"She only wanted to borrow a pipe wrench, Sis. Fortunately, Armando had one."

Sissy glanced toward the two front windows. "There's Sweet Pea! She just pulled onto the gravel."

Christopher tasted acid as he brought his leg off the ottoman, pushed down on the arms of his chair, and stood. "That's her all right."

"Chrisy, quick, finish what you were telling us earlier about the chances of going overseas."

Bill rose and strode past his son toward the front door in his alligator boots.

"Fifty-fifty," Christopher replied. "Of the million troops sent to Iraq and Afghanistan in the last three years, the Pentagon says twenty-five percent are coming home with major depression or post-traumatic-stress-disorder. The result on families will be devastating and the financial cost to America huge. We haven't seen this magnitude of psychological damage since Vietnam."

"What in hell does all this have to do with you?" Bill called across the tiles.

"The White House wants counterterrorism teams from Cholla Labs and Livermore to fly into the war zones to reassure troops that we're protecting them from . . ."

Bill wheeled as the chimes sounded. Heather's face appeared above the Anderson-Windows label on the glass. Grinning, she waved a bouquet of lilacs. Her ponytail swished from the right side of her head.

Bill pulled the door open.

"So sorry I had to work!"

"We're just glad you're here now, kiddo."

"Hello, Sissy." Heather lifted the sweet-smelling blossoms and fluttered them.

"C'mon, I've got a garden to show you." Bill wrapped his arm around her shoulder.

Heather had knotted the tails of a lavender blouse above her skirt. She had only a second to shake the drops from her rain hat before her father-in-law began propelling her past the dining table toward the hall.

"Hey, whoa, Bill. These are for you, Sissy." Heather freed herself and put her hat, boa, and shoulder bag on a chair. Without a word to Christopher, she approached the piñon sputtering in the kiva, handed her mother-in-law the flowers, and bent to kiss her cheek. "I love that fragrance," she whispered.

"Lilacs are my favorite."

"I don't mean the flowers."

"Oh. The new Balanchy." Under her powder Sissy blushed.

Heather kissed her again. "You and Bill should have seen the double rainbow over Atalaya Peak. Hello there, Christopher. We're like ships in the night, aren't we? I got the backgrounder whipped into shape and e-mailed to Genesure."

"Yeah?"

"I did."

"Señor Bill?"

"Oh, goddamn it, now what?" Bill said as Armando appeared in the entrance to the hallway, cap in hand. Behind him Tony held the collar of the slobbering chow.

"We have run out of wallpaper paste."

"There's plenty more to do—get those labels off the windows for starters."

"We have the dog. Outside without us, he'll bark."

"You've explained that. Keep him with you."

"But we don't like to disturb your family on the Lord's day, señor."

Bill shot his breath out. "Go patch and tar the roof over the kitchen sink, go finish up the trellises."

"It's raining, señor."

"Actually," Heather offered, "the rain has stopped." She gripped her ponytail and drew her fist down it. The short white scar that curved across the back of her neck shown under the ceiling halogen. The bulb spotlighted one of Sissy's collages, a rose-petal sunrise garnishing a photo torn from *Better Homes & Gardens* of a stone manor crowning a mountaintop.

"I'd better get our game hens stuffed," Sissy said, rising. "I'm trying to learn your city's vaunted style of cooking. Tonight, two hens in mole sauce and chili polenta."

"Can I help?" Heather asked.

"Not yet you can't, kiddo. I enticed you here to see what you make of my rose idea. You tail along, too, Chris. Achoo!" Bill's chin dropped to his breastbone. "Armando! Get that cur away from me. Take it into the guest room and scrape off those labels while I'm showing the kids my plan. And roll up the rug first, you understand?"

Bill backed toward the fireplace as Tony and the chow followed Armando across the room.

"Let's go!" Bill muffled a sneeze with his fist. He led Heather and Christopher down the hall past the powder room into the master bedroom.

Plywood covered the corner window that Tony had broken above Sissy's desk. A quilt appliquéd with rocking horses and lightning bolts covered the king-size bed. Its headboard, rising halfway up the wall, consisted of three dozen strips of alder glued to each other. A pink strip showed tiny goats; a green strip showed violets; a third, only blue; a fourth, prickly pears; a fifth, orange.

"God, I love this incredible bed," Heather said as Bill pushed the glass slider aside.

"Hard for me to fall asleep in, though, it's so lively. Handcrafted in Truchas, Sis says. Chimayo? I can't recall where. See?" he said, throwing out his arms.

"The double rainbow!" Heather cried. "Look how it loops past the clouds to Atalaya." She knocked her shoulder against the slider's leading edge and clutched her chest, gulping the rain-scented air. Its freshness whisked her to her tearful conversation with Sissy two days ago about the lawn that Heather's father had trimmed for the wedding reception.

"Wise up, Heather. Dad's not talking about the rainbow, he's talking about his rose garden. Well, garden-to-be."

While wind teased their hair, the trio stood on the aluminum threshold gazing at a plot twenty feet square. The joints of a six-foot wall were already whitening because again Tony had neglected to underlay its stucco with wire and tar paper. A gate featuring a wooden-barred window opened to a path that wound to the graveled drive past the bedroom and Bill's office. Half a dozen outsize lattices of redwood—four oblongs, an oval, and an oblong sprouting a two-foot slat— soared among dirt clods and gopher holes and tufts of buffalo grass. Rosebushes, a few bearing blossoms, waited in polyethelene pots around the base of each trellis. A slope of stones that Bill had wheelbarrowed off the home's acre rested against the wall.

"Those stones," Bill said, pointing, "will top the rims of the big water basins Tony needs to dig. Our neighbor across the street, the poor gal Sis suspects me of doing I don't know what with, said yesterday that her deceased husband grew tree roses successfully, floribundas and hybrid teas. She's going to search his files to find out how he amended the soil up here, alkaline and too dense because of caliche, she tells me.

"Anyhow, you kids, can you picture it? Double Delights shaped into an eight-foot-high processor, its two DVD slots rendered in red rows of Mister Lincolns. And here's my plan for an iPod—white John F Kennedys and rose-colored Nancy Reagans, reconciled at last."

"It's original, Bill, I'll give you that."

"Thanks, kiddo." He turned to pat Heather's cheek.

"How about a few Tibetan lanterns to hang in those aspen your contractor planted outside the wall?" she asked straight-faced.

"Jeez, this isn't your project, Heather. Dad, it's starting to sprinkle."

Bill heaved the glass slider shut behind them.

Sissy appeared in the doorway where the hall dead-ended, biting a fuchsia-glossed lip. "Heather, dear? Is there a supermarket open close by, do you think? I forgot to pick up peanut butter to add to the mole. Oh, drat! Dinner's going to be late and Christopher said he's got to leave for the Labs at dawn. Will you forgive your mother, Chrisy?"

"Johnnie's Cash Store on Don Miguel may be open," Heather said. "When I'm feeling too corralled in Rancho Viejo, I drive up to buy his homemade tamales. There's a shortcut if the road's not too muddy. But it's Sunday and he and his wife are probably Catholic."

"You certainly know a lot about this area," Christopher said. "No wonder you're always behind in your work."

"Christopher!" Sissy exclaimed. "That was uncalled for."

"I'll say," Bill added.

Heather felt her neck and shoulders heat but kept her voice low and eyes on Sissy. "I'll go right now. If Johnnie's is closed, Wild Oats isn't much farther."

"May I come?" Sissy asked. "I'd like to get to know the local merchants."

"Of course."

"You men," Sissy began, but rolled her eyes toward the ceiling of latillas as a wave of light-headedness engulfed her. She exhaled and, blinking, started down the hall toward the living room. "You men can talk business in peace now," she said over her shoulder.

Heather retrieved her hat and burlap shoulder bag from the chair near the table. Sissy turned off the sauce and brought an umbrella and felt hat from the cloak closet. Heather led the way down the steps toward her Honda hybrid beside Christopher's BMW and Baca's dented pickup.

Bill strode across the tiles to wrench open the guest-room door. "Come on out, you two, and get those last trellises up." Pinching his nostrils, he backed to the dining table. Christopher waited in front of the chair his mother had been using, his forehead a washboard of furrows.

"All is well, señor," Armando muttered, squinting across at Bill. From his denim jacket he pulled a pack of Luckies and, clutching it, moved toward the hall. The leashed chow shook itself behind Tony. Like decaying leaves, its prints glistened on the living-room's tiles.

"I'm about to go loony-tunes, Chris," Bill said when the contractors had disappeared. "Armando tells me worry over his wife's crack addiction and the cost of repairing his truck is slowing him down here. He claims he can't focus. You know what? I'm gonna pop another hang-in-there pill while your mother's away. Hey, that Mexican chocolate sauce smells pretty good, doesn't it? More sherry?"

Christopher extended his lower lip and shook his head.

"Join me in a cigar from Honduras?"

"No thanks."

Bill unstoppered the decanter and poured out another finger. He lifted his hip to extract his pills, teased out one, and downed it. "Supposed to take one every four hours but guess what. I don't give a rat's ass anymore."

He plucked a petit corona from the cedar box on the end-table's shelf, pulled a lighter from his pocket, bit the cigar's end into the cut-glass ashtray he'd brought from Palo Alto, and sucked in the flame. He blew smoke toward the ceiling, squeezing his eyelids shut. "That's more like it, hey?"

"What are those pills, Dad?" Christopher pulled the ottoman toward the chair, lowered himself to the cushion, hoisted his left leg to the ottoman, and leaned forward to massage his knee.

"Half milligram of lorazepam."

"Yeah? What's that?"

"Mild tranquilizer. Supposed to lessen the itching on my back."

"Itching from what?"

"This is a quiz? I supposed your mother would have told you."

"Not a peep."

"Hives, Chris. Nerves."

"Father and son, Dad."

Bill narrowed his eyes at him. "But I'm too old to be putting in seventy-hour weeks. This year we're dealing with an upstart out of Santa Cruz called Microcurity. Their chip has some features Silidyne wants. Hyperthreads to goose the software's multitasking capabilities, plus designs to grease the linkups between audio and video."

"Yeah?" Christopher picked up the desert edition of the May *Sunset Magazine* off the coffee table and began to leaf through it.

"Just before flying out here we closed a three-hundred-million-dollar deal to ensure access to Microcurity's patents. That kind of money ought to keep their best people from bolting." Bill puffed on his cigar. "Cat got your tongue, Son?"

"I'm happy for you," Christopher muttered, gazing at a sun-dappled photo in *Sunset* of a couple sipping tea in bed. He and Heather never stayed in bed mornings. He and Jessie used to every Sunday, sipping Bloody Marys.

"You're happy, Son? Because I'm on tranquilizers? Because you and your second wife aren't getting along?"

Christopher glanced up. "Happy that you're so successful, Dad. And look, worry not about Heather and me. We'll probably stick it out in spite of her little animals crawling and swimming and flitting all over the house. No one wants to divorce. It hurts too much."

"But it was imperative, wasn't it? That you and Jessie split up? She refused to seek help."

"The tragedy with us was that drunk or no drunk, she and I were compatible. Mathematicians I can relate to. Left brains communicate. Though I admit that sometimes I wanted to hang her by her thumbs."

"I'm glad she's out of our lives, Chris. The truth is that I never liked her much. She was too damned serious and she had no chin."

"What's that have to do with anything? Divorce sucks and so does staying put. But you pump a lot more stress into Heather's and my life when you tell us not to have children."

"You've already covered that! You think I'd dare utter the words again?" Bill yanked out the cigar, closed his lips, and drew his thumbnail across them.

Christopher shrugged. "Tell you what . . . this crap-o knee." Sliding his leg off the ottoman, he got up, limped over to Bill, poured himself a couple of fingers, set the decanter back down, returned to his chair, and emptied his glass. "Let's talk about a sharper bone that's gotten stuck in my throat."

"What bone's that, Son?" Bill drew air through the cigar, reddening its ash, and exhaled with a burbling sound. White smoke curled toward ceiling vigas thick as phone poles.

Christopher aimed his forefinger at him. "Keep your fucking hands off my wife."

"My fucking hands off your wife? What are you accusing me of?

You watch your language there. What's what with you? Sometimes you baffle me. However you think you feel, you need to know, through thick and thin, I love you. It pains my heart—"

"Oh, can it, Dad." Christopher felt his chest muscles tremble. He coughed. The cigar's odor was making him gag.

Bill put it in the ashtray. "Exactly what is your accusal here?"

"You know very well what my accusal is. Don't harass me."

"Harass you!" Bill jumped up and, swaying, planted one boot in front of the other.

Christopher sprang up, threw out his right arm and leveled his forefinger. "Keep your hands off my wife's thighs." He threw out his left arm. "Keep your hands off my wife's knees." He threw out his right one. "Keep your hands off my wife's face." Beginning to wheeze, he threw out his left. "And don't put your arm around her shoulders."

"She's my daughter-in-law, Chris. This isn't the workplace."

"You have no right to touch her."

"You don't own her! When someone feels affectionate—"

"She doesn't like it! And I wonder what Mother thinks when she sees you paw her. You understand? Heather doesn't like your handling her and she doesn't like the stink of those cigars."

"I never smoke when your mother or Heather's—"

"Your breath's always foul, old man!"

"Oh, my God. I don't handle your second wife and I don't need to take this. You're a guest in this house." Bill's jaw bunched as, clawing under his collar between his shoulder blades, he lurched forward. He jerked his head to the side. "What's that stink? Did that cur throw up? Oh, goddamn it." He wobbled into the hallway.

Christopher laughed in spite of himself, worried he might burst into tears. He pinched up the stub of cigar and flung it into the glowing teepee of piñon. Grasping his hands behind him, he crossed to the window beside the front door, shoulders as hunched as his father's.

He stood gazing at raindrops spattering his sedan until he saw Armando, Tony, and the chow round the corner and hurry toward

Baca's truck. Armando lugged a green bucket. Tony followed, cradling a hammer and a couple of saws across bare forearms.

"What fools we all are," Christopher said to no one. He shut his eyes and twisted to lean against the St. Peter carved into the door.

FLIGHT
MONDAY 16 MAY 2005

The next morning at The Teahouse, Derek glanced at the clock framed in wood—Chad's work?—hanging beside a painting of two pears whose stem ends seemed to be kissing. He clasped his fingers to warm them, only to discover that the tips weren't cold. His heart pounded. Had Heather lost her nerve? Already she was ten minutes late. An hour ago he'd shaved off the five-day bristle he'd been growing for Greer. How gullible. Now twice?

The noise of pickups and SUVs gunning up Canyon Road mixed with the clatter of plates and the voice of a woman on her cell phone. Derek stood, took a handkerchief from his trail shorts, and placed it on the table near a huge, arrow-leafed plant cradled in terracotta.

"I'll be back," he said to the chubby waitress who approached, and pointed to the folded handkerchief. He headed for the door to fetch the poetry manual left by mistake in his Neon. What had happened to the Derek who'd assured Chad a week ago that marriage gave him stability? That Derek had vanished like the steam rising from the teacup at the next table.

A red-headed finch fluted from the Russian olive rising beside Jake Gerson's ramshackle art gallery. Moses Said Buy Cowboy Paintings read the sign, which Gerson had set among a stand of iris. A long-haired graybeard strummed his guitar on a bench nearby.

Where is she? As he crunched over the gravel and headed for his car, a Honda Civic hybrid crackled down the dirt driveway and swung in close. His heart started knocking again. Rather than the lopsided pigtail worn to the gym Wednesday, Heather had let her hair flow to her shoulders, as it had at Chad's house. It was the same dark brown as his own.

She pushed open the door, scrambled out, and threw her hands wide. "I'm really sorry. My cat knocked over the fishbowl and tore through the great room and freaked my two birds."

"Birds?" Calm thyself, Derek counseled. Under his shirt he felt his chest warm. What a perfect outfit she had on: white, ruffled skirt and V-necked sleeveless top, gold-fiber belt and wooden buckle. More inspiring than anything he'd seen Greer wear. Was Heather to be his true muse? He clenched his jaw.

"Lovebirds," she said. "I've got a couple of horned toads, too. Oh, this is so cool. Live music to greet us! Moses says buy cowboy paintings? Look at that robin fluttering in the puddle. What a change from having to churn out biotech backgrounders—this is why I moved here. Where do we go eat?"

The sun, rising through wisps of clouds, burnished her hair. She brushed a strand from her forehead and took a step, but didn't see the stone. "Bat guano!" Derek grabbed her shoulders as she pitched toward him. She sucked in her breath, raised her green eyes to his gray ones, and choked out a laugh.

"We're heading this way," he said, pointing past a woman breakfasting under an apricot tree. "First I need to get something for you out of my car."

"Like what?"

"You said you wanted to talk poetry."

"I do! I brought you one I just finished." She patted the burlap bag slung from her shoulder.

"Shall we sit outside?" she asked when he came back, the manual tucked under his arm.

"I saved a table inside for us next to a big philodendron."

"Oh . . . those mouse heads on your shirt crack me up."

"They're the good-mood part of me," he said as the screen door flapped behind him.

They pulled out chairs facing each other and sat down. He placed *A Poet's Handbook* on the table's walnut top, picked up the handkerchief, and stuffed it into his pocket. The waitress lumbered close, a roll of tummy exposed above the band of a miniskirt.

"I love your T-shirt," Heather said to the young woman.

Handing them menus and a twelve-page list of teas, she pulled the orange cotton from her breasts. Happiness is Pillow Talk, the slogan read. "Back soon," she growled and squeaked off in thick-soled sneakers.

"I hate cells," Derek announced, the curls on the left side of his part bouncing as he tossed his head toward the woman at the next table who wedged a phone between her jaw and shoulder. She tapped on a laptop while she talked.

"Want to move?" Heather asked.

"Always some annoyance, isn't there?"

"But Derek, I like this place! Look at those birdcages above us with teacups perched in them."

"Let's decide what to order so we won't be interrupted."

"Sure, fine." Was he going to be more controlling than even Christopher, she wondered?

Beth Orten's song of woe accompanied by electric guitar came from twin speakers set among the track lights.

"I guess I'll have the breakfast pie, fruit salad, and an Americano," he said. "A good choice when I discovered this place a couple of weeks ago."

"No tea?"

"I need coffee caffeine. I like this place too, especially when you're here."

Her shoulders trembled as she quickly looked down at the menu.

"See anything?"

"I need a minute. But call the waitress. That'll help me decide."

He waved. She shuffled over and plucked a pencil from behind her ear.

"You go first," Heather murmured.

The woman took his order.

"Okay, for me," Heather said, "Scrambled Eggs Parma with proscuitto and some kind of tea, my goodness, all these pages . . ."

"Want me to recommend?"

"Would you?"

"Try the Sencha Gyokuro. It's Japan's best green."

"I'll do that!"

An instant later, Heather pulled a spiral notebook from her bag and ripped out two pages. The handwriting looked cramped except for her flaring ascenders.

"Here," she said, thrusting the sheets at Derek. But she released them an instant before he could grab hold and they fluttered to the floor. She jumped up, knelt to retrieve them, and moved back to her chair.

"That's your poem?" he asked.

"About a rag doll escaping a hut I wove from red willows. Oh, there's so much I want to tell you."

"I'm glad," he said, smiling.

"But I'm nervous."

For himself, he felt no guilt. Natalie seemed the puff of a dandelion blown far away. "You're thinking we shouldn't be breakfasting together?"

"Maybe that's right but here we are, aren't we? Talk to me before I show you what I wrote. I hardly know anything about you! How did you become a poet?"

"Oh, boy," he sighed. "All my life I've loved to make up sentences and say them aloud, especially if no one's there. Something like the way my sister loved to dress up dolls. When I graduated from Cal Berkeley, my dad left my mother for a Mister-America black mechanic and I decided to become a priest. A la Gerard Manley Hopkins and Pierre de Chardin. Do you know about them?"

Heather shook her head. Yes, she did like this man! Didn't she? Fuck you, Christopher.

"Catholic writers. I started at the Jesuit School of Theology three blocks from the UC campus, but found I couldn't accept the God of Intelligent Design. So after a year I drifted here and joined the New Mexico Book Association, where I discovered a big need for indexers. And that this town is crawling with poets. Oh, hang up!"

He glared at the green-slacked woman hunched over her laptop. "I'm telling you I need two bedrooms!" she barked into her phone.

"You don't want to find another table?" Heather asked.

"The only one free is next to that guy who brought his fold-up bicycle in. He's got a phone, too. Santa Fe's changing too fast. Maybe I should go back to the Bay Area to look for my pocket of peace."

"Are you kidding? Oh, but your mother's there."

"She died of an intestinal blockage after my father left."

"God, Derek! Where's he now?"

The waitress approached with a lacquered tray holding drinks, paper napkins, and silverware. "The Americano?"

Derek touched the tabletop in front of him.

She set down his coffee and Heather's tea. The leaves lay at the bottom of an infuser poised in a clear-glass mug. "Food's coming up," the waitress said and turned.

"So where's your father?" Heather asked again. She plucked the infuser from the saffron-colored liquid and placed it in its top. Drops scattered onto the poem's first page. "Shit," she muttered, picked up the page, and waggled it.

"Your prayer flag."

"What a klutz."

"You said you're nervous."

"I can't help it, Derek."

He nodded and gulped from his steaming cup. "I get postcards sometimes from Pop. He's still picking up car-repair work and reading the classics. He used to love to read to me from *Don Quixote* and Burton's *Arabian Nights*."

"Lucky you. My dad's always been tight-lipped. So how did you and your wife meet?"

A squawk stopped all the room's conversations.

"Look!" Heather exclaimed.

A woman shuffled through the low archway, her rope-belted dress hanging in shreds. Half a dozen needleworked badges festooned her bosom: Iraq Quack, Iran Kazaam, Syria Teary-uh, Saudi Lawdy, Babble Kabul, Qatar Babar. She displayed a grin of ash-colored teeth and swung her arms like a drum majorette returning for her fiftieth high-school reunion.

"Awk, awk, awk," she prattled, mimicking the great white bird whose claws gripped her shoulder. Its scarlet eyes gleamed as though sightless. With each round of squawks, the white crest flipped skyward and fanned out like wings.

Rrrrawk!

The woman spat at the man with the bicycle and approached Heather and Derek. She dipped toward them. Her cockatoo hung fast.

Rrrrawk! The black beak clacked shut.

"These are for you and Charles, Maud," came the waitress's bass voice. She carried two polyethelene bags. "Baguettes with Brie and leftover apple crisps." The soles of her sneakers sounded like suction cups lifting as she stepped around Heather.

Maud grabbed the proffered bags, white hairs curling from her chin. "You're good," she rasped, cocking her forefinger with its split nail at Derek. She pointed to Heather. "Stick with this one."

Rrrrawk, the bird protested.

"Let's not quit before the miracle, Charles." Maud reached to smooth a free hand down the bird's feathered back. No longer shuffling, she strode past a girl who entered through the rear doorway, black-knit dress distended with child. As Maud and the bird left, the mother-to-be took a freed-up window table, unzipped her boots, and hauled them off. She curled her toes around the bottom rung of the chair opposite.

"I want to be like her," Heather said, sitting.

"Pregnant?"

"No! Like the old woman. Sibylline."

"Sorry about that," said the waitress, returning with their breakfast. "She's the owner's mother, not as ancient as she looks. She crept to the end of the limb five years ago after the Taliban kidnapped her son near Kabul. There's been no word from him since."

"It's a terrifying world," Derek said.

"Scrambled Eggs Parma?"

Heather nodded.

"Breakfast pie, fruit salad."

The crust was soft enough for a fork but Derek used a knife to slice off the wedge's tip. "You look through *The Courier* this morning?" he asked and began to chew.

"I did. These eggs smell heavenly!" Heather took a sip of tea.

"The guard at Guantánamo who flushed the Koran down the john?"

"Typical of us."

"The stabbing death at Santa Fe High?"

"That one I missed."

"The North Koreans threatening underground testing?"

"Yes."

"The Kansas school board insisting that Intelligent Design be taught alongside Darwinian evolution?"

"I think so."

"The thirty-eight corpses found last night in Baghdad with their throats slit?"

"Derek, stop!"

"You're right."

"I know everything's bad. I'm already about to crack up."

"I just wanted to show you why poetry's become my refuge. I don't really care if the words make sense. What makes sense is that we're hardwired to sabotage each other. Poetry lets me create true beauty—beauty in the real world's a sham." He knifed free another bite of pie, thrust it between his lips, and took a gulp of coffee.

"Why sham?"

"Because it distracts us from the major reality that our fate is to overpopulate, humiliate, and maim."

"I wonder."

"The major reality needs changing and no one's been able to do it."

"What about acts of kindness, Derek?"

"There aren't enough to matter." Wrapping his upper lip with his lower one, he picked up the gray-covered handbook and offered it to her. "This is what started me writing poems at the seminary."

She laid the paperback next to the peony rising from a funnel-shaped glass. "First I want to know about your wife."

"Why do we need to talk about spouses?"

"Does she know you're here with me?"

"Does the guy with the crew cut you're married to?"

"No."

"Neither does my wife."

"Might she come looking for you?"

"Might your husband?"

"He works in Albuquerque."

"My wife thinks I go to Starbucks off the Plaza every morning. As mostly I do. You're saying now you're too uneasy to stay with me?"

Heather shook her head, staring at the strange way his hair bristled on the right. She picked up the book and flipped its cover.

"Heather, you know what? I've told you a lot of things—how about telling me about that scar on your neck?"

"This is the first time you've used my name this morning, do you realize that?"

"I guess I do." He felt perspiration wetting his shirt.

She slipped her poem inside the handbook. "No one except my husband and our parents know anything about that scar."

"You'd rather talk about your poem?"

Heather took a bite, swallowed, and sipped before looking across at him. "By seventh grade I knew I wanted to be a writer. I couldn't think what to write. So I decided to find out what trying to kill myself would be like. It felt so damned good to imagine the pain I'd cause Mom and Dad. Our lives were too monotonous. Mom raised sheep and did Tarot readings and Dad grew wine grapes and proofed *The Mendocino Beacon*. It's what they still do. I found Dad's Xacto knife and . . . did this!" She drew the uncolored nail of her forefinger across the right side of her neck. "Can you believe it?"

"Of course!"

"As soon as I saw the blood push out I started screaming. Mom came running from a session. She grabbed a Kotex from the bathroom and told me to use it as a compress. She drove me to the ER. The blade had missed my carotids. I'd lucked out."

"Whew," Derek whistled and paused. "My sister had a neck scar."

"Yeah?"

"Fell on the bent lid of a soup can when she was a toddler."

"Wait a minute, had a scar?"

"She didn't luck out. Or maybe she did."

"What happened?"

He swallowed the last of his pie and thrust his fork into the bowl of strawberry and banana slices. "You sure you want to hear this?"

"I asked, didn't I?"

"About the age you cut your neck, I showed my sister how I'd learned to make my penis stiff."

"Oh."

"Shall I keep going?"

"Why not?"

"We started fondling each other. I keep telling myself it wasn't incest. But we couldn't quit until she got into the film program down at UCLA and into therapy. She overdosed on prescription uppers six years later. She was a year younger than I am and she never married."

Heather bit her lip and dropped her gaze.

"I'm with the wrong woman now," he muttered.

"You may be right."

"I mean my wife, not you."

Heather spread the fingers of one hand across her chest and pushed her chair back. "It's a lot for one morning, Derek. I'm feeling dizzy. Will you pay for us?" She flipped her wrist. "Almost nine-thirty!" Pulling a twenty-dollar bill from the wallet in her bag, she leaned toward him. "Look how my hand's shaking!" Heather tossed the bill his way. Her thumb hit the handle of his fork, flipping it and a slice of banana to the floor.

He bent to retrieve them. "What about your poem?"

She extracted the two pages, tossed them at him, clamped the handbook against her ribs, and hurried away.

Natalie swung her blue van into the life coach's driveway an hour later, under a sky now mottled with clouds.

As she stepped onto the gravel, the breeze blew the stench of dog shit into her nostrils. She saw the pile buzzing with flies near the entrance to the garage Meredith had had converted into an office. Natalie spied the muscular jaw of a smallish dog through a barred window.

"Welcome, dear heart!" Wearing her usual black shoes and slacks, Meredith hauled the door inward and threw her right arm behind her. "I've named this doggie Saint Paul. A woman at the shelter introduced me to him three days ago. He's only a year old."

Natalie shrank from his growl. She noticed scabs at the tips of the ears that jutted near the big woman's ankles. Silently she thanked Meredith for remembering to wear no perfume this morning, though a musky odor rose from the dog.

"You saw the poop by the bench? Last night I brought it over from the forsythia on a trowel. It's the German shepherd's from across the street. Once his stool lures him to my door, whammo, meet Saint Paul the Apostle, here to avenge little Shadow's death. He's a pit bull mix. Come on in."

That morning Natalie had resolved to stay upbeat the whole day by wearing bright colors—orange sandals, an orange-and-white-striped shirt, a flounced Mexican skirt, and her blue-jay feather. She stepped inside. Saint Paul's chest muscles knotted at the tinkling of ankle bells. Meredith shortened her grip on the chain she'd snapped to his collar. "Don't worry, he's a creampuff with people."

But would he spark an asthma attack, Natalie wondered? Shadow never had. "Oh!" she exclaimed, "you got a new washing machine. Black!" Her fancy re-formed it into a crouching bear. She began chewing the gum she'd stopped working when she'd seen the dog.

"This baby's industrial grade with a ten-year warranty. Shall we get started?" Meredith snapped off the ceiling fixture and settled into the armchair in the corner. She leaned forward to set the timer for the preliminary five-minute meditation, holding onto Saint Paul's chain.

Sunk in the couch, Natalie stared at the wooden, eighteen-inch Archangel Gabriel standing near the water heater. She recalled that Meredith had carved the angel under Chad's guidance. What last week had seemed Gabriel's Nazi salute today seemed a command to relax. She shivered in the room's chill and closed her eyes. The pit bull began to snore, though it sounded more like purring.

Natalie gripped her knee and cried out, caught up by thoughts that had been plaguing her since Saturday. Six feet away, the dog responded with a noise like a feeding hog.

Meredith made no comment until the timer dinged. Then she placed Saint Paul's chain under her sole and smoothed the sides of her hair. "Let's have it, woman." She retrieved the chain, hefted her bulk, and moved with the dog to the Confrontational Chair. Her fingers gripped the two carved heads of the cougars.

"You and that pit-bull thing frighten me, Meredith."

"You yelped. Why?"

"Two evenings ago at his gallery Chad Hopp made a pass at me. I wanted him to go further but he backed off. I keep playing out what could have happened and I want to scream. My husband's told me he doesn't love me."

"Good!"

"Good?"

"Keep talking, dear heart."

"I asked him to call you for an appointment but he won't do it. Chad wonders if Derek's seeing another woman. Sure he is! Monica, his dead sister. He was growing a beard to please her—oh, I don't know. He certainly wasn't growing it for me." Her head dropped and she began to tremble. Should she keep to her plan to search this afternoon for a military outfit like Derek's sister wore in the photo on his desk?

Meredith released the dog's chain and clumped over. She gripped Natalie's shoulders. "Did you tell your husband what you need?"

"He doesn't care anymore!" Natalie started sobbing. "I wish I had the courage to leave him."

Meredith returned to her chair, pinned the chain with her heel, and rubbed her hands along her thighs. "Leave him for Chad Hopp, you're thinking? Mr. Chad Hopp may himself be in for a surprise."

"What do you mean?" Natalie sniffled.

"I'm not at liberty to reveal that. His wife's a client. I will share, however, that if you plan to start an affair with him, watch it. He has a violent streak. Two weeks ago, while he too was a client here, he started shouting down my Christianity. Nobody with smarts does that. Everyone knows a new world's coming. The evidence for Jesus Christ's return is overwhelming. I sent Chad Hopp into the bathroom to find some peace."

"He may help me get space in his gallery, Meredith."

"You're not strong enough to end up in a love snarl, missy. Even if you leave your husband, what makes you think Sir Chad will leave his wife?"

"They're having problems."

"I can't discuss it."

"There's also another man I fantasize about."

"Oh yes? Who?"

Just then through the window above the couch came a rahr rahr — rahr, rahr, rahr.

Meredith leaped up, grabbing Saint Paul's chain. "All right, Lord, bless us with a glimmering of Your Rapture. The sucker's sniffed the bait."

The pit bull's nails slid along the faux oak as she dragged him to the door, pulled it open, and kneeled to unsnap his chain. She locked the squirming dog under her arm like a white-patched football and hurried out to the step.

Natalie's knees indented the cushion as, forearms pressing the sill, she peered between the window's black bars. Across the street, the man she'd seen Tuesday stood at his opened gate, arms akimbo, feathered fedora slanted across his brow. He watched his shepherd bound over Meredith's forsythia and, barking joyfully, gallop through her patch of dandelions.

Meredith came back in, slammed the door, and moved to the end of the couch, standing on tiptoes to watch Saint Paul yipping near the pile of poop. His shoulders shook as he confronted the shepherd, who had paused five feet away.

"Slay him," Meredith muttered, "right where he snapped

Shadow's neck. Do that and I call off my lawyer."

Ruff, ruff. The shepherd inched closer, wagging its head and lowering it. Suddenly the pit bull rolled to his side, rolled over, wriggled upright, and charged Meredith's door.

"Porg! Stay!" White feather bobbing, the man came marching up her drive.

Saint Paul rose on his hind legs whimpering, and began a frenzied scratching through the door's blue paint.

"You little chickenshit!" In three strides Meredith had reached the door. She flung it open to let the snot-nosed disappointment slink inside, sidewinding like a rattler.

"I keep telling you Porg's a kitten," his owner chuckled. "But letting your mutt's excrement pile up is not what we do in this neighborhood. C'mon, angel, you've had your romp."

"There's a lawsuit heading your way," Meredith shouted after him.

Saint Paul glanced up, drool streaming from his lips. He slunk across the floor to the bowl of water she'd placed next to the chest Gabriel stood on.

Meredith threw the chain onto the armchair's cushion and sank into the Confrontational Chair. Natalie resettled herself on the sofa. Again tears sprang to her eyes but this time from laughter.

"What's so funny?"

"Saint Paul. You. Me. Everything."

"I'm sick of this town," Meredith announced.

"How ashamed your poor little dog must feel."

"Who the hell knows? Tell me about this other man you imagine playing licky-face with."

"Licky-face." Natalie burst into giggles. "I'm sorry, Meredith." She stuck her wad of spearmint in a tissue. "He's a tall, curly-headed Jew—an acupuncturist. I told my husband I wasn't going to see Yuri again, but I've let our session for Thursday stand. Last week after he put the needles in and left the room, I began to turn myself on. I must have tossed my head because a needle buried itself in my scalp."

The life coach's bosom started to shake. "There's no needle pain when you let a woman do you," she guffawed.

Saint Paul gazed mournfully at them, ears at half prick and jaw resting on his paws.

"When I started to yell, Yuri came running. He made me feel important. I don't know what to do anymore, Meredith."

The life coach pushed herself to her feet, trotted over, and clasped Natalie's cheeks. "Let me show you how to enjoy painless orgasms," she whispered.

"Huh?"

"Run away with me, dear heart!"

"Run away with you?"

Meredith gripped Natalie's wrist. "Let's go where the winters are warm. I can make a fortune on this house. We'll go to Merced! Shall we? The homes there cost half what they cost here."

Natalie felt herself trembling. "Go where?"

"To the golden state's fruit bowl and gateway to Yosemite. There's a new University of California opening in September. Merced has the same population as Santa Fe but thirteen fundamentalist churches and twenty-six Mexican restaurants. Loads of landscapes for you to paint, dear heart, and it's lousy with losers who need coaching. Though no one follows my advice, not in the long run. I may just chuck this game, get me a real estate license, and sell santos to illegals on the side."

"Your fingers are hurting my wrist."

"I want you to be my companion!"

Natalie's right temple began to throb. "Meredith, please! I'll think about it, okay?"

The life coach lumbered across to the armchair, shoved the dog's chain aside, sat, and grasped her black-rayon-covered knees. "Not think. Know."

"Just like that?"

"This room is for decision-making and I need yours now."

To Natalie the register of her coach's voice had become a foghorn's. "But I've told you I don't think I'm gay."

"No more thinking!" The heave of Meredith's breasts pulled her blouse tight.

"All I know is that I long to have men touch me."

"Then get out!"

Saint Paul raised his head and growled.

"Shut up, you."

Natalie rose, tonguing rouge-caked lips.

"Wait right there, missy. Fifty bucks. No, wait, I owe you ten minutes because of the interruption. Take this hair-ball failure with you and I'll let you out of here free."

"But the smaller ones are so needy. Most of them give me asthma. My mother's Lhaso apso does, anyway. And Derek hates small dogs. He wants a dalmatian."

"Oh, Christ, go!"

"Now the ax falls," Abigail whispered to herself, tousling her pixie cut and squinting. An hour ago Meredith had praised the wisdom of stashing keys, license, and credit cards in a tummy purse and delivering her news to Chad in full daylight. He'd disappeared into his shop after a mostly silent breakfast. Through the wall came the muted roar of his band saw.

Abbie gazed out at the catkins of elms sparkling motionless against the sky, set Chad's glass of iced coffee on the mat, and returned to the kitchen to fetch two platters holding the special salad.

She clicked off the flame under a pot of black-bean-and-chorizo soup on the six-burner range, ladled it out, stepped down into the laundry, and pushed open the door to the garage.

"Lunch, ChaCha."

He loped past her through the kitchen in his gray dungarees, the frayed cuffs of his shirt speckled with sawdust, and took his chair at the dining table's end.

She gentled his salad aside to serve his soup, a moment later returning with hers, and sat as usual at his left elbow.

"What's the occasion, Ab?" The triangle between his nose and ends of his brows deepened. "Trying to turn me on with that fiesta blouse? Hey, I'm yours whenever. And why fix our wedding-anniversary salad three months early? Are these nopalitos fresh?" He spooned up a mouthful of soup, swallowed, and jiggled his head. "Hot!"

Abigail's heart drummed behind breasts immobilized in their D-cup bra. Could she manage to get anything down? She twisted the blouse's Egyptian cotton near her navel. "The nopalitos are fresh, ChaCha. Don't they smell scrumptious? I had Kaune's shave the spines off. A clerk told me a farm in Dixon grows the cactus and the onions and the tomatoes. The limes come from Guadalajara."

"But why today?" Chad tried another spoonful of soup. Half a bean stuck in his grizzled beard and he swiped it free with his napkin.

"Wasn't *The Courier* full of bad news this morning?" she asked. "We don't need a second supersized Wal-Mart. And a convention center for forty-two-million bucks? Figure seventy-two million, I'm sure. What about that piece on New Mexico's rivers? Development and grazing are polluting them. Worst was the article on global warming, don't you think? Our spring has advanced six days over the past thirty years because—"

"Bag it, huh?" Chad parked his spoon in his soup and smacked the mahogany on each side of the mat. "What's the deal, Ab? Our anniversary salad to persuade me to abandon Santa Fe? I thought we'd beat that horse to death. This is home."

"Yours, maybe, ChaCha. I'm pulling up stakes." Oh, God, she'd said it. She raised her eyes to his scalp.

"Pulling up stakes? You're not pulling up stakes. What do you mean you're pulling up stakes?"

"Greer is leaving Kullman College and we're taking off."

"Greer? Huh? What about our lovemaking Friday night? What about those daisies in your hair the next morning?" He slapped his thighs. "Greer?"

He shoved his chair back and stood wordless until his panting slowed. "Where are you two going? Nova Scotia mon amour? She's taking those dogs of hers?" His mind had become a cloudland of whistling winds and into it, like a jumping jack, sprang Natalie in the gallery last Saturday, pressing his palm to her nipple.

"We hate it here, Chad. Greer's had enough agony in her life, that father who fucked her mother and her, a husband who started wearing dresses. The dogs'll ride in her minivan and I'll drive a rental. We're going to Maine, I'm not telling you where. I'll find a divorce lawyer there or perhaps we can do mediation. The Subaru's yours."

Hitting the table, Chad shouted, "We've been married almost twelve years, Ab!"

A sudden realization exploded in his mind. "You're lovers! That's what this is about!" He lurched around the corner of the table and, wrists grown thick from using a lathe, grabbed the sides of her head. He pinned her gold hoops and ears to her skull. "Lovers! Aren't you?"

"Let. Me. Go. We'll be out of your hair—what's left of it—by this weekend. I need to move my things. Let me go."

She wrenched her temples free and flung herself up, the chair tumbling to the floor as her elbow smacked her bowl, propelling the hot liquid and slices of chorizo across the mat and onto her blouse. The air came alive with the soup's fragrance. She flinched but stood her ground.

"This weekend?" He jerked his chin to the side. "Oh, no, Ab. Right now." He pushed her shoulder.

"I'm not splitting until I'm ready."

"You're ready now. And I'm going to help. You see?" He hit her left shoulder, the right again, and blocked her swing with his forearm. "I said out, Ab, before I do something I'm sorry for. Get out!"

She bit her lip and wheeled, leather sandals slapping the planks as she hurried around the far end of the table.

"Did Friday night's lovemaking count for nothing with you? Are you just a whore, is that it? Have our years in this house been some kind of puppet show?"

She ran to the front door and jerked it open. Ear hoops swinging, she wheeled and snarled, "Your stained fingers stink of oil, you never-has-been!"

He leaped at her but she backed onto the porch.

She stumbled down the three steps and along the path onto the street. Her tears welled as, hearing his feet pound the steps, she sucked in the scents of grape hyacinth and the yellow roses she'd planted. Where could she escape to?

As she skirted the outside corner of their guest bedroom and turned into Chavez Lane, the toe of her sandal stubbed a chunk of granite. The high-school kid must have left it there while ringing the neighbor's patch of ivy across the street. She plunged headlong into the dirt, stretching her arms forward.

Her wrists burned and she spit out a piece of gravel.

In a moment the birthday socks she'd given Chad last month loomed a foot from her face.

"I married a lesbian," he hissed, sending a kick under her ribs to her right breast.

"Ahhh!" she shuddered, rolled to her hip, and drew her knees to her chest. "Help! Somebody help me!" The kick hurt like a hammer blow.

The lace curtains in the multipaned window above the neighbor's ivy parted. She squinted at the triangular face above the white turtleneck until the man drew the curtains shut again. A stagecoach lamp on the dark adobe wall next to his carport still glowed, though the day had edged past noon.

Pain jackhammered her breast. She heard her husband's footsteps recede toward the driveway. Was he going to take the car?

As her breath slowed, she felt a brush fire of rage flare in her belly and spread to her back and shoulders. She clenched her jaw, straightened her legs, and sat up. Bits of rock stung her butt. She rocked her breast in both hands, as if it were a howling baby.

Was that noise from the garage his lathe? Drill press? The band saw? Grinder? After she managed to stand, she reached back to brush the dirt off her skirt's homespun. Dizzy, she risked a step and tried to picture where she'd propped the rake.

She hobbled past the neighbor's carport. A tangle of aspen, two giant cedars, and an unpruned locust obscured the structure's flaking white. An ancient Olds 98 rested beside paint cans lining the wall. The car faced the blue door leading into what she supposed was his kitchen.

Abbie crossed the lane and passed the Subaru's front bumper with its When Women Vote, Democrats Win. The mid-May sun warmed her face and neck as she brushed the honeysuckle blossoms that camouflaged the guest-room.

She saw Chad—earmuffed, gloved, goggled, and wearing his canvas jacket—standing at his band saw, grasping the slab of walnut he'd praised to her indifference last night. As he proceeded to cut the wood into an octagon, the squealing seemed like hot needles puncturing her eardrums.

She edged along the honeysuckle to where the garage door met the kitchen, hiding her from his view. She peered around the jamb to see the rake leaning near the sheet of fiberboard set on sawhorses that held his finished bowls. A batch of picture frames sprouting wooden vases stood against one end.

The pockets she'd sewn on the back of his jacket to hold gloves faced her. She doubted she could withstand the screech of the saw much longer. What could she damage quickly? She grabbed the rake's handle and stepped forward to roundhouse the bowls off their perch, then caught a couple of birch frames in the rake's teeth and flung them behind her onto the drive. Reaching the drill press, she hooked its top and, straining, hauled it off its steel table into a bed of sawdust.

Chad twisted around. After the second it took to grasp her intent, he yanked off the earmuffs and switched off the saw. "That equipment was custom-crafted in Czechoslovakia, you bitch!" He flung his goggles aside, dodged the table holding his buffer and grinder, and came at her.

She tumbled the vise onto the fallen press and thrust the rake at his face. He grabbed it in his glove and snatched it away, leaving a splinter in the heel of her hand.

He dropped the rake and charged forward as she ran to the fifty-gallon drum accumulating tung oil that dripped from bowls drying on the grate, and with her forearm swiped them and the grate to the floor. She seized the drum's rim and leaned against it until the open drum toppled in his direction.

"Hell's fire," he bellowed, losing his footing in the spilled oil. "Ohhh!" His shoulder hit the corner of the cast-iron foot supporting the lathe's base and he sprawled onto the concrete.

Abigail fled the garage, nauseous from the stink that never failed to remind her of the castor oil her mother had once force-fed her.

"You're doo-doo, Ab," she heard behind her back.

"Help! Please!" she cried, jumping over the picture frames and streaking alongside the Subaru. When she'd crossed the lane, she looked to see Chad quitting the garage, his raised fist clutching a chisel.

She ran into the neighbor's carport, its gloom smelling of turpentine, and pounded on the door at the rear. "Call nine-one-one," she shouted. "Help me, sir!"

Chad had reached the carport when the door opened.

"What's all this?" The old man in red slacks and the turtleneck balanced himself on two canes.

"Call nine-one-one, my husband . . . look!"

"Beat it, you!" the man shouted at Chad. He lifted a cane and shook it.

"You'll pay, you know that, Ab," Chad rasped. "Say bye-bye to your Nikon."

The splinter from the rake was causing the flesh at the base of her thumb to sting.

"All right, lady, c'mon inside. Better make it quick."

Two hours later, Abigail slouched in the wicker armchair in Greer's office, striped skirt torn at the hem, the pocket half ripped from the blouse. Greer sat at her desk facing her. On the side table stood a stack of unread *Library Journals* and Greer's 'guardian-spirit', the papier-mâché scorpion.

The afternoon sun beamed onto the crested head of Carlos the hairless, his neckerchief imprinted with tricolor Mexican flags. Lids closed, he lay sprawled on the towel in the corrugated box Greer kept under the table. The scent of mango lotion that she'd rubbed into his skin before driving to work filled the room.

Greer fingered one of the dogs' heads on her charm bracelet as she listened to Abbie's story. The blue-denim shirt draped over her slacks seemed too large for her boy's figure. She looked glum.

"So this crippled Good Samaritan across the way—whom Chad and I hardly know—let me lie in what's to be his music room," Abbie continued. "The old dude's determined to learn to play drums and form a rock 'n' roll trio. It's never too late, is it, darling? You got rid of a cross-dressing husband and I'm dumping a rageaholic."

Carlos began to snore.

"What about the cops?" Greer asked.

"A guy and a woman drove up five minutes after our neighbor called nine-one-one. The woman stayed with me while the guy went over to our place. He persuaded Chad to lend me the car since I'd told him I wouldn't press charges. He brought back my Nikon and lenses. Thank god Meredith had warned me to hide them before I delivered my blow at lunch."

"So what do we do now?"

A knock stopped Abbie's reply.

"Yes?" Greer called out in her sepulchral contralto. The door pushed inward.

"I saw your Think Before Bothering Me sign, Miss Eddy, but the assistant dean said to remind you about your appointment in half an hour with the candidate for your job." The student had dyed one side of her spiked hair orange. She stood massaging the opposite hip.

"I'll be here waiting." Greer waved toward the phone on her desk. "You've forgotten how to use this?"

"No, Miss Eddy, I thought—"

"You thought wrong." Greer pointed at the doorway and the girl, biting her lip, turned.

"Close it, please."

It clacked shut.

"I wish we could lock it," Greer said. "Saturday afternoon's lovemaking at your place was paradisiacal, sweetheart."

"I need to hang out with you until I can bring over my photos and clothes. Damn that I trashed his shop! He'll retaliate somehow. Will I need a restraining order? Maybe I ought to . . ."

"Stop it, Ab!" Greer left her chair, came over to take the older woman's temples, and, bending, pressed her lips to hers. Greer's straight hair swung against Abbie's ears. "He assaulted you!"

"He could sue me," Abigail whispered.

"Tell him you'll sue for worse. He'll keep his trap shut."

Carlos dragged himself from his cardboard cave and began to bark.

"Take this, amigo." Greer hauled a handful of kibble from her slacks and placed it next to his water dish. "I can't wait until this day's over, Ab. In two weeks you and I and the kids'll be in a farmhouse twenty-five hundred miles from here, and I can start work at the county library."

"If I get my stuff to your house by Sunday."

"You can, sweetheart." Greer glanced out the window. "Damn, that looks like Tony's father."

"Tony?"

"A student I've been mentoring. Keep Carlos quiet, will you? I've got to see what's going on."

She hurried out the vestibule's double-paned doors and turned right along the bricks under the portico until she stood in the sunlight.

Armando kneeled on a foam pad he'd placed on the walk, facing the banks of daylilies that emblazoned the slope below the cafeteria. Beside him sat two polypropylene pots holding butterfly bushes. Their spikes sprayed bursts of purple blossoms. He'd set a third bush in a hole packed with compost. The sides of its gallon pot spread open near his boot. He looked over his shoulder at Greer's approach.

Greer filled her lungs with the bushes' lilac-like odor, hoping to calm herself. "You're Tony's father," she said.

Armando stood, pulled the cap off his white hair, and plucked an unfiltered Lucky Strike from his lips. The backs of his hands seemed cracked leather. "Thank you, señorita, yes, Armando Trujillo."

"Where's your son, Mr. Trujillo?"

"At home studying for tomorrow's oral."

"And what are you doing here?"

"I am planting three shrubs on instructions."

"From Tony?"

Armando dipped a grizzled chin. "No, on instructions from Señor Berland."

"Our head of buildings and grounds."

"Exactly so. He has hired me to assist my son."

"Hired you."

"Last Friday. Until Saturday's graduation. There is much to be done."

"I'm Greer Eddy, the library director at Kullman."

"I know of you! The woman Tony speaks about so often." Tobacco had browned Armando's grin.

"This is my last week at the college and I need to tell him."

"Your last week? Why is that? But no!"

A gnat had landed on the side of Greer's neck and she slapped at it, feeling the heat that had lodged in the wisps of her hair. "I'm leaving for a better job on the east coast."

"But, please, you must not do it." He jammed the Lucky between chapped lips, wiped his palms on his vest, inhaled, and pulled the cigarette free. "Tony's mother has relapsed, she has a situation with cocaine, my boy worships you, señorita! Can you not wait?"

"No can do, Armando. Hello, Carolyn, hi, Jeremy." She nodded to two sophomores starting up the steps, the girl's arm draped around the boy's shoulder, rings on her right thumb and each finger.

Greer felt Armando's own fingers curl around her wrist.

Startling, she flipped it free and stepped backward onto a swath of lawn.

"Miss Eddy, he must maintain his scholarship. We need to feed his mother every sort of good news."

"Tony's perfectly able now to handle his sophomore year. Besides, I doubt he still worships me. I told him something last week he didn't want to hear."

"He said nothing."

"Tell him to come see me tomorrow. Fuck!" she blurted, spotting Derek in flip-flops and green shorts striding around the cafeteria's far corner, pack strapped on his shoulders. She rushed back under the portico.

She raked a sheaf of hair behind her ear and pushed her office door open. The plywood, don't-bother-me sign jumped and swung back with a clap. Abigail sat hunched cross-legged on the carpet near the window, cradling Carlos. "Derek Johansen's heading this way," Greer said.

Abbie's hand slid from the hairless's spine and he jumped off her lap. "I can't deal with another specimen male today! Chad's probably told him everything about what happened this morning." Abbie's right breast throbbed like a toothache. Cupping the right side of her bra, she rose to a knee and stood.

"Sweetheart, you're shaking."

"Of course I'm shaking! I can't absorb any more. What'll I do?"

Greer sprang to her desk, opened the bottom drawer, pried her purse apart, felt for her keys, and dragged them out. She slipped one off its ring. "There's no screen in my office window. Take this house key and scram."

Abigail zipped it into her tummy purse and heaved at the sash. Greer joined her. The window lifted with a screech, catalyzing Carlos into a series of high-pitched yips.

"Steady, hombre," Greer panted to him. She pushed at Abbie's fanny.

Abbie had managed to secure one knee on the sill when four knocks shook the door.

"Can't you read?" Greer yelled out.

"This can't wait." Derek burst in and tilted his head up. "Who's that?"

"I'm calling security right now, Derek." Greer sidestepped toward her phone.

"Abbie Hopp? What's she doing here? Abbie, what is this? Greer, I'm saying please, don't lift that receiver."

"My skirt's caught on a nail," Abigail moaned, her neck stretched under the sash that hovered like a guillotine.

Greer glared at Derek. "She's trying to re-fasten one of the wires holding my chipmonk feeder and it's none of your business." She went to stand beside Abbie's shoulder, then stretched her arm to release the skirt's hem.

"I don't see any chipmonk feeder."

"Oh, shut up, you meathead."

Gasping, Abigail eased her knee down, turned to face Derek, and leaned against the sill. She smoothed her hair and waited for his accusations to begin.

"Perhaps it's good that you're both here because I've got some news," Derek said. "But Abbie, your pocket's torn, your skirt's a mess. You fell somewhere?"

Realizing that Chad must not yet have talked to Derek, "Yes" was all Abigail answered.

"Derek, goddamnit," Greer said. "I've got to meet with someone in a few minutes, speak your piece, will you?"

He spread his flip-flops to steady himself and shoved his fists into his pockets. Abigail moved to the armchair and scooped up Carlos.

"All right. I need to tell you that Natalie and I have decided to separate. Very bad vibrations. But I've met another woman. Abbie, it's the woman who came to your front door a week ago with the poem about Chad's bowl."

Abigail guffawed.

"That's amusing?" Derek asked.

"Weird, like everything."

"I'll give you that. Listen, Greer, I have to know that what you told me last Thursday is how you really feel. My life is too complex and I need to simplify fast. Excuse me, Abbie, but I have to say this." His eyes shifted. "I want to stop fantacizing sex acts with other women and especially with you."

"With me?" Abigail managed, clapping a palm to her chest.

"With Greer."

The two women stood speechless.

He freed his fists from his pockets, bent his knees, and clasped his hands behind him. "Well?"

"Just what was it I told you?"

"That you hate men and I'm supposing hate me most of all."

Greer rolled her eyes toward the plaster ceiling and back down to his. "I have no words for what you are to me, Derek, except an unbelievable jerk. Get out."

He tried to steel his voice into a monotone. "You won't see me again."

"Good!"

Quivering, he grabbed a strap, heaved the pack from his shoulders, hoisted the professor's manuscript she had given him to index, ripped off the rubber band, and slung its four-hundred-plus pages across the carpet. "Not worth my time. The prose stinks. No charge."

He wheeled, opened the door, and stomped past the glass case displaying editions of Goethe's *Faust*.

"Sweetheart!" Greer cried, beginning to laugh. She ran to Abbie, crouched to grasp her knees, and pushed her cheek against Carlos's wet nose. "Gone! Good for us, Ab. Oh, dear Derek, thank you."

Within five minutes the orange-haired student led in a public librarian from Cleveland—buffed loafers, slacks with cuffs, his tie's knot protruding like a second Adam's apple.

WILTING
WEDNESDAY 18 MAY 2005

Christopher pulled up in front of the gym about seven the next evening. He beep-locked his BMW, then tugged one of the building's glass doors open. His right hand clutched four tulips in green tissue that he'd bought for Jan Gray just ten minutes before. He clenched his jaw against remembering the tulips he'd brought Heather the night he'd asked her to marry him.

Brazilian salsa blaring from loudspeakers and the annoying scent of disinfectant filled the warehouse-size space. He stooped to pluck up a discarded paper cup and crumpled it. Straightening, he spotted Jan at the back of the room talking to a woman in black tights who had dropped a barbell to the mat. He tossed the cup into a wastebasket beside the stepper and, in jersey shorts and striped shirt, hurried across the gym's vinyl.

"We'll end with a dead lift, darlin'," Jan was saying. The spandex of a sports bra peeped above the undone button of her halter.

A new inked sign hung on the wall behind her, Use Apparatus At Your Own Risk. Because of my fall on the trampoline, Christopher wondered?

"Watch me close so you don't hurt yourself," Jan said. "Head up, butt down, spine arched, arms vertical. Keep them away from your waist. Steady and slow, like this." Jan's blue-denim skirt rode far up her thighs as she squatted. The bar rested on its weights inches above her running shoes. She pulled herself straight until the weights hung just below her knees. "Now you do it," she said, releasing the bar. Its weights thudded on the rubber mat.

The woman stooped and blew out air. She squeezed her eyes shut, groaned, and heaved the bar up. Her belly button showed as the Work It Out With Jan & Gerry shirt rose. She opened her eyes and jerked her face toward Jan, forehead furrowed, white hair dangling over an eye.

"Good-o, Amelia; terrific!" Jan enthused. "Twenty reps on the pyramid pull to stretch out those dorsals and you're done. Hello, there, Christopher. Whadaya got?"

The woman dropped the barbell and hurried off toward the drinking fountain.

"These are for you, Jan." Christopher thrust the red and pink blooms at her.

"How sweet! But why?" she asked above the hum of an evaporative cooler. She took the bouquet.

"For the vases on the frame Gerry gave you for Mother's Day. I thought the flowers he bought might need refreshing."

"I haven't had time to notice. Gerry's been home with a pulled ligament in his elbow. We'll go for a look-see in a sec." Her gray-blonde curls shook as she bent in front of the barbell and slid off one of the rubber-rimmed weights. "How's that knee, you terrorist-exterminator, you."

"Almost healed."

"Didn't bring the wife tonight?" Jan removed the second weight, shoved both onto a branch of the weight tree, and hefted the bar to its rack.

"I got back from the Labs to find she hadn't fixed dinner because of some poem she was scribbling. Okay, I lost it when she started opening a can of soup. So I charged out for roast duck at Joe's Diner and picked these up for you."

"Let's go give them a home."

"Oh, crap, look who just walked in." He pointed to the figure in the far corner in a muscle tee and shorts.

"Derek Johansen? What's the prob?"

"Bad blood between that yo-yo and me."

"Really? Gerry told me to have him sign a release so he can get started on the trampoline. I'm glad at least we found your form."

Christopher scowled and smoothed his eyebrows with the tips of his forefingers. As the CD player in Gerry's office switched from salsa to Ry Codder's "Bop Till You Drop," a man on the nearby VersaClimber let out a grunt, his pompadour bouncing in sync with his thighs.

Derek scurried toward the standing-leg-curl machine.

"I better go grab that boy before he starts in. Hey, Derek!" Jan hallooed.

Derek looked across the room as she threw her chin up and crooked a finger at him.

"Chris?" she said. "You're a take-charge kind of guy. You keep an eye on these dweebs while I'm gone, will ya? I 'spose anyways you'll want to get in a full workout, to lower that stress level before you head back home."

She tucked his gift under her arm and said to Derek, who stood by, "C'mere, sport, we've a job to do." She reached for his elbow and led him toward the rear wall, then twisted her head and waved the tulips. "Mucho thanks for these." Preceding Derek, she pushed at the steel door to the hallway that led to her office.

Christopher swallowed hard as an afternoon in Eugene five years ago flashed in his mind. His mother had begun to demonstrate how to fix corn bread for a surprise birthday dinner for Heather, newly his fiancée. But his father had burst in, eager to show Sissy the city's public rose garden, and she'd abandoned Christopher to an opened *Joy of Cooking*.

The hell with them all. He headed toward the stationary bike for his warm-up.

Jan waited for Derek to enter her office. "Sit there, honeybunch," she commanded, indicating a chair on the near side of her desk. She skirted the couch where she napped and the filing cabinet. The soft sculpture topping it was different from the one displayed a week ago when Gerry had barged in. This new creation of hers looked phallic, too—half a dozen ropes knotted and shellacked, rising from three rainbow-speckled egglike objects molded from plasticine. A length of electrical wire veined each rope.

She yanked Gerry's drooping blossoms out of the carved vases flaring from Chad's frame, threw them into her trash basket, and replaced them with Christopher's bouquet. She took the chair behind her desk near the life-size skeleton. "Chris Ryan's thoughtful," she muttered. "I'll change the water later. Gerry tells me Chris's wife may be signin' up here before the month's out."

"That creep doesn't deserve the woman he's got," Derek said, setting his palms on bare thighs.

"You know her?" Jan bent to grasp from a drawer a form headlined Jan & Gerry's Trampoline Release. She placed it in front of her.

"We've met."

"Oh? The night Chris fell?"

"A couple of days earlier, at the home of the guy who made that frame." Derek's eyes turned to the photo of Gerry about to start a clean and jerk, New Mexico State Champ lettered on the sign beside him, sunflowers circling his neck.

"Chris's wife's pretty, don't you think?"

"Sure." What is this, Derek wondered? He stretched his lungs with the warm air, looking away from Jan's crinkled gaze and back again.

"I don't think they're gettin' along. But you know what? You're a lot sexier than he is."

"Why did you bring me in here, Jan?" Derek's lower lip enwrapped his upper.

"I need you to fill this out." She slid a pen and the paper across the desk. "Gerry tells me he wants you strengthenin' those calves on the—"

"Where is Gerry, by the way?"

"He hurt himself tryin' to show a client how to use our new but too-complicated power trainer. Derek," she said, stationing her elbow beside the phone and propping her jaw on her palm, "you've developed a great body workin' with my son. Why don't you two get along?"

"He baits me." Derek lowered his eyes to the form.

"Then I'm gonna talk to him. We both love how you've built up those deltoids and pecs. And your willinness to show them off, wearin' shirts like that. Nice."

Embarrassed, he scrawled his name at the bottom of the sheet, lay the pen on it, and pushed the assemblage back toward her. As he gazed at the full lips smiling at him, he began to feel randy. "Anything else?"

"There is. I'd like to clear the air from a week ago."

"It does still stink in here," he countered, hoping to sidetrack what he assumed she planned to say. He started to rise but, worried that his half-erection would show, plopped back down.

She tossed her head and laughed. "That's the solvent evaporatin'. Friday I got new plasterboard and cedar panels in here. Gerry scared the bejeez out of the shyster that put the originals in. I can hardly smell the scent anymore. But it bothers you?"

"Well, yeah, it does, and I better go, Jan," he said, relieved that his cock had collapsed.

"Give me a minute, sport. Last week you claimed you're a committed man and I intend to honor that. You recall our talk?"

He blinked at her. "I do. Yes."

"Can I ask you a personal question?"

"I suppose." Bolt, you fool, he told himself.

"Do you find me attractive, Derek? I work hard on my bod, too, and I try to keep my skin lookin' young at the salon." She smoothed her palms across the denim and down to her knees.

"You're in good shape, Jan."

"And how do you feel tonight?"

"About what?"

"Where is that wife of yours, anyhow? Wasn't she goin' to start workin' out?"

"She's probably changed her mind."

"How come?"

"We're separating."

Jan's eyes widened. "Well now!" She strummed the skeleton's fingers as if they were wind chimes, jumped up, rounded the corner of her desk, and grasped his head. "I haven't had a good man's hands on me for a long time, Derek."

Her aroma seemed that of someone who'd been tumbling inside a drier. Though he smelled fresh sheets, he saw the yarn smile of Heather's rag doll.

Jan stepped to the door, closed it, and stabbed the knob's brass button. "I want to see all those muscles, honeybunch."

His balls began to ache. As he sat staring up at her, his memory replayed the long-ago Sunday in his bedroom that his sister had first squeezed his erection. Their parents were at Mass. The scene changed to thirty years later, Natalie throwing him over the arm of her couch, the scrape of his zipper as she tugged at it, her painted lips descending.

Jan mashed her lips against his and thrust her tongue into his mouth. She pulled back, jerked him upright, and hauled the sleeveless shirt from his shorts. "Help me here, Derek," she panted.

He pulled his gray shirt over his head, hating himself but aroused.

She tossed it to the seat of his chair, and shoved his hand under her skirt until it pressed the fabric covering her vulva.

He could feel his heart knocking as she undid his shorts and yanked the zipper down. "Here's trouble," she whispered, reaching in and patting his bulge. "Though we'll manage, won't we? Got a condom?"

Snorting, he shook his head.

"Maybe you better come outside of me." She pulled the elastic of his jockeys away from his belly and lowered them to his ankles. "You want to get me naked yourself or shall we speed things up?"

"Jan, I'm not divorced yet."

"Huh? What century do you live in? Get your shoes off."

He hobbled to the chair and sat on his crumpled shirt, penis jutting like a bowsprit. He tugged his shorts and the underwear off his sneakers, watched her undo the last button of her halter, strip it from her back, and unhook the bra. It fell to the carpet, revealing peach-size breasts, their nipples poking from pocked areolas.

The solvent was making his nose buzz. God help me, he snuffled, praying to a Being he had no belief in, then raised his right ankle to his knee and untied his laces. She stepped from her skirt and black panties. He forced his gaze off the triangle of blonde hair and the kidney-bean-shaped birthmark beside her navel, and swiped his nose with his forearm.

"Come and get it, big boy." She lay herself along the couch's three cushions, propped a foot on its further armrest, and pushed her breasts together.

"Jan," he sniffed, "I—"

"What's the prob, afraid to ask for head? Is that what your wife does? I used to be real good at it."

Wilt, he begged, staring at his organ. Mucus was causing one of his nostrils to tickle. He wiped it and blew out air. Help me start fresh with Heather or someone like her or help me live like a hermit, he prayed.

"C'mon, I gotta get back out there. Whadaya waitin' for?"

Wilt, he commanded. Gorging his lungs with the sour air, he slapped his erection.

"Whadaya doin', Derek? Oh, screw it. You're too strange."

As she elbowed herself upright, he felt the blood drain from his shaft.

"Limp!" he cried. "Look at that!"

"What are you, anyways, gay?"

He laughed and wrapped his arms around his ribs. "You're a good-looking woman, Jan, but you see? I can't do it." He patted the organ drooping over his balls. "What am I? A poet!" He leaped up and clomped over to her, gripped her tanned shoulders, and—as fervently as she had minutes ago—pushed his lips to hers.

"You pig," she sputtered, twisting away and grabbing her bra. "You won't be thinkin' of comin' back here, will ya."

"I've paid through the end of May, Jan." He shook out his shirt, raised his chin to snuffle down more mucus, and reached to fit the sleeveless cotton back over his chest.

The setting sun inflamed the trunk of the weeping birch as Derek wheeled into his driveway behind Natalie's old Chevy van. The blue-glass tulips of their living room's chandelier glowed, as did the light above the porch bench.

He drew open the screen and turned his key in the doorknob. Though he'd exercised at the gym until closing time, his groin still ached from the close shave with Jan. Nothing, he felt, could stop him now from telling Natalie that he was moving out.

"Sweetheart!" she cried, jumping from the chair at the table under the chandelier. She ran toward him in a square-billed khaki cap, camouflage jacket like the one Monica had worn, creased khaki slacks, and combat boots. No feather swung from her earlobe. Her lipstick matched the porch bench's purple; the familiar scent of witch hazel preceded her. The pile of underwear and sheets to be washed had vanished from the kitchen doorway.

A canvas enlivened by blossoms and what looked like two heads leaned against the floor lamp. Derek just had time to notice the new work before Natalie collided into him. She pressed her face to his, squeezed him tight, stepped away, and threw out her arms. "Tah dah! I'm your sister. You like it?" Her eyes flashed above their bags.

In spite of the heat she'd turned up, he shivered. "You've flipped," he replied in monotone.

"For you. I don't want us to break up, Derek! I bought the outfit two days ago after seeing Meredith. I thought it might turn you on." She lurched close to cup his genitals. "I guess not." She withdrew her hand.

"Where'd you find all that?"

"Armijo's Army and Navy."

"Don't those boots hurt?"

"So what? Oh, Derek, let's be tight again. I know you hate large breasts. So did my father! I'm going to get them reduced. We can pay for it. Can't we? You see how I've cleaned up the room, darling?"

She tried to pry his lips apart with her tongue, failed, and tossed a hand into the air. "I draw the line at playing touch football, like my father hoped I would after my brother went lame. But, sure, we'll get a dog. Would you go for a pit bull instead of a dalmatian? Meredith has a pit bull named Saint Paul."

Derek wiped his forehead. His nose had dried but the pain in his groin had spread to his belly, and his back had begun to ache. Saliva flooded his mouth. He swallowed. "Dogs give you asthma," he managed. He sidestepped to the chair, longing to lie down.

"We're a couple, Derek. Couples cooperate. I'll get an inhaler and maybe you'll finally go get your front windshield fixed."

"No way. That windshield says everyone I know has gone crackpot."

He felt dismayed at seeing her ape his dead sister and averted his eyes to the table, spotting for the first time Heather's poem about the rag doll. The two pages she'd torn from her notebook at The Teahouse lay half under Natalie's health-supplements catalog. He grabbed them up. "What are these out here for?"

"I cleaned the whole house for you, Derek. Including your office."

"I've told you not to mess in there."

"I didn't mess, I dusted and vacuumed."

"Stay out of my space!" He arched his spine against the pain. Maybe he'd better go see the chiropractor whom Chad called his best customer for bowls.

"Who wrote that nonsense about a waterlogged doll drowning in the Rio Grande?"

"It's not nonsense."

"And that's not a man's handwriting."

"No kidding."

"So Chad's right! This cap's too damned hot." She plucked it off, liberating her shoulder-length hair.

"What do you mean, Chad's right?"

The ends of her hair quivered. "That you're seeing someone. Who is she, Derek?"

His fingertips went cold and he curled them into his palms. "I'm helping a person with some poetry and it's none of your concern. But it's my concern that you and Chad are talking behind my back."

"We can do whatever we want."

"That's it! I'm looking for my own pad tomorrow."

"Pad?"

"Apartment, quarters."

"You're—

"Ending this marriage."

"No!" Her eyes became slits. "You're making me sick, Derek." She staggered back until the wall braced her.

"You make me sick. From now on, everything you spend on that fat neocon Rapture-monger, thinking she's helping you get better, is your expense."

"I'm not—"

"I can't hear you."

She coughed. "I've changed my mind. I'm not seeing Meredith anymore. I'm sticking with Yuri."

He glanced at the gold-plated studs the acupuncturist had punched into her right ear. "Whatever you and Chad are up to isn't enough? You know what you are, Natalie? You're a floozy."

Vising her skull between her thumb and little finger, she started chuckling. "Floozy," she managed to repeat.

"It's not funny."

"I'm sorry." She pushed herself from the wall, unable to stop the laughter from rising. She stepped over the fins of the heat register, swiping at the wisp that had fallen over her forehead, and marched across the oak planks to the floor lamp. Its tin shade funneled light onto her new painting.

Pink and orange ruffles of begonia blossoms and the five-petaled reds of hibiscus filled the canvas. Among them at the lower left nestled the face of a woman ringed in curls who reached toward the face of a man directing a hatchet at her. Her smile seemed to welcome the blow. An eye, lashed and browed and three inches across, stared at the viewer from the upper right.

"What I'm doing, behind your back," Natalie said, "so you can process it while you're looking for your pad, is taking this painting to Chad tomorrow for his appraisal. He's offered to talk to his gallery about giving me space."

Derek reached to press his hand to his spine. "Of course you have no inkling that Abigail's leaving him."

"What?" she frowned. "Leaving him? It's Abbie you've been seeing?"

"Get a grip, Natalie."

"That shit about the drowning doll's not Abbie's?"

"She's no writer."

"But she's leaving Chad?"

"I just told you that. You had no idea of course."

"No, I didn't!"

"Chad's learned that the librarian at Kullman has been Abbie's lover for years. The two women are relocating to Maine to start a new life."

"Abbie's gay?"

"That brought a smile."

"Oh, zip it, Derek."

So why four days ago, Natalie brooded, did Chad recoil from her in his gallery's storeroom? Had he lied about his being so damned loyal to Derek? Did Chad simply find her unattractive? In her fancy Chad and Derek loomed as twin balloons, Tweedledum and Tweedledee, rising in bow ties and waistcoats until bang. The shreds lashed her face.

"God help me," she groaned.

She let the Army cap fall to the throw rug, grabbed the lamp pole she'd painted purple, lowered herself to one knee, then the other, and clenched her eyes. Her long lashes curved up from the yellow bags under them.

The thermostat clicked to let more heat rise through the registers as Derek pulled the pages of Heather's poem onto his lap. Right now Heather seemed as much phantasmagoria as Greer. Sneering, he found himself regretting he'd not plunged into the reality of Jan Gray's come-on. "I've got to use the bathroom," he muttered, rising. "I'll sleep on the daybed in my office."

Natalie heaved herself into a sitting position, palms pushing the floor. "When someone needs to retch they go first, Derek." She lurched into the hall, pressing the starched shirt to her tummy.

Christopher drove his BMW into the garage in Rancho Viejo fifteen minutes after Derek had returned home. He punched the remote clipped to his visor, stepped onto the concrete slab, and opened the kitchen door.

The garage light winked out behind him. In the kitchen a

fluorescent bulb turned Primrose's scales a Day-Glo orange as she circled her underwater castle. Why hadn't Heather turned the heat on? Christopher rubbed his palms together and strode into the great room, grateful that he and that poet pest had not had to work out near each other after the asshole emerged from Jan's hideaway.

The black cloth Heather had had a seamstress hem draped Pity's and Merciful's cage on the credenza. Only the lamp beside his mother's photomontage given to bless their firstborn—what a laugh!—lit the great-room's dark.

What sounded like an acoustic guitar drifted from the short hallway opening to the baby's room, the guest bath, and Heather's office ahead. Was someone in there with her? For crap sake, Christopher, get real.

Unable to stop himself, he glanced into the guest bath, pretending that the nightlight wouldn't show the baseboard he'd had to rip off behind the toilet, to expose the brown splotch spreading above it. The mustachioed horse's ass of a contractor refused to return his call? He decided to bug him with back-to-back phone messages before leaving at quarter to six tomorrow morning.

He brought his gaze forward to spot Heather in her chair facing the lit-up cactus garden where she'd buried the horned toad. She sat hunched at her desk in a vest he'd never seen, reds and blacks zigzagging down its back. Over a shorty nightgown? Above work boots? The gooseneck lamp burnished the strands of her lopsided ponytail.

He approached the doorway where Trixie lay curled on the rug that his wife had brought from the guest bath. What a bad mood he was in. He wished a man were with Heather so that he could punch him in the eye. "Out of the way," he snapped, launching the toe of his shoe against Trixie's hindquarters.

Heather whipped around as, with a shriek, the tailless Manx leaped up. From the great room came the lovebirds' squeals, obbligato to the strumming that issued from the CD player perched beside the desk lamp.

"What the hell was that for?" Heather demanded, swiveling toward him. "Yes, I heard you sneaking down the hall. Here, baby." She left her chair, glaring at her husband. The silver stars and gold crescents on her nightgown shimmied as she bent to scoop up her pet.

Christopher straight-armed the jamb, his right hip jutting toward his wife.

"You know what?" she said, returning to her chair and stroking Trixie's fur. "You're as mean as the little boy who'd shoved a pencil into her eye two weeks before we brought her home. If we were ever to have children, I'd pray for girls."

"That's some costume," Christopher said. "Halloween's five months away." He stooped to pluck up a tangle of cat fur and stuck it in the pocket of his T-shirt. "Why aren't you catching up on work that pays? You had that *Poet's Handbook* out when I left two hours ago."

"So?" She stared at Christopher's combed eyebrows and the crew cut he gelled each morning. How she wished Derek would phone, tell her that the line, "Her rouge ran down like rain" or "Raggedy as a fledgling," —or any line in her poem—stirred him.

Christopher tucked his fists into his shorts. "Look, I'm sorry. But as long as we're together, I expect certain basics. Dinner when I get home, for one. My work slacks creased. And your share of keeping our income stream flowing. We've got a monster mortgage to whittle down. Even showing me something sexier than that. He thrust his open palm at her.

"Get lost, Christopher."

"We've got to discuss some things. It's too cold in here."

"Go put on your robe."

They held each other's stare as the CD of guitar music ended. The great room had grown silent as well. He turned to go, then turned back. "I take it you're not planning to follow through at the gym."

"The owner's son's too oily for me. I'll stay in shape walking and gardening." As she reached to knead her neck, Trixie jumped off and hopped toward her basket, pausing to lap water from her bowl. "You through talking?" Heather asked.

"How long can we keep this up?"

"This? Meaning?"

He dipped his head to the side. "Staying together."

"Without counseling, maybe a week. I'm making a trip to Genesure next Wednesday. I'll add a couple of days to explore San Francisco. It'll give us a chance to think."

He gazed out at the cactus she'd planted—hen-and-chicks, teddybear cholla, strawberry hedgehog, porcupine prickly pear—and remembered how she'd squeezed his hand just a month ago, leading him along the S-shaped path and sharing the plants' names.

He blew out his breath, moved to her rocking chair, and sat.

"Afraid I'm going to leave you before you leave me, babe?"

"Where'd you get that poetry book, anyway?"

"I might have bought it, you know."

"But you didn't."

Why lie, she asked herself? "I was talking to a man near Canyon Road who carves bowls. A friend of his is a poet. He lent it to me. You think I'm shacking up with him, maybe?"

"Oh, c'mon, Heather!" He paused, thinking back. "This poet isn't that guy at the gym, is he?"

"What guy?" How she hoped he'd not seen her talking to Derek near the entrance doors, the night Christopher had lain beside the trampoline with a hurt knee.

"Forget it, I can't picture you wanting to spend time with that asshole."

Both startled as her desk phone rang. She twisted her face toward it.

"Not going to answer that?"

She bit the corner of her lip. "Someone at Genesure working

overtime. Voice mail's got it. Why are you sitting there? Don't you have to leave early tomorrow?"

"Same as every morning."

"If you can't read yourself to sleep with one of those counterterrorism workbooks you cart home, go bead another pair of moccasins."

He'd half-finished beading the collar of the blouse he'd bought for her birthday next month. He felt like throwing it into the garbage. "Right now I'm trying to figure a way out of this mess."

"Wishing you'd never divorced Jessie?"

"Quit it, Heather!"

"Then quit hounding me. I'll turn into a worse alcoholic than she was."

"I think we should try counseling."

"You'd never stick with it."

"You don't know that."

"Go away, go away, go away!" She paddled the air as if demonstrating the breaststroke. "And fold out the sofa bed again. Your snoring's gotten unbearable."

He stood shivering in his shorts, feeling as if caught in a riptide. "It's because I've got too much on my mind. Mother's dizziness—"

"She's just not used to the elevation."

"Maybe. That and our own fucking situation; my dad's moods; that Hispanic contractor's chow uprooting Dad's roses; and now my team needs to come up with a chemical grenade to flush the Sunnis out of caves north of Baghdad. So our interrogators can force them into telling lies by shoving a nozzle up their asses. Or rolling them in a drum with broken beer bottles."

"Ugh! I don't want to hear about your job."

"I've got to talk to someone."

"No way that's going to be me, babe."

MUSICAL CHAIRS
THURSDAY 19 MAY 2005

Natalie spotted workmen in hard hats and orange vests peering into a hole jackhammered in the parking lot that fronted Dr. Yuri Livnat's office. Like what's happened to my life, she thought. Above her, clouds scudded across a cerulean sky. She left her van under a cherry tree and stepped out. Blossoms blew past her shoulders. Though she'd left the traffic noise of St. Francis Drive behind, she clamped her ears as a backhoe dropped chunks of asphalt into the bed of a pickup nearby. An empty can of Bud Light rolled against her sandal.

She hurried from the din to the acupuncturist's door, anklet tinkling and blue jay feather swinging. She turned the knob and walked in.

A surprised Yuri jerked his face away from the seated nurse's. His mass of black curls jiggled as he straightened. He brushed his palms down his lab coat and examined his watch. "Fifteen minutes early, Mrs. Natalie." He backed from the desk toward the glass-topped table holding magazines and extended his right arm. "Welcome to getting better. That's a beautiful outfit to match a beautiful Thursday."

Blushing, Natalie looked down at her yellow art jacket that exposed two inches of belly above fitted jeans. After lunch it had taken her twenty minutes to decide what to trade her bathrobe for.

"One for you?" Yuri extracted a twist of red licorice from a coat pocket.

She shook her head. For today's appointment she'd even decided not to chew gum.

"Not feeling well, shiksa? But I see that all three ear studs have stayed in place. A good sign!" His silver necklace shook over the hairs darkening his collarbone as he bit off an end of the twist. "Jolly will get you ready."

He'd half turned toward the hallway's entrance when Natalie blurted, "Yuri?"

"Yes?" He faced her and threw his cleft chin forward.

"Is that receptionist's position still open? I'm going to need some income. Last night my husband told me he wants out."

"Oh, how awful!" The nurse reached past the edge of her desk to touch Natalie's arm.

"Perhaps this change will mean less pain for you?" Yuri asked. "Let's see how we can help. Jolly can tell you about the job opening and please enjoy the lavender she's brought us from her garden."

He vanished past the hall's archway.

Natalie had been relishing his musky scent, so the sprays of lavender perfuming the room came as a surprise. But it was the crash of asphalt on the window's other side that made her jump.

"Another break in the water main," Jolly said. "That's twice in five weeks. The landlord tells us the pipe is twenty-five years old. Ouch!" She twisted the embroidered sunflower she'd pinned to her white blouse. "A gift from the doctor. Sometimes the catch pricks."

Natalie pressed her palm to her jacket, hoping to slow her heart. "Jolly, what about the job?"

"Oh, sure. Ten dollars an hour to start, eight to four-thirty, Monday, Tuesday, and Thursday. Limited health benefits kick in after twelve weeks. Your take-home works out to a little under a thousand a month."

"That may not be enough. I'll know more after talking to a friend this afternoon who hopes to get my acrylics into his gallery. When do you need an answer?"

"We have two other applicants. Are you familiar with Excel?"

Natalie shook her head.

"Can you type?"

"A little."

The nurse puffed out her already-plump cheeks. "I'm not sure. But let's get you started healing."

In the procedure room she wrote down Natalie's weight and blood pressure and left. Now Natalie sat barefoot beside the pillows on the edge of the padded table. She faced the glass-fronted cabinet that dominated the room and listened to the jackhammer breaking up more pavement. Suddenly she linked Yuri in his lab coat with the attendants who, thirty years ago, had arrived two weeks after her mother called the cops. Her father had been "having relations with" his secretary on the dining-room rug. Or so her mother kept insisting from inside the sanatorium.

Natalie's left temple started to throb. By the time Yuri strode in she was trembling. This man must take care of her! Carrying his clipboard and chewing his licorice, he approached the cabinet and removed the tray of throw-away gloves, stainless-steel needles, and the battery-operated console sprouting red and green wires.

"No need to insert more ear studs," he announced, washing up then heading toward her. "Unbutton, please, and on your back. Place the pillows under knees and neck."

She felt a buzz in her crotch. She started to free the loops from her jacket's silver buttons, then exclaimed, "Yuri!" and goggled up at him.

"What is it?" He had set the tray on a chair and, gloved, was ripping the polypropylene wrap from the first needle.

"I have to tell you something."

"Do so, please."

"I've known for a long time that my husband had tired of me. He writes poems. I'm a painter."

"These are big differences?"

"They've come to be. There's something bigger." She loosened her jacket's third loop.

"Yes?" He bent to place the half-exposed needle on the tray.

She turned from his gaze to focus on one of the vinyl tiles. "I may be falling in love with you, Yuri."

"Meshuga." He cleared his throat.

"What's that mean?"

"It's Yiddish for 'crazy'."

"Crazy is right! Remember last week after you'd hooked up the needles and left? And came running back when I screamed? It wasn't because I'd had a nightmare about my husband. It was because . . ." She drew in air and stopped.

"Go ahead." He took the chair and set the clipboard and tray across his thighs.

"Because . . ." She freed the remaining loop and clasped the jacket's flaps to keep her breasts hidden. "Because I fantasized that you loved me. Cherry blossoms rained on us, Yuri. I, well, had an orgasm, and wrenched my head around, and jammed a needle into my scalp."

"It's time you stopped coming here, shiksa."

"No! I want to work with you. Jolly can teach me the computer skills. I'm smart, Yuri. And suppose we are compatible. Let's find out, why not? You'll be glad."

"Impossible." He shook his curls and stood up.

"But why? Don't you like me at all?" She released the jacket and grasped her throat. With her other hand she held onto the pad's edge.

He circled the table's end in his custom-made boots, dropping his gloves and the exposed needle into a wastebasket. "I am privately involved with two people now and need a third like a hole in the head." He shoved the tray onto a shelf and clacked shut the cabinet's door. "Jolly will help you dress."

"She's one of them, isn't she?"

He hauled open the room's door. "Jolly!"

"Does she know about the other?"

"Don't make me phone the police, Mrs. Natalie. There'll be no charge for this afternoon."

"You bastard!"

Lab coat flapping, he disappeared.

She hurled the cylindrical pillows after him. They skidded across the floor as the nurse filled the doorway, sunflower pin askew. Jolly stooped to pick them up.

"I don't need your help dressing. God, it's hot in here!" Natalie pressed both temples, eased herself from the table, and began to fasten her jacket's buttons. "He's cheating on you, Jolly, do you know that?"

The nurse's broad forehead wrinkled, turning the mole over her eyebrow into a sliver. She reached back to click the hall door shut.

"He's sleeping with someone else!"

"He told you?"

"He implied it—don't you care?"

"What do you think?" Jolly returned the pillows to the table and patted them as if they'd fluff up. Her double chin wobbled under lips rouged as heavily as Natalie's.

Natalie slipped one high-heeled sandal on, then the other, and moved close to the nurse. The warmth Jolly radiated calmed her. "Why do you keep on with him?" Natalie looked down into the shorter woman's eyes.

Jolly scratched a rash on her forearm. "Doctor Livnat's AC/DC. He spends a couple of nights a week with his realtor cousin who talked him into leaving Israel. Look, I'm gonna tell him I need to leave early. Let's go find us a couple of gin-and-tonics. The first round's my treat."

"Oh, Jolly, I can't!" Natalie wheeled to throw both arms around her, pressing her own to the nurse's ample breasts. She released Jolly as if the other's thumping heart were a bomb, and ran to the window ledge to grab her purse.

"Mostly what I love to do is moosh the colors around," Natalie said to Chad an hour later. "So you honestly like the new painting?"

They had turned onto Calle Corvo from Delgado near Canyon Road, strolling back to Chad's home two long blocks away. Corner clumps of chamisa spread their faint scent of turpentine. The wind had died, and to the east, cotton-ball clouds dappled the Sangre de Cristos. Chad had traded his garage-shop dungarees for knee-length shorts. A cell phone hung from his belt.

"That knife blade glinting among the blossoms in your painting creates a leap forward in impact," he told her, his voice a rasp smoothing hardwood. "I know Buddy at the gallery'll want to see it. When will you have more?"

She pushed the bridge of her sunglasses against her nose with her forefinger, trying—because of her headache—to shut out more light. "I'm not sure, Chad, I'm so unhappy. And how pathetic is that in the middle of all this beauty?"

They could hear the pickups and SUVs negotiating Canyon Road and Paseo de Peralta. But the old Russian olive trees behind ivy-matted walls, the wooden gates, the occasional pots of geraniums, gave this half block of Calle Corvo a peacefulness that Canyon Road and its lilacs no longer had.

Chad pulled the brim of his sombrero down against the sun. "So your acupuncturist's nurse says he's bisexual? Too many surprises, aren't there? Only forty-eight hours ago Abbie informed me she's gay and plans to hightail it to Maine with her hiking pal."

Natalie guffawed, grateful that she still had laughter in her. "Sorry, bud, I win. It's less than twenty-four hours ago that Derek told me he's splitting. And has been seeing someone, just like you hinted Saturday."

"Actually," Chad said, "she's the second woman Derek's gone loony tunes over in the last couple of weeks. No doubt there'll be more."

"The second?"

"The first is the librarian at Kullman College, Ab's hiking buddy."

"She's Abbie's lover?"

"Yep."

"Oh, God, everything's so tangled. What about the other one, do you know her?"

"She knocked at our door last week, gaga over a bowl of mine she'd seen at the gallery."

"The bowl I liked?"

"That's my memory. She wanted to show me a poem she'd written about it. Derek had come over to tell me how miserable he's been. We'd invited him to stay for lunch."

Natalie ducked under a branch of a locust, rattling a couple of seedpods. She shook out her hair. "Don't tell me what she looks like, okay? Maybe Derek's and my splitting is for the best. Less pain, like Yuri said." She chomped her half stick of spearmint. "I've told you that our sex life sucks and you know what? I've never been able to make heads or tails of his poems. Listen to this: 'How would we play, careening between the jaws or scrambling in the cavern of the brain.' What does that mean?"

"Can't tell out of context."

"The rest was no help. I found it on his desk while I was vacuuming. So now starts your and my search for divorce lawyers."

The cracked sidewalk ended. He took her elbow as they stepped into the street. "Watch the busted bottle."

They skirted its brown shards. She wished she'd thrown her walkers into the van. On the undulating asphalt her sandals were making her feet ache. "I'm just afraid I'm bad company," she said. "My head hurts terribly."

"Those Advil I gave you before our walk didn't help?"

"A little."

He slipped his arm through hers and without thinking she pressed it to her ribs.

"I thought in the gallery storeroom that you didn't like me very much," she said.

"Why?"

"You backed away at the end."

"Because of my friendship with Derek. I told you that."

"You've changed your mind about him, then?"

"I love hearing those ankle bells tinkle," he replied.

"Want to know why I wear them? To get men to look at me. I'm sure no man would bother otherwise. Would you?"

Before he could respond, she asked, "What does your taking my arm mean, Chad?"

"I'm not sure yet. Too many changes coming too fast. I know I find you intriguing."

"You do?" Feeling her cheeks warm, she stepped ahead to pass between a parked truck and a crevice where the asphalt had split open. She skipped back toward hollyhocks soaring along the curb. A maroon sedan zipped by.

"I do. Even so, what I told you in the storeroom remains true. I've been obsessed with woodworking since hanging around my grandpa's shop up in Missoula. I worshipped the old guy. My dad ran a Texaco station seven days a week and evenings he pampered a hothouse full of orchids instead of me."

"Where was your mom?"

"Most of the time sick in bed with sciatica. Forty years later, all I long to do is shut myself in the garage and, trying to create beautiful things, relieve my growing distress about being in the world. That gnawing to push the world away, feel joy rush in—you must know it. If I lost my hands I'd lose the reason to get out of bed. Mostly I love carving bowls, their simplicity. The dark loveliness of mesquite burls, myrtlewood's golden streaks . . ."

She paused on a patch of gravel and risked taking his hand, relishing his rough skin. His clipped beard sparkled like the aspen leaves behind him.

"What I long to do," she said, "is reveal the world's dark realities in the midst of its beauty. And to teach again, one-on-one to conserve energy. But I also want a soul mate. Is that asking too much? My father hoped I'd become a brother for Sammy. But I yearned to be a man's dance partner, a woman! That's all my mother ever wanted to be. Is that why Dad focused his anger on her breasts? 'Don't ever let a man do this to you, Nattie,' Mother confided the day I started menstruating—and unhooked her bra. I ran to the bathroom to retch. She lived with his beatings until he brought his anorexic secretary home to demonstrate what sex positions pleased him. Isn't that incredible? 'Your in-the-flesh training manual,' he told Mother. She got a big settlement in the divorce but not before her breakdown."

Natalie started to move along the curb toward a house whose oaken gate declared Beware of Dog. But Chad took her elbow again and stopped.

"I need to tell you something."

Her brows lowered past the rims of her sunglasses. She tugged at the long bill of her cap and faced him.

"Two days ago just before Ab trashed my shop . . ."

His cell phone dinged and he hauled it from its holster. The voice was Abigail's.

"I'm on my way in Greer's van to pick up my clothes. You okay with that?"

"Is she with you?"

"No. What's it matter?"

"Are the dogs with you?"

"No, why?"

"I'm nervous."

"You suppose I'm not?"

"Are you still sore? From the kick, I mean?"

"Make a guess."

"I feel pretty bad about that, Ab. Just your clothes, right? You're not planning more mayhem?"

"Clothes and my computer, and the folios, unless you've destroyed them."

"I haven't touched your photos."

"You know I'll pay for the equipment in your shop."

"You sure as hell will!"

At the click he sucked in his breath. Squinting, he clenched his jaw and strode past Natalie.

She caught up with him as Calle Corvo curved left toward Atalaya Elementary's chain-link fence and the basketball poles beyond. "What's that about a kick, Chad?"

"Okay, look, I'm no angel. After you said how your father hit your mother, I decided I'd better tell you the whole story about what happened Tuesday. As Abbie was running toward the shop, she fell and I kicked her."

"I don't believe you."

"I connected with one of her breasts."

Natalie gasped and slowed behind him.

Sawing his upper teeth across the hair on his lower lip, Chad waited for her on the corner of Acequia Madre. Motor oil splotched the asphalt in front of him. Ten feet to his left, on the road's other side, a sign marked Dead End announced his own street, San Antonio. He pulled back as a Pontiac hauling a flatbed loaded with steel posts jangled by.

She followed him across runoff from the city's reservoir that gurgled through a corrugated drain beneath a little bridge. Separated by fifteen feet, they emerged from under a cottonwood and headed along the dirt road toward Chad's.

He paused until she reached him. "If you and I are going to build a friendship," he said, "I thought we should start getting our secrets out of the closet. I guess you gathered that Ab's heading over here to collect her clothes and photos. Oh, nuts!"

"What?" She grabbed his wrist but, worried now that she'd better stay cautious, released it. They were passing the split rail that guarded the blossoms and red leaves of an ancient weeping cherry. A Townsend's Solitaire warbled from one of its branches.

Chad threw a hand toward his adobe home at the end of the block. "That's Meredith Dewsbury's pickup in front of your van. I forgot she's been scheduling Thursday afternoons for carving lessons."

"Chad, I'm not sure I can handle it. At our last session she put the make on me."

"Yeah? No surprise there. Maybe she's waiting outside my shop and you can drive off before she comes round or Ab shows up."

"Let's hurry."

Natalie forced herself to match his stride. The last yellow sprays of forsythia fronted the home of the neighbor who had tracked down the drill press crafted in Czechoslovakia. It still lay on its side in Chad's shop.

"That's Saint Paul!" Natalie exclaimed, pushing at her sunglasses.

"Who? Don't freak me out. This neighborhood's already become a never-never land."

"In the front seat, Meredith's new pit bull mix, Saint Paul the Apostle."

"Perfect! I'm glad her window's up."

"He's a fraidy cat, Chad."

Breathless, they arrived at the adobe.

Natalie heard the crunch of shoes before she saw the life coach striding around the corner, cradling an odd-shaped hunk of wood.

"What're you doing here?" Meredith bellowed, moving close.

Natalie tried to keep her voice calm. "We've been discussing the new painting I told you about Monday."

"Going to get snarled up with Mr. Chad Hopp despite my warning? Your funeral, missy. We ready to begin, señor?" The wooden crosses on her bracelet clacked as she rotated her forearm to glare at her watch. "You're late."

"The shop's a mess, Meredith. Maybe we ought to—"

"No sir!" She planted her ridge-soled shoes beside the jonquils and hefted the block of walnut in front of her face. Its curves bore chisel marks. "Brutalized Eve needs to emerge. You see her begging us to get her anguish right today? In a month I'm lighting out for California and gotta learn as much as I can double-quick. My tools are in the truck."

She thumbed her remote, unlocking the pickup's doors.

"Don't let your dog out," Chad said. "A pit bull ripped my wrist open once."

"He's not my worry much longer." Meredith's fingers, nails bitten to their quicks, curled around the truck's door handle. "Gotta return him to the shelter by five. This little chickenshit is about as dangerous as Lazarus dead."

"You're taking Saint Paul back?" Natalie asked.

The piebald mutt had risen to claw the driver's window, his slobber dribbling down the glass. A fold of flesh dropped over one eye.

"Like I said, lady."

"Let me have him."

"I thought dogs gave you asthma."

"I don't care, I want him, Meredith."

"Good Christ, he's yours, though you may have to readopt the flea-bitten hair ball. Now who's this coming, complicating things?"

A white Chrysler minivan flaunting a bashed-in front bumper rattled toward them.

"That's Abigail!" Meredith blurted. "What'd she do, buy herself new wheels?"

The minivan squealed to the left into Chavez Lane and swung around in a horseshoe, stopping catercorner to the life coach's pickup and Natalie's blue van. Across the lane, lace curtains parted and the triangular face of the old man who'd rescued Abigail two days ago appeared.

"That's not Abbie's car, it's her lesbian lover's," Chad informed Meredith.

Abigail clambored out and stared at the three of them, palms planted on hips almost as beefy as the life coach's.

Meredith lumbered around the hood of her truck. "What's this about you and a lover? You're not cutting loose on your own? I've been cranking up to talk you into heading west with me."

Abigail responded by high-stepping over the grape hyacinths onto the red-dirt path. She faced her husband. "You and your best friend's wife, ChaCha? That was fast."

"She—"

"Forget it." Abigail twisted back. "Hello, Meredith. Lesson time? Good luck in the shop."

"I told her it's trashed," Chad said behind Abbie.

Meredith clamped Abigail's arm. "Say, you been deceiving me, lady? There's another woman in your life?" Meredith's bosom swelled.

Abbie jerked toward the steps, ear hoops swinging. "I don't have time to explain—go ask him." She flipped her thumb toward Chad.

"You're ordering me? You nympho, false Jezebel, mealymouthed hypocrite, Machiavellian crock of shit." Meredith waved her arm and the old man across the lane yanked his curtains shut. "Atheists! All of you! Judas Iscariots, devil-worshipping swindlers, Pharisees, idolaters, smooth-tongued perjurers . . ."

"I'm history," Natalie whispered to Chad.

"Go fast," he whispered back.

Natalie ran the few paces to the pickup, flung the door open, and reached for Saint Paul. He leaped into her arms, short tail a blur. The chain fastened to his collar clanked against the gearshift. "Umph," she grunted, kissed his massive jaw, and rushed him to her van.

She gunned the engine. Dirt spewed from under the rear bumper as she accelerated toward Acequia Madre. In the mirror she saw Chad at Meredith's back, immobilizing her with a bear hug, while Abigail hurried between the bushes of yellow roses and up onto the porch.

STOP RIGHT THERE
FRIDAY 20 MAY 2005

At noon the following day, the year's hottest so far, Heather saw Derek's Neon sitting empty beside the bicycle racks of Monsignor Patrick Smith Park. She spotted him staring down the bank of the Santa Fe River, hands clasped behind his back. As she neared the park's entrance, a gust billowed cottonwood fluff and the creamy seeds of Chinese elms up from the curbs of East Alameda.

Heather turned right over the bridge into the graveled lot and stopped next to his car. After he'd phoned two nights ago, would he like the outfit she'd put together from a couple of shops off the Plaza, she wondered?

Thunderheads loomed behind the Sangre de Cristos. The breeze that shook the Russian olives bordering the parking lot ruffled the silk of her new pants imprinted with cattails. For a moment Heather leaned against her hybrid's sun-warmed door, closed her eyes, and filled her lungs with the sweetness of grass wafting from beyond the swings. A ball slapped the backboard closer by. She stepped over a low steel cable and hurried toward Derek. Pulling the linen top taut over her bra, she spoke to his back. "Guess who."

Startling, he pivoted and grinned.

For the first time Heather noticed hairs sprouting from his ears and discovered herself longing to touch them. "Hey, I love that cap!"

He removed it, tilting his head. The bill and crown were black. Turquoise spelled the word Slaphappy across its front. "Can you believe it?" he asked. He pointed down at the yard-wide pretend river gurgling past the boulders, coyote willows, and shrubs of box elder toward downtown. Paper cups and beer bottles littered its banks. "It's been seven years since the river's had water. This year Game-and-Fish has stocked it with trout. Hungry? Let's go eat."

He touched her upper arm and started toward their vehicles, his flip-flops smacking bare heels.

"Where'd you ever find those red shorts?"

"Yesterday at Santa Fe Hemp," he said over his shoulder. "I wanted something special for our picnic. I love that get-up you're in."

"I bought this yesterday, too."

"No guilt today?" He crossed the cable and waited for her.

Her happiness and the heat were making her dizzy. "Not so far. You?"

"I've told my wife I'm splitting."

"You didn't say that on the phone!"

"I've retained some sense about what not to leave on voice mail, even though you said it's your own line."

As he unlocked the car trunk, she waved away gnats flitting around her face. He pulled out his backpack, a light quilt, a Styrofoam cooler, and a packet of brown paper. "Here are the two tamales I promised from Johnnies." He handed the packet to her.

She shrugged her shoulder bag toward her back. "They're hot!" she exclaimed. "Let me wrap them in the quilt." She shivered as her fingers brushed his.

"I picked them up ten minutes ago. Let's head over to the elms near Canyon Road."

He led her past twin jungle gyms and a teenager pushing a toddler in a swing. A man in dark glasses and sombrero lounged against the trunk of a cottonwood, watching.

"Oh, God, Derek, look!"

"At what?"

"That little girl. Is she Asian?"

He set the cooler down and, frowning, turned toward her. She lifted her chin toward the furthest of three concrete tables at the park's other end.

A nun in a white wimple and brown dress leaned over a perhaps-six-year-old with pigtails. They looked much like the twin ponytails Heather had gathered her own hair into in grade school. The nun cupped the child's elbows from behind, guiding her through a patch of dandelions. Stays that glinted in the sun rose from the girl's black shoes to under her pinafore. A buckled leather band wrapped each leg below the knee.

"Polio? Is it still possible?" Heather asked.

"She looks Asian. There's a Tibetan community here."

"You have no children anywhere, right?"

"That's right."

"I want kids and I don't want kids. Pets are easier. They're my babies."

"I'd love to own a dalmatian."

She felt impelled to race to her car and drive where? She didn't know—to a ranch that raised dalmatians. Buy him a puppy, tie red yarn around its neck, hurry back, offer it to him. Instead, she said, "Listen, what's that bird?"

"A chickadee? There's a flicker, you see?" As a motorcycle roared out of the parking lot, he pointed to the bird with rusty head and black bib that had landed on an elm's low branch. Its breast of polka dots heaved and stilled.

They proceeded through weedy clumps of foxtails to the green slope abutting the path that issued from Canyon between lengths of chain-link fence.

"How's this?" he asked.

"Oh, yes!" She smoothed out the quilt and, kneeling, set down the parcel. He overturned the cooler's cover and took out minibags of salt-free tostada chips, plates, napkins, stainless-steel knives and forks, and a couple of Granny Smiths he'd washed after Natalie had left that morning to get her hair cut. He sat cross-legged, feeling the perspiration cool the creases under his knees, and waved a fly away. He screwed the caps off the bottles of green-tea cola and handed Heather one.

She folded her legs to the side, fanned herself with her floppy straw hat, replaced it at a slant, and started peeling paper from the tamales. "Ummm, these smell lovely!" She placed the bulging corn husks on plates he extended.

He gave hers back with an apple and chips. "So many foxtails. We're sailing in a sea of them."

"And wild roses. See? Up against that wall?"

Over his shoulder he glanced at the thicket of tiny pink blossoms. He pulled the strings from his tamale and bit off an end. "Nobody can beat Johnnies."

"I wonder if we've ever been in his store at the same time and never knew it."

"You come up here often?"

"My in-laws are building a retirement place about a mile away, near Kullman College."

He blinked at her, dappled in shadows from the elm canopy. He sighed.

"What's the trouble?"

"I'm leaving home and you're not."

She started to answer but he said, "Let's talk about your poem."

"Okay. Be gentle."

He unzipped his backpack, pulled out the two lined pages she'd given him at The Teahouse, and laid them next to his plate.

She fingered the beads of coral and turquoise on the necklace she'd bought yesterday, waiting.

"Do you read aloud after you've composed?" he asked.

"No, why?" She lifted her tamale. The tang of chile flooded her mouth.

"Think of the words as musical notes and you as their singer. The more you practice, the more the words you put together will sound euphonious or harsh, whatever you intend. You've got the gift, Heather. Here," he pointed, "where your doll slips—mud, malodorous, manic, misfit—nice alliteration. And your vowel sounds where the snow goose spirals down—altogether, balked, shock—great assonance. Do you have a thesaurus?"

"*Roget's International.*" She ripped open her bag of chips. "I use it to draft marketing copy, mainly for my biotech client in San Francisco."

"Your use of image verbs is strong."

"Image verbs?"

"The motors that rev everything up. 'Raggedy thrashed the reeds, desperate to locate the nest.' What if you'd written instead, 'Surrounded by reeds, Raggedy felt desperate to locate the nest.' No image verb. Wordy. Faulty rhythm. Limp," he smiled, remembering his encounter with Jan two days ago.

"What's so funny?" Her ponytails stirred as she raised her chin.

"Someday maybe I'll tell you." He tore open his bag of chips with his teeth. "Right now I can show you how to strengthen the poem, if you like."

"Of course I would! How?" Her heart raced as she realized that though his eyes were gray and hers were green, her brown hair matched his exactly. She drew her fist down one of her ponytails.

"Similes and metaphors boost a poem's impact." He lifted the pages. "Yours uses similes: 'Her rouge ran like rain' and 'raggedy as a fledgling.' Metaphors are stronger because they don't need prepositions. For instance, 'Desire's brambles' or 'iron will.' Add three metaphors to your poem and let's talk again. And see if you can use smell and, even better, touch. They're stronger than sights or sounds."

She longed to spring up and embrace him, run her fingers through the hair curling on the right side of his head. She took a deep breath, held it, let it go, and dug *The Poet's Handbook* out of her bag. "I ordered my own copy from Amazon the night you called." She handed it to him. "Derek?"

"Yes?"

"Look at all the fluff floating down. Pinfeathers."

"Metaphor," he laughed, pointing his finger at her.

"Let's both write a poem about it, okay?"

"We can try."

For a moment they listened to the shouts of two couples tossing a Frisbee near the river. Along the path off Canyon came another couple pushing what looked like twin boys in a green stroller.

"Think of the reality those kids are growing up to face, Derek. Global warming's going to be worse than the Black Death."

"Why I write poetry." Derek crunched a bite from his apple.

"Derek?"

"What?"

"Does your wife know we're together?"

"I told her I'd be gone all day looking for a place to rent. This morning I found a studio apartment in that building over there." He swung to point at a two-story adobe on Canyon. Three brick-silled windows flamed in the sun. "It's shabby but I'm starting to miss deadlines in my indexing jobs. I've got to get situated."

"It's a great location."

"True."

"Derek?"

"Yes?"

"I want to learn more about your wife. I want to know how you met." She brushed a gnat from her arm, wiped her forehead with her wrist, and took another bite of tamale.

He sighed. "I'd lost faith in my ability to craft poems that seemed to matter and discovered a fascination with the subtlties watercolors are capable of. Natalie taught a course in technique at the community college."

"Natalie. It's a pretty name."

"We did fine for a while."

"What happened?"

Should he mention his wife's jealousy of his dead sister? No. "Natalie became a hypochondriac," he said. "And she may be having an affair with the man you met last week, whose bowls you called 'poems in wood'."

"But you told me he's your best friend!"

"I don't know. How about you and your husband, how did you meet?"

"Professor of chemistry at the University of Oregon. I was editing the customer newsletter for a biotech start-up in Menlo Park. We'd both signed on for an art-therapy weekend at Port Townsend. Afterward, we started e-mailing each other. But this may crack you up—guess who I've bonded with most over the four years we've been married? His mother." She bit into her apple and wiped her lips with her napkin.

"At least you've found someone in the family to relate to."

"She's such an optimist, Derek. Global warming, AIDS, the disaster of Iraq, preparing Los Alamos for more pit production. . . she paddles through it all. Exasperating! And I think I'm going to miss her more than my own mom."

"Then you are leaving!" He bent toward her.

"Oh, boy, how I yearn to! Two nights ago, when you called, I was working on a poem about what it's like flying to San Francisco once a month, stomaching early business breakfasts with the biochemists and marketing types in my major client's cafeteria. Just like Rilke wrote, I tell myself I've got to change my life. Doesn't mean I will. But you know what is true? Oh, bat guano!"

"Bat guano?"

"I just set my elbow in the last of my tamale. At least I missed staining my sleeve. Have you got another napkin?"

She cleaned bits of beef, celery, onions, chile peppers, and cornmeal from her forearm. "What I was going to say is, guess what, we've been here half an hour and nothing really bad has happened. What are you doing?"

He had leaned over the quilt's edge and was pulling up a fistful of foxtails. He stretched his other arm to yank up more, bit off the weeds' heads, spit them onto the grass, and severed some stems in two. "A three-word poem, dedicated to us." He arranged the stems on the checked cotton. THIS IS FUN, the words read.

Heather clapped her hands. "Look at me, I've started crying. I need another napkin."

He pulled one from the cooler and handed it to her.

She snuffled and blotted her eyes. "Give me the rest of those stems." Slowly she spelled out the word HARD, then plucked a sheaf of foxtails from among the tufts of grass, bit off the heads, and in a couple of minutes finished up. HARD TO TAKE, the words read.

He nodded. "Heather? I've just decided I'm going to put myself in therapy."

"Why?"

"You know that story I told you at The Teahouse, about what my sister and I did?"

"How could I forget?"

"I keep missing her."

"You mean sexually?"

"That's part of it. I want to break free. You happen to know anyone good?"

"Good therapist, you mean?"

"Yes."

"Afraid I don't. How many years have you and Natalie been together?"

"Eight. They seem like sixty."

Staring into his eyes, she picked up her shoulder bag. She braced herself on her right palm, raised a knee, paused on the other, and rose. "Your sister and your wife—am I to be the next idol you set on a pedestal? I want to be, of course I do! But not really. That old crone at The Teahouse told me to stick with you. I want her to be right. But as your companion, not your muse."

"Dear Heather." Derek clambered to his knees and gathered up their unfinished colas and plates. "Would you . . .?"

"Yes," she whispered, "I would."

"You don't know what I was about to ask."

"I think I do. I hope so. No one's at our place except the animals. And you could look around the development afterward. I bet rentals down there are a lot less than here."

"All right, Sam Bradford's a smart guy, accept it," Christopher told himself aloud. He lifted the thermos of coffee he'd refilled in Albuquerque forty-five minutes ago from the BMW's cup holder. He tilted it and sucked from its spout. Ten miles from the crest that looked past the rest stop down into Santa Fe.

He wheeled his sedan into the interstate's fast lane to avoid a Buick struggling up Cochiti Grade. Even though he'd shut the windows and turned on the air conditioner, he could hear the Buick's muffler clanking as the BMW roared past. On this unseasonably hot day he remembered seeing snow that morning still mottling the Santa Fe Ski Basin. Maybe he should head there first instead of going home to tell Heather what his new boss had said:

"Chris, I want you to start taking Friday afternoons off. We're not offering this raise and a Section-Two team of eight to a new manager on the brink of a breakdown. Stemming chemical-weapon proliferation is core work at Cholla Labs. Square yourself away."

With the thirty-percent boost in pay Sam had detailed at lunch, Heather could stop working if she wanted. But Christopher felt that couples counseling had become a must.

186

Should he call her? He lifted his phone but, fearful of her retort that the marriage was kaput no matter what, he jammed the phone back into its holder and slowed the car. Sam had ordered him to relax. Yeah, good idea, chill out with a drink and snack up at the Basin.

As Christopher drifted back into the right lane, twenty-five miles to the north Heather swung onto their driveway's pebbles, beeped open the left-hand garage door, and rolled in. Though her chest muscles fluttered, she was determined to pursue romance with a man who actually liked her! Who shared her love of words. She deserved it, damn it all.

Heather had asked Derek to park in the drive. She punched the remote and watched his Neon stop catercorner to her descending door.

She ran into the kitchen and threw her hat onto the doll's hut on the coffee table. Pity and Merciful began squealing. She paused on the foyer's slate to take two big breaths, then opened the front door.

Derek glanced at her and gazed past into the great room. "You and your husband make a lot of money."

"I guess we do." Her belly tightened. "Does it change how you feel?" She shaded her eyes against the glint off the pots of nasturtiums with which she'd lined the porch.

"No."

"So come in."

She stepped aside and closed the door behind them. Sun turned its stained glass oval to a red and violet glow. She faced the birdcage and threw her finger to her lips. "Shhhh, I've brought home a poet."

He pulled a handkerchief from his shorts, patted his forehead, wiped the back of his neck, and looked up at the opaque-glass blossoms dangling from the brass wheel chained to a viga. "That's some chandelier."

"My background's more like yours, although it must not seem so." How she wished he'd wrap his arms around her. "At least the place stays cool when we have a day like this".

He heard a soft growl and looked down. "And who's this?"

"C'mere, baby, meet my friend." Her shirt billowed as she bent to scoop the tailless, orange-and-white Manx into her arms. "Trixie, Derek. Derek, meet Trixie." She cupped the cat's jaw and turned it toward him.

"Her eye's gone!"

"A little boy at the shelter stabbed it out with a pencil."

"The poor animal. Machismo's generic, I guess. Hello, there."

Trixie shrank back against Heather's necklace.

"C'mon, I'll introduce you to my other pets. My husband hates them all. Let's meet the squealers first."

Would he and Heather truly be making love soon, Derek wondered? "That's a big cage," he said.

She pursed her lips to create kissing sounds. A bird started chattering from the miniature ladder's top rung. "That's Pity; blue breast. I think he impregnated Merciful a week ago, it looked like that's what was happening." Should she ask Derek to forgo using one of the condoms Christopher saved to keep himself clean? For the rare times he wanted her during her period? Don't be crazy. She released Trixie and headed for the kitchen. "See my rag doll? Careful of those tiles. They've come loose. The workmanship in this place is pretty slipshod, despite its look of privilege."

Derek's rubber treads slapped the floor. "Hey, wow. Your kitty hops like a rabbit and growls like a dog."

"Isn't she funny? Manxes befriend dogs and they never get fleas. This is Primrose." The goldfish was finning over the Java fern as Heather bent under the sink for a can of chopped liver. She pulled the tab, grabbed a spoon from a drawer, and took Derek's hand.

"This is the baby's room, only my husband can't get me pregnant. Over here meet Ruby and Harold. How are you guys?" She set down the cat food and spoon and left the terrarium's top on the changing table. She lifted out one of the horned toads, tickled its belly, returned it to the sand, and replaced the aluminum top.

"Okay, Trix, follow me. You, too." She smiled back at Derek.

"So this is where you hide out," he said as they entered her office.

"My blue grotto. Where I worked on the drowning-doll poem." She knelt to spoon the mashed liver into Trixie's dish. "Shall we have some music?"

"Let's do that."

"I was listening to Segovia when you phoned." She flipped the player's lid and pinched up the CD. "Trixie may follow us in a minute. She likes to stay nearby when I'm home."

"I've got to use the bathroom a second."

"The guest bath around the corner's a mess. The timber behind the wallboard's started to rot. The master bath's going, too, but not as fast. C'mon."

Heather led him across the great room into their bedroom. Christopher's robe with its University of Oregon duck quacking on the pocket drooped from a hook on the bathroom's half-open door. "There you are," she said.

She flipped the cover of a CD player on her side of the bed, fitted Segovia to the pivot, and turned the volume low.

Don't close the drapes, she told herself and drew her hand back. After their picnic, she yearned to prolong the sense that nature smiled on whatever she and Derek did. The thunderheads that rose smoky and white over the Sandias seemed castles from dreams. Closer by, the mid-afternoon sun made fireflies of the thousand blossoms trembling on the pear trees. Behind them along the backyard fence, junipers and piñons screened the window from joggers using the web of trails.

"Too warm for this," she murmured, turning down the blanket as Derek emerged. "I need a hug."

He came to her and she shut her eyes, luxuriating in the strength of his arms pulling her against him.

"I'll go change," she said.

Was this really happening? He watched the bathroom door close and curled his fingers into his palm to discover that their normally-cold tips were warm. Even his lower back felt fine. He shook off his flip-flops, pulled down the red shorts and his jockeys, and unbuttoned his shirt.

Oh, dear Heather, let this work for us! He filled his lungs, slipped under the sheet, and turned onto his side to stop his erection from serving as a tent pole. "Hello!" he said to Trixie who'd appeared from beyond the bed's iron foot. She lay on his clothes and tucked her front paws under her chin.

"I bought this after I called you last week." Heather approached in her shorty nightgown festooned with silver stars and crescent moons. Hair no longer gathered into ponytails fell to her shoulders. "You like this scent?" She bent over him.

He reached to hold her cheeks and bring her lips to his.

Straightening, she supposed her grin stretched all the way to her ears. "It's called Kiss of the Dragon. Mostly gardenia. Are you a dragon, Derek?"

How could she know he was drafting a poem about dragons from an article he'd read in *The Smithsonian*? "A Chinese dragon," he said, "beneficent, fecund, king of heaven. That perfume of yours is from heaven, too, Heather. Come to bed."

She paused to soak up the sunlight, then walked to the other side and sat. She lifted the gown above her head, shook out her hair, let the satin fall, and opened the bed-table's drawer. "He keeps some lubricant in here but you know what? I'm not going to need it. You'd better use a condom, though. For you I'll bet I'm fertile."

Her fingers touched what felt like the slippery surface of a photograph. She turned to grin before pulling it out—Derek had reached up and was massaging her shoulders. She twisted back. "Damn, will you look at this?"

"What?"

"It's his first wife! He's been getting off gazing at her before he climbs onto me."

The dog-eared, black-and-white image showed a woman standing in slacks, checked shirt, Dutch-cut hair, and glasses, hoisting her breasts for the camera.

"That's it, buster!" Heather ripped the photo in two, reached into the drawer again, and handed a foil packet to Derek.

He placed it on the CD player and rolled back, watching her stretch herself under the sheet.

"Aren't you afraid he might come home early?" He drew two fingertips across the hollow of her neck.

"Never. Seven p.m. seven days a week."

"What about the drapes?"

"No! What we're doing isn't about guilt. We don't need to hide. Besides, the light outside's too glorious. Let's not talk anymore. Just hold me, okay?"

"I want to."

She squirmed close. They shut their eyes. The kiss was drawn out and delicious.

"Oh, God," she whispered, "I'm so happy."

He edged lower, pushing his erection against her nest. "Your breasts feel lovely."

"They're hardly there," she murmured, swirling her hands across his back, marveling that, unlike Christopher's, no fuzz edged his spine. She brought her palms to his buttocks. "Isn't there anything about me you wish were different?"

"No."

"Is it too soon to call you darling, Derek?"

"It's how I've been thinking of you for hours."

He wrapped her shoulder with his right arm. She pulled his pelvis as close as she could while he took her lips again.

The sun variegated their faces, and the rising and falling belly of the Manx, through the massing clouds. They could hear Pity and Merciful squealing merrily from the great room.

As Heather and Derek lay together, Christopher decided the

hell with it, he might as well face his wife early, before he lost his nerve. Having left I-25, he steered the BMW right from Cañada del Rancho and, squinting into the hide-and-seek sun, wheeled past the neighbor's sumacs toward his home half a block away.

Whose wreck was that in the drive, for crap sake? Had Heather finally hired a cleaning woman? He'd seen that cracked windshield somewhere. The car blocked entry into his side of the garage. Bristling, Christopher parked half up onto the buffalo grass that—yes, yes, he'd get to it—needed trimming. He left his jacket and briefcase and laptop on the front seat, intending to bring his sedan in out of the heat, once the housekeeper or whoever it was cleared the driveway. What a relief to shed his shirt and tie, kick off his loafers, step out of the slacks Heather again had forgotten to iron, and flop for a few minutes on their two-thousand-dollar Swedish mattress. Then he and Heather would talk.

He climbed out, pulled the knot of his tie loose, and unbuttoned the top of his button-down.

Why did this jalopy strike a chord? Tassels like those on his father's loafers flopped as he plodded over the pebbles toward his front door. He stopped beside one of the Neon's windows and peered in, keys balled in his fist. Three Styrofoam cups lay strewn across the floor. The tan upholstery had ripped above the back seat. Suddenly he stiffened. Next to a cap lettered Slaphappy lay the poetry book Heather had been studying before Christopher had run off to Joe's Diner and the gym Wednesday. Derek Johansen! The poet Jan Gray sucked up to.

His chest knotted as he sawed his lower teeth against the others. He couldn't believe it. Heather had lied to him. Hadn't she sworn Wednesday night that she didn't know this yo-yo? Who last week had warned Christopher not to get 'chummy' with his wife? They were writing together here?

He stood outside and peeked into the kitchen, having meant instead to unlock the front door and shout, "Somebody move that car!" Only the goldfish showed life. He strode past the baby's room to the big window fronting Heather's office. Vacant.

How debasing to tiptoe along the path bordered by Heather's cactuses. He passed the horned toad's tombstone and the door to his own office and glanced in the window. Of course no one's in there, dummy.

Heart, throttle back!

He rounded the corner where Heather's crabapple threw its branches up and slowed approaching the great-room's picture window. He wiped his palms on his slacks and craned his neck to look inside. The lovebirds were hopping from ladder to water dish, down and up. But the sofa bed, the ladder-back chairs at the dining table, and the four armchairs shouted, Not here!

They could be taking a hike. Poets like to tramp about, don't they? His knees began to tremble. Jesus! Did he now have an adulteress to deal with as well as her fucking pets? His teeth scraped each other as he yanked the phone from its leather holster and flipped the cover up. He jabbed his thumb to the Camera ikon, hit the OK button, and inched past the pears to the bedroom window ten feet away. From overhead came the roar of two fighter jets crisscrossing each other's contrail.

He took two more strides and wheeled. The pain stabbing his gut confirmed that he saw what he thought he did.

He gripped his right wrist to steady the camera and snapped a photo, hit the Save button, snapped another, and saved it. Neither Johansen nor Heather noticed. He stumbled forward and rapped the glass, backed off, snapped and saved a third photograph.

At the sound of his knuckles, Trixie leaped from the pile of clothes and streaked through the doorway to the great room. Heather pulled away from Derek, covered her mouth with both hands, jumped from bed, scooped her nightgown from the carpet, and held it to her chest. Through the glass Christopher heard her yell, "Lock the outside door by the drapes!"

Derek peeled off the still-empty condom, threw off the sheet, hurried to push down the door's lever, and thrashed the heavy cotton until his hand found the cord. He yanked it downward.

As Christopher stood goggling at the drapes' gray backing, the sun emerged from a clutch of clouds and beat the back of his neck. He jammed his phone into its holster, shaking beside the spade his mother had left against the stucco. Should he bash in all of Derek's windshields? Deflate his tires? Tear off the bedroom's door and pummel the asshole senseless?

Think, Christopher! If the son of a bitch can't drive away, you can't get into your garage. And what if he pummels you? Keep your head. Sam Bradford expects control. You're the terrorist if Heather files suit because you've broken all her fingers.

But you'd better do something fast or Johansen's long gone.

Yet rather than rushing to the front of the house, he staggered to the piñon that beetles had browned months before. He hung onto a couple of branches and rammed its trunk with his head. The pain thundered through his chest and arms. He butted the trunk again, again, again, and rested his forehead on the bloody bark.

His eardrums clanged and his head throbbed as if a hammer were whacking the inside of his skull. But the pressure behind his eyes had eased. Feeling strangely calmed, he straightened, brushed his palm across his brow, and wiped blood onto his slacks. Control. He closed his left eye and wobbled through the strawberry plants to the far corner of the great room. Just shy of the crabapple, he spied a crumpled wrapper from one of Heather's energy bars and managed to stoop low enough to pluck it from the dirt.

Reaching his office, he fisted his keys from a sticky pocket and tongued lips that now seemed rolls of sandpaper.

He slipped in through the glass door, ordered his hand to shut it, and moved past the rolltop desk his father had bought and had had refinished for his and Heather's move to New Mexico.

The counterterrorist executive soon to manage a crack team

of eight, shown demonstrating control, steadied himself against the jamb that separated his office from the great room. He watched Heather in her nightgown move barefoot behind Johansen out of the bedroom. They paused beside the TV perched on an oak table next to the fireplace.

"All right, yo-yo," Christopher cried out, hoisting his thumb as he used to after school, trying to hitch a ride. "For the next thirty seconds the front door's yours. Not yours, Heather. Return to the bedroom."

"What happened, did you fall somewhere?" She clapped a palm to her mouth.

"Turn around and proceed into the bedroom."

"Don't you lay a hand on her, I'm warning you." Derek said, edging past the doll's hut.

Beneath the birdcage Trixie lay twitching her ears, one, then the other.

"You're warning me?" Christopher guffawed. The pain cracking his head made him wince.

"Touch her and your happy days are gone."

"Out, asshole."

"No way I'm out of your life." Derek passed the entrance to the kitchen and disappeared into the foyer.

Christopher heard the doorknob clack against the wall. A loose tile shifted under one of his loafers as he forced himself to follow. "Crawl back in your hole!" he shouted at Derek's flaming shorts. The door closed.

"I found that photo of Jessie you've been using," Heather blurted.

He pivoted to see her in the bedroom doorway again, pulling at the usual single ponytail she'd gathered her hair back into.

Outside, the Neon's engine raced.

PAIN
SATURDAY 21 MAY 2005

"What a nice surprise that was, stopping for tea at your gracious St. Francis Hotel. Thank you, Chrisy."

"But it's hot in this car, Mother. Let's go on into the gym."

"Not until I discover what you're worried about. I think it must have something to do with those awful cuts on your forehead."

"I tripped over the horned toad's tombstone yesterday hauling gravel for Heather's cactus. I told you."

"And I don't believe you. I never remember your shoulder twitching like that."

"My boss says I'm working too hard."

They sat in the BMW with the windows lowered. Instead of his usual T-shirt, sneakers, and shorts, Christopher wore tooled black boots, wrinkled khakis, and a short-sleeved, checked button-down. His eyes followed an empty water bottle that the four-o-clock wind was rolling toward Johansen's Neon parked three slots away. Just Christopher's damned luck. With that asshole here, how could he endure the upcoming appointment?

He felt his mother's palm settle on his thigh.

"I've been counting on meeting your Jan and Gerry for a week, Chrisy. And seeing what sort of program I might start out with after we leave the Bay Area. But unless you can settle down, you drive me home this minute. I'm your mother and I need to know what's wrong."

"Nothing's wrong!" He stared at her wrinkled neck and at the gray showing in her helmetlike hairdo. He recalled the wedding photo in his parents' bedroom in Palo Alto. Then her hair fell to her shoulders. "The salve that Heather put on my wound," he lied, "stings. Plus I had a long morning at the Labs and now I'm sweltering. So what? I'm relaxing. Can't you tell?" He pulled in air and grasped the door handle.

"First give me a kiss. While I was growing up in Pasadena, my mother insisted I kiss both cheeks whenever I left the house and whenever I came back. To steady us both. I believe I've told—"

"You have, yes."

"I'm hereby reviving the practice with you and Sweet Pea. To bring all of us good luck. The kiss, please, each side."

"Oh, crap, Mother!"

"You see? A bad case of nerves."

He twisted his head and pushed his pursed lips to her cheek.

"The other one, please."

While kissing it, he reached to turn the key in the ignition. He swung from her and fingered a switch near the gearshift to raise the windows.

They climbed out into the afternoon heat. As he beep-locked the doors, she said, "It's an impressive building, but I don't like to see those words spray-canned in red and that scrawl of the man with a knife. Is this a dangerous neighborhood?"

"Taggers range all over the city, Mother. You must have them in Palo Alto."

"Not so violent, I should hope."

Inside, the Beatles were belting out "A Hard Day's Night" through loudspeakers bolted to the gym's ceiling grid. Everywhere evaporative coolers hummed. Near the water fountain, a woman about Sissy's age was attempting partial push-ups. An artery in her forehead bulged. A teenager stood at the wall catercorner to the men's locker room, forcing his shoulders toward the rack of wooden stretch bars, one sneaker lifted to a high rung.

"It certainly smells clean, like a hospital," Sissy said. But Christopher was looking for Johansen. He saw him in back with the barbells and weight trees near the steel door that led to Jan's office. He lay over a physioball, fingers clasped behind his head, raising and lowering his torso. Gerry stood above him gesturing, a toothpick between his lips.

"Chrisy!"

"What?"

"Have you forgotten me?"

"Of course not. There's Jan in Gerry's office."

Jan sat at her son's desk writing. Gerry's full-color photos of TV wrestlers on the attack loomed on the wall. Christopher rapped one of the office's interior windows, waving when Jan looked up.

She hurried out in short-shorts and a lime-green blouse that revealed the top of her sports bra. A red hibiscus blossom perched in her curls.

"Hi! I'm Jan Gray and you must be Chris's mother. Did you fall, Chris?"

"Helping my wife."

"It looks painful. What a gorgeous dress, Chris's mother!"

Sissy clapped her palm to the square-necked bodice of the linen sheath that she'd purchased two days ago, following a phone call about the shop from Heather.

"Are you celebrating—" Christopher started.

"Oh, thank you!" Sissy cut him off in her enthusiasm, coyote earrings swinging.

"And that bracelet and necklace. You've sure enough caught our Santa Fe style," Jan added.

Sissy's turquoise and silver beads rattled as she lowered her hand to her hip. "All from a shop called Originals on the Plaza near the St. Francis Hotel. My daughter-in-law tipped me off about it.

Christopher tried again. "Are you celebrating something, Jan?"

"Me?"

"That flower in your hair."

"Oh, yeah, in fact, I am." The sinews on each side of her neck tightened.

"A birthday?" Sissy asked.

"A favor my son Gerry's goin' to see to this afternoon. I've promised to keep it secret."

"I've a few secrets of my own but there is one I can share. Chrisy's father has informed me that, God willing and the creek don't rise, we may push our move date here to October."

Christopher's left shoulder jerked.

"Chrisy's father and I are eager to be closer to our children." Sissy took Christopher's hand.

Mother, please, I'm not a kid! he fumed in silence, pulling free.

Jan patted his upper arm. "You know, Chris is one of our favorites here. Good-lookin' boy you've got. Some of our gal clients are regretful that he's hitched. You must be proud of the work he's doin' to keep us Americans safe."

"Jan," the woman who had been doing partial push-ups interrupted. Christopher lowered his glance from the woman's cracked lips. "I'm planning a hike with my granddaughter tomorrow and I'm worried. I just picked up some discomfort." She clamped one side of her neck.

"What exercise you on, Lois?"

"Moving to the rings. But this hurts!"

"You go take yourself home and put an ice bag on it and again tonight and that ornery sternomastoid'll be fine, darlin'." Jan reached to pat the woman's rump.

Soon we'll be doing that to each other, Christopher said to Jan in his head. I know Dad's been faithful to you, Mother, and I've managed to stay faithful to Heather. But don't move to Santa Fe early. Everything's about to change and you're not going to like it.

"Chrisy, does your stomach hurt?"

He realized he had placed his right boot in front of him and was leaning forward.

"You okay there, Chris?" Jan asked.

Not until you're underneath me, he thought. "Hunger pang," he muttered, straightening. "Smelling the rack of lamb my wife's serving tonight."

"She is?" Sissy asked. "How delicious!" But the lines at the corners of her eyes deepened.

From the loudspeakers came the Mamas and the Papas crooning "California Dreamin".

"Let's see if I can't catch my son's attention for a sec. We try to turn Jan and Gerry's into one big fitness fun house, and I want him to hear how you think we might be helpful." She waved both arms at Gerry. "Will your husband also be wantin' a program?" she asked Sissy.

"Oh, my, I don't know. I'm not sure that he's ever joined a gym. He may ship his exerciser from California to the home we're building here."

The three of them watched Gerry nod to his mother. He pivoted to face Derek, who had gotten up from the physioball, and pointed to a shiny bar free of weights that lay on the rubber mat.

Gerry crossed the cushioned vinyl, blond curls jiggling. He removed the toothpick as he approached. "Hi, there! Mom said Chris was bringing you along. Welcome to our city different."

Gerry's voice always reminded Christopher of his own squeaking left sneaker.

Jan wrapped an arm around her son's waist. "Pretty pleased with this one. State champ last year, three-hundred-pound clean and jerk."

"I beg your pardon," Sissy said.

"For what?" Jan asked.

"I don't know what—"

"Clean and jerk means? Here you go." Gerry arched his back

and dipped until his knuckles reached his calves. He threw his right leg forward, his left one back, and raised his fists to shoulder height as if they hoisted a steel bar. He brought his lifting shoes together and blew out air. Now, arching his back, he bent his knees again and raised his fists high, once more throwing his right leg out and the other one to the rear.

He dropped his arms, crooked the right one behind him and the left across his belly, brought his shoes together, and bowed.

"Oh, I see, a weight-lifting thing," Sissy said.

Gerry aimed a thumb at Derek. "I'm setting up a clean-and-jerk prep for our client back there right now."

"Liftin's a primo conditioner for any age or sex, you name it. Gerry'll be startin' a program at the gym this summer for elementary-school kids. "

"I'm impressed," Sissy said.

"Mother, this is Gerry Gray. Gerry, my mother, Sissy Ryan."

"Wholly forgot my manners!" Jan exclaimed. "But Gerry's been lookin' forward to meetin' Sissy. May we call you that?"

"Call me what?" Sissy felt herself growing light-headed and hoped it was simply her increasing worry about Christopher and Heather. Never had she heard Sweet Pea say she wanted to attempt something so complex as rack of lamb.

"Call you Sissy," Jan said.

"Well, my real name's Cecilia but everyone does say Sissy."

"Okay if we do that?"

"Oh, certainly."

"And what is it you'd like us to be helpful at?"

"I think I'd like to take off some weight."

"Mother believes she's fat."

Jan and Gerry looked at each other and laughed.

"Actually, it's my husband who's been urging me to begin working out."

"Mother's also getting dizzy spells."

"Now that could be our elevation. Not a long-term problem," Gerry said. "You need six months, usual, to toughen up those red blood cells. Meantime be sure to get down your ten glasses of water a day."

"I'm planning to go for a complete physical after we fly home on Monday."

"Good thinking. Tell you what, Mom. Let's us write out a suggested program for Sissy and have it ready for our buddy Chris to pick up tomorrow. Then her sawbones can have a look-see and we'll modify according to his input. Sound like a plan, Sissy?"

"It's very nice of you."

"Mom here can ask you the right questions. I better hustle back to our client or he'll have himself plumb tuckered out. Focus on his shoulders, right, Mom?"

"Not too much, remember."

"I'm with ya. Good to meet cha, Sissy, and welcome to our lair."

She shook the hand he extended.

Had Christopher seen Gerry wink at Jan? When Christopher stopped by tomorrow, he resolved to invite her to join him for roast duck at Joe's Diner some evening soon.

Derek stepped closer to a cooler at the room's other end. The whirring fins fluttered his shorts. Balls, I'm tired, he thought, eying Christopher follow Jan and the older woman—the mother that Heather claimed she'd grown so fond of?—into the office and shut the door.

He watched Gerry swagger toward him. The trainer was being super-courteous this afternoon. Jan must have realized, after failing to seduce Derek Wednesday, that she and Gerry had better not harass him. In any case, Derek planned to quit the gym, as Jan had urged, at the end of May, when his next quarterly payment was due.

When Heather called this morning to reassure him that Christopher had not hit her, she and he had agreed to meet at their park tomorrow for an early-morning walk. Why did he need to keep proving his prowess here, anyway, maximize his conditioning, as Gerry kept insisting, with weights? Walks were great exercise and cost nothing.

Gerry clapped his shoulder. "Hey, hey, Derek, you all set there? We been working toward this day for weeks, haven't we now? Strengthening that back and those thighs up. If you're ready, let's get the hang of the dead lift today and by next Saturday you're on your way to the C and J. You hear that? I'm rhyming like a poet." He extracted the toothpick from his shirt, shoved it between his lips, and shifted it to a corner. "Go get yourself two fifties and two twenty-fives."

"That much?"

"Do it like I tell you and you bet."

Derek removed two orange and two black weights from the weight tree, set them on the mat, and fitted them to the bar at his feet. "What's next?" he asked. After making love with Heather less than twenty-four hours ago and absorbing Natalie's shrieks this morning, he wondered how long he could keep his eyes open.

"Go on and get some chalk."

Derek trudged to the bin perched on a pedestal, dusted his palms, clapped the excess off, and returned to the bar.

"Squat yourself down and get a good grip."

Derek complied.

"Now don't bend those knees too far. Shoulders rounded but not too much. That's the way. Chin down a teensy bit. Good. Arms in toward the waist. All good. Don't forget to breathe. Now lift!"

"Ahhh!" Derek's chin jerked up as the barbell thudded to the mat. Still in a crouch, he threw a hand behind him. "Oh, God," he groaned.

"Jeez-o, I told you to keep that back arched."

Glaring at him, Derek shuffled toward the chair, palm pressed to the erector muscle at the left of his spine. He started to sit but repeating jolts of pain kept him stooped like an old man.

Gerry lowered his voice. "I'm sorry you didn't hear me there, Derek. Maybe you'd better hustle yourself to a chiropractor fast. No telling how long he'll want you to stay away from the gym. But what a chance to make lemonade."

"Ahhh." The pain shot into Derek's left buttock, causing him to lower his brows until they fringed his eyes. "Lemonade? What are you jabbering about?"

"All those poems you'll have time to write. But you'll leave Mom out of them, right? She says the other day you came on a teensy bit too strong."

"You creep, I'll sue you both."

"Because you heard me wrong? Your call, buddy boy. You see that new sign there? Use Apparatus At Your Own Risk?" He grinned and his toothpick tumbled out, flipping when it hit the bar. He headed toward the door to the hallway and disappeared.

Derek was gasping. He limped across the vinyl, palm pushed to the spasming muscle.

In Gerry's office, Jan brushed her hands down the side of her blouse, stood, and peered through the glass. "Wonder what happened there to Derek Johansen? Looks like maybe he didn't follow my son's instructions."

"Johansen's always been a know-it-all with me," Christopher said.

"I better go talk to Gerry."

"But the poor man!" Sissy exclaimed, rising from a metal armchair. "Look how he's bent over. I hope it isn't serious."

"Ice often helps. These longtime clients who think they know better . . ." Jan wagged her head. "Chris, we'll see you tomorrow, say mid-morning?"

"It's a date." He watched Derek struggle to open one of the outside doors. That takes care of that asshole. Now how to deal with Heather. Christopher, control. Think consequences. But his left

204

shoulder jerked as four words, No Wife No Life, appeared in his mind like a pop-up on his lapotop's monitor. Had he the courage?

"What nice people your Jan and Gerry are," Sissy said in the heat, waiting for Christopher to beep open the BMW.

"I'll start the cold air, Mother." Feeling downright jaunty, he slipped inside and turned on the engine and air-conditioner.

"You must, must, must listen to the experts, not go off half-cocked." She slid onto her seat and closed the door.

He let the engine purr. "Who are you talking about?"

"Anyone at all. Now you listen to me. When we reach home, I want you to come in and nap, even if the workmen are still there. Will you do that for your mother?"

He released the hand brake but before he could reply, she gathered breath for more.

"I'm going to phone Heather to bring that lamb over to our house and I'll fix the trimmings. We have only a couple of days left to spend with you two, Chrisy. Perhaps I'm being selfish but I insist."

He placed fingertips on her wrist, guiding the car with his other hand across the lot toward Zia Road. "Mother, by now she has the whole meal fixed," he lied. "She began after lunch. She'll really be upset if I don't go home. We're trying super-hard to bridge the impasse I told you and Dad about Sunday. We really want a child, okay? For you and us and for Heather's folks. You're already fixing a farewell lunch for her and me tomorrow. Okay?"

"Oh, dear, I don't know. You're my two chicks and you seem so far away."

———————————————

"Crap, look at this mess!" Christopher steered the sedan along the drive past the contractor's revived Dodge-RAM pickup. The driver's door looked new, though the rear bumper hung wired to the bed and the left taillight was still smashed.

A couple of broken windowpanes jutted among empty buckets

of stucco and wallpaper paste above the rim of the green dumpster that Armando had had brought in. Splintered trellises, shards of stucco, and scraps of roofing paper littered the pink gravel beside the path leading to Bill's rose garden.

"Armando and Tony finally got the double-pane or thermopane or whatever-you-call-it windows in," Sissy said. She opened her door. "Oh, gosh! No wind and it's still a furnace out there, even up here in the foothills. All right, we'll expect you and Sweet Pea by eleven tomorrow. Two kisses, please."

A moment later she stood outside smoothing her dress, then bent to peer across at him. "I want you to take a couple of Tylenols and lie down when you get home. I don't like the way those cuts look, Christopher."

"I can't feel them any more, Mother," he lied.

"Hoo-ee!" he heard a woman's voice call as Sissy shut the passenger door.

He steered around the dumpster, watching the woman whose Lincoln Navigator had bashed Armando's truck cross the street. She scurried along the gravel in white shoes and a fluted tennis dress—a widow, he recalled his father saying. She waved as Christopher rolled past. He turned to head down toward Rodeo Drive and the blue-plate special at Joe's Diner.

"May I help you?" Sissy asked, stopping at the bottom of the portal's steps and shading her eyes against the sun. A whiptail lizard scampered in front of her into a patch of groundsel.

"Hello! Is Bill still in?" A sapphire encircled by silver glinted in each ear under her straw hat.

"I'm sure I don't know."

"I wanted to tell him that I've found another of my husband's folders about how to prepare the soil for roses."

"Oh?"

Taller than Sissy, the woman removed her hat and shook out a ponytail streaked with gray that streamed halfway down her back.

She lowered her eyebrows. "I'm sorry, am I disturbing you?" Her baritone sounded like a chain-smoker's. But even in this hot weather she carried no scent.

Go away, Sissy felt like blurting. Instead, she said, "I just got home. Come back, can you?"

"Sure thing. I'm Sheila. And you are?"

"Sissy Ryan, Bill's wife."

"I'll tootle back in a bit, Sissy."

Sissy flashed a false grin, hurried up the front steps, and shoved down the door's cast-iron latch.

She heard Bill's shout before seeing him jump from the armchair near the corner fireplace. He yanked a petit corona from underneath his white mustache. "You're telling me now that the kitchen cabinets are light because they're birch, not maple?"

It must have been for Sheila that, while Sissy was gone, he had changed into those awful yellow shorts and wore loafers without socks. "I've grown used to the cabinets' color, Bill," she called across the rug. "It's fine. And the dishes are already in their places." Let Armando be, she pleaded in silence.

The contractor reached behind his head to remove his cap by its bill, rose from the bear-clawed sofa, and twisted toward her. "Thank you, señora."

He turned again as Bill snarled, "The cabinets are fine as a rat's hemorrhoids. You go out and buy some stain." He shoved the cigar into his mouth, sucked until the end glowed, and pulled it free. "Half my trellises need rebuilding, thanks to the gophers and Baca's chow. Tony's got to dig the basins, the slate capping the mailbox needs cementing, and four of the canales are still missing their sheathing. Plus the grounds need cleaning up. You have until sundown and all day Sunday and that's it! Or I pay you nada." He riffled his fingertips against his thumb. "You clear on that?"

Sissy backed against the Saint Peter carved into the front door. Bill's shorts and yellow knit had started burning her eyes. She shut them, dropped her head, and slowed her breathing, feeling unable to walk to the hall, vanish down it and into their bedroom.

"I understand," she heard Armando say. "Tomorrow my boy will accompany me."

"He'd better not bring along a hangover or that mongrel dog."

"All will be taken care of after Mass, Señor Bill."

"What time's that?"

Oh, Billy, stop it.

"Perhaps eight-thirty."

"That's too late! God blast these hives."

"I've told you, señor, that Tony's mother has returned to Brighter Days and that Tony has just found out his mentor at the college leaves forever in a week. My head's a watermelon split in two. In order to accomplish all you ask I must go home and rest."

Sissy opened her eyes and stepped aside. Armando shuffled across the rug, hunched as she'd never seen him. He nodded at her, depressed the latch, and left.

Bill splashed more whiskey from the bottle of Wellers over what remained of the ice. He took a gulp and swept his left hand close to suck on the cigar. As Sissy started for the hall, he narrowed his eyes.

"Nothing's working, Sis." He laid the corona in the ashtray on the end table and took another swallow.

"Least of all this threadbare marriage." All at once she veered right to snatch the ashtray up.

"What's what, here? Give me that." He grabbed the glass edge but was unable to break her grip.

"I don't like your smoking and I don't like your drinking and you know that—and you know that, Bill." She wrested the ashtray free, stepped to the fireplace, and tossed in the cigar. She hesitated, then pitched the ashtray, too. It clunked against the charred remains of oak.

"Christ on the mountain, what are you doing, woman?" He took a stance as if about to cock his fists. "If you'd been reading what I've had to pour through at work and then fly here to deal with bozos like Baca and the Trujillos, you'd be drinking and smoking, too."

"Please let me pass."

"No! Not until you hear me out. No one wants to listen. We're in an end time, Sis." He reached back to scrabble manicured nails between his shoulder blades.

Sissy retreated to the wall. "Have you taken your tranquilizers?"

"They're no longer helping, can't you see that? You've got your head in the clouds like everybody else. I'm fed up searching for patent openings for an outfit that's not going to exist in thirty years. And why is that? A runaway particle experiment at Stanford could squeeze this planet down to the size of a marble. Gene splicing could juice up monkeypox into a pathogen more lethal than smallpox. Sea levels have risen twice as fast over the past ten years as they did over the previous century. We spend more on our military than the rest of the world put together. Rotter, Sis. Extinction's certain! Before it comes I want to be sniffing my hybrid teas and floribundas and that's not going to happen"—he raised his right fist—"if the Trujillos don't show up tomorrow because the son's soused himself into a stupor because he can't make his grades."

Bill drained his tumbler and goggled at her.

"Who's the drunk around here?" Sissy steadied herself against the wall under one of her photomontages. "This marriage is one catastrophe you forgot to mention, Billy. But haven't we covered it up well?" She pressed a liver-spotted hand to her neck. "I'm sick of your women, your drunken mea culpas over the years, sick of fibbing for your sake, of knowing that the real reason you want to move to Santa Fe sooner than later is because your current playmate at the office has started pestering you to divorce me. How does she stand your rants? I stopped listening when I stopped loving you long ago. Now, while you waste my time lying that you're going to change, I envision montage after montage of how I thought life with you would be. And you see? I no longer cry about it. When we get back to Palo Alto, I think I'll buy myself a pretty bowl and goldfish like Sweet Pea's. And a little dog to cuddle. Let me pass."

Chin high, she launched herself toward the hall.

"I'm starved," he mumbled at her back. "What's for dinner?"

She couldn't believe that once again she'd hoped to prove, with the filets of Kobe beef she'd picked up this morning at Kaune's, that the way to a man's heart is through his stomach.

The front chimes sounded before she could decide what to say.

Bill clutched his tumbler.

"I'll get it," Sissy snapped. "What's for dinner tonight? Cowboy beans and rice."

"You're kidding."

"Not kidding. And shredded lettuce." She fought light-headedness by gulping and blowing out air as she tramped across the room and flung the door wide. "He isn't home."

"Of course I am. Hello, you," Bill said behind her. His breath smelled like cream gone bad.

Sheila moved her head for an unobstructed view. "You're not home? You are home?"

"Sis thought I might be too tired. Not true."

"I found another box holding his files on roses if you'd like to take a second look."

"Surely would."

"But I don't want to disturb your dinner." She pulled at one of the sapphire earrings. "These things hurt."

Sissy pivoted and aimed for the hall, her flats clicking on the tiles.

"Too damned early for dinner," Bill said.

"Have you a moment to come over now?"

"I'll go grab my sombrero."

THE TERRORIST
SUNDAY 22 MAY 2005

The previous night Christopher returned from Joe's Diner to find Heather locked in their bedroom. He'd slumped on the sofa bed watching slasher movies on Showtime until he fell asleep at two-thirty in the morning.

He woke now in his boxers to the rumbling of a garage door. Knuckling his eyes, he flung off the blanket, shook his head clear, and sat up. The lovebirds, still under the black cloth shrouding their cage, started squealing at the muffled racing of a car engine. A sheet of paper lay on the shirt, khakis, socks, and boots heaped at the base of one of the sofa-bed's arms. He sucked in breath and reached for it. The familiar cramped handwriting with its flaring ascenders read:

> My friend hurt his back and I've gone to help out. Home at 11:00 so
> we can drive to your folks. Let's not tell them about us until they've
> left. Fewer emotions to deal with up close.

She dared tell him how to act? The bitch hadn't even signed it. So fate had designated this morning for him to proceed. Had he the nerve, he wondered?

His hand trembled as he crumpled the sheet of paper and carried it to the wicker wastebasket beside the TV. Tomorrow he'd give two weeks notice, find a motel close to the Labs, and early in June go live with his parents in Palo Alto, until he could secure a position to teach college chemistry again.

Sounded simple. But he'd better make a to-do list. Already

doubts about what he planned for the next hour were making his hands shake.

He swallowed and carried his clothes into the bedroom. He pulled a pad off the bed table and printed out *1. WASH & DRESS FRESH 2. BREAKFAST 3. GROOM 4. TRIXIE GOES FIRST 5. MOTHER'S PROGRAM (FORGET JAN) 6. PARENTS AT 11:00*

He pulled the spread up from the bottom of the bed, stepped out of his boxers, balled his wrinkled clothes against the footboard, and for the moment set his boots on the dresser beside the closet.

He avoided eying Primrose as, a few minutes later, booted and decked in clean khakis and a green plaid, he carried Cheerios and blackberries from the kitchen to the breakfast nook. Across the street's dead end, the neighbor and his wife were planting butterfly bushes next to their driveway. He closed the curtains and wolfed his food down.

He rose and strode toward the door leading to the garage, pausing to grab the apron inscribed I Love You, Babe, Now Get To Work from the pantry that Heather had given him last Christmas.

He returned with two garbage bags and a couple of twist-n-ties, left them next to the doll's hut, hurried into the master bath, and faced the mirror over the sink, glancing up at the reflected corner above the toilet. Soon he'd no longer be the one needed to cajole the contractor into ripping off the wallboard and replacing the rotting timber. He licked his fingertips, smoothed his eyebrows flat, buttoned his collar flaps, and took his electric razor, toothbrush, and hair gel from the cabinet.

Back in the bedroom, he smoothed an emerald bath towel crosswise over the spread and fluffed his and Heather's pillows against the headboard. Through the window he spotted three runners in shorts beyond the piñons, headed as if in stroboscopic motion along the asphalt trail. Draw the drapes? But why? They couldn't see in.

Having slipped a sheet of cardboard from a new shirt, he penned the words that had popped into his mind before leaving the gym yesterday with his mother:

He propped the sign against the headboard on top of the pillows.

Go! He jogged into the kitchen, stuffed one garbage bag inside the other, poked the ties into his shirt pocket along with a paring knife, and headed for Heather's office.

Trixie lay curled in her basket. He pulled the lips of the green bags apart, and to her rrrranhh! pounced before she could spring, snugging her down into her polyethelene shroud.

Damn! The ringing phone caused his heel to upset her dish. Water darkened the beige carpeting. He managed to place the Manx's empty dish against the wallboard while fisting tight the top of the thrashing bags.

He scurried back to the master bedroom, spun the bags, and twisted the ties around their tops. Trixie's cries seemed to come from a well.

"Easier now," Christopher said aloud, squinting at what seemed kittens batting the green plastic. He placed the bundle on the towel.

Wheezing, he left the bedroom and stopped at the willow hut. He turned it on its side, lifted the knife from his pocket, and slashed the rag doll's mouth open. A wad of cotton burst through the red yarn.

In the kitchen he took a see-through sandwich bag from the drawer beside the sink. The wall clock showed he had plenty of time. He shook the tension from his arms and upended Primrose's bowl. The goldfish splashed out with the last of the water and flopped into the sink's strainer.

How slimy she felt! He firmed his grip, shoved her into the bag, and slid his thumb and forefinger along the top to seal it.

Cradling the bag and refilled bowl, he grabbed the doll on his way to the bedroom and deposited everything on the towel. Fewer thrusts distended the garbage bags.

He flexed his belly muscles, hoping to ease a burning that had begun. Back in the kitchen he put the knife back in a drawer and pulled out more sandwich bags. He carried them to the room with the two pink walls and two blue ones that Heather and he had painted after Thanksgiving. Could he swallow the lump in his throat yet? No.

The terrarium's fluorescent-lit top came easily off. He set it on what was to have been the baby's changing table. Heat lamps glowed at each end of the tank. No trouble plucking out one of the toads except that—goddamn it!—a spine punctured his thumb. He sucked the wound, spit into the handkerchief he pulled from his pocket, and sealed the beast in a bag. Its belly swelled as it stared at him with eyes as dark as his own.

Only the head spines and nostrils of the other reptile showed above the sand. But when he dug his fingertips under its belly and heaved it out, a stream of blood shot from the corner of its eye, spattering Christopher's cheek and dribbling down. Without thinking, he flicked his tongue to lick it. Bitter! He dropped the toad to the carpet, hauled out his handkerchief, spit into it again, and wiped his face. "You little bastard!" The toad was scrambling toward a chair leg. He stooped to clutch it in his handkerchief and forced it into the other bag—which the pet reddened with another squirt of blood. Nausea mixed with the burning in his belly as he replaced the tank's aluminum top and held the two closed bags stiff-armed away from his side.

In the bedroom the garbage bags hardly moved. He set the horned toads beside it, sank to the mattress, and stared at the wall, hyperventilating.

Get up, Christopher!

In Heather's office he unlocked the door that opened to her cactus garden and plucked two hen's-egg-size rocks from the gravel. He locked the door, proceeded to the kitchen, and found the twine Heather used to bind for trash pickup the biotech journals she'd read through. He cut foot-long lengths, wrapped and knotted an end around each stone, took them to the bedroom, deposited them on the spread, and strode out.

Morning light flooded the great room, giving the montage his mother had created for their firstborn the glints and gleams of an Eastern Orthodox icon. He approached the six-foot-by-three-foot-by-three-foot cage, ripped off the cloth, and tossed it onto the dining table.

Squealing, the blue-breasted Pity fluttered up from pecking a Cheerio off the litter and settled on a rung of the ladder. Merciful stayed wide-eyed on a scallop of her dish and created a similar racket.

"Steady there, steady." Christopher yanked out the nail catch and reached for the wire-handled net that hung in a corner. He swooped the net over Pity and twisted it to keep the struggling bird enmeshed. As he drew Pity out through the doorway, he squeezed the tiny body and poked the green tip of a wing back under his fingers. But before he could secure the door, Merciful dashed herself against the back of the cage, dropped to the litter, and, screaming, rocketed into freedom.

Christopher staggered backwards as one of Merciful's wing feathers whisked across his neck like a blade. His anklebone struck the leg of an armchair. "Ouch, goddamn you!" He seized the writhing net with both hands.

Merciful whirred in and out of shadows that the vigas formed on the white-plastered ceiling. She settled on a blossom of the chandelier and began to squeak as Christopher carried Pity to the bedroom.

He managed to extract Pity's legs from the net while avoiding the bill that kept trying to jab his fingers. He tied the legs with the twine's loose end, held the stone above the fishbowl, then lowered it into the water. The chill on his hand surprised him. When the stone clunked against the glass bottom, he disentangled the bird and lifted the dripping net out.

Control, Christopher. You will not be sick. Take a deep breath and tidy up.

Massaging his belly, he turned from the beads of Pity's eyes and the water that sloshed against the bowl's sides as the bird struggled. None of the bags on the bed moved as Christopher smoothed wrinkles from the towel, sat Raggedy Ann beneath the sign he'd made, opened one of the three sandwich bags to haul out Primrose, and stuffed her corpse in the gape he'd made of the doll's mouth.

Merciful let out a scream from the great room. Christopher's left shoulder jerked as he opened the bottom drawer of the dresser and hauled out the blouse he'd bought for Heather's upcoming birthday. So far he'd beaded only one cuff and half of the collar with turquoise. He extended the blouse's arms on the spread below the towel, pulled out the horned toads, and, careful not to prick himself on their spines, placed them over the blouse's pockets. By now the pets' eyelids had closed. He set the net and second stone on the pile of yesterday's clothes.

He gripped the one clear sandwich bag and the one splattered red, stepped to the bed's foot, and appraised his tableau: *NO WIFE NO LIFE*, doll propped against a pillow, fishbowl and cat on the towel, blouse with its spiked breasts below. Don't tell him he had no artistic gift. But Trixie needed shifting to balance out the doll. He grabbed the cat's shroud and discovered that a front paw had managed to claw through the two layers of polyethelene. He set the bundle against the other pillow so that her stiffened foreleg jutted into the air.

The twine holding Pity to the stone had stayed taut, though his lids had closed white. Christopher's thighs felt waterlogged as he centered the fishbowl on the hem of the blouse. He stepped to the dresser and jammed his University of Oregon cap over his crew cut. He opened the top drawer, hoisted his apron to hook the camera phone to his belt, and crammed wallet and keys into his khakis. Ugh! His saliva still tasted bad. He spit again into the handkerchief.

Merciful made no more cries. "Where are you?" he called from near the bathroom doorway. The answer came flapping in. He ducked as the yellow-breasted menace swooped close to his head, circled the bowl, and whizzed back into the great room.

Brandishing the net, he ran after her, but she sat squawking on the bracket that held the spotlight aimed at his mother's montage. "Then starve, you devil!" Christopher cried out and shut the cage's door.

He carried his dishes from the breakfast nook to the nearly-full dishwasher and crammed them inside while the refrigerator hummed across the room. At the base of the sink he noticed a puddle gleaming on the floor. He pulled a towel from its brass holder, wiped the tile dry, and washed his hands.

He hung up his apron and, consulting his list, decided first to visit the florist next to Joe's Diner to pick out flowers for his mother.

Though he knew the carnations he'd bought Sissy would wilt in the BMW's back seat, they now seemed too falsely cheerful to present.

The two-day heat wave had broken. He stood on one of the portal's big slate tiles, biting his lip and waiting for one of his parents to open the door. Where was the contractor, he wondered?

"Why, Chrisy, you never need to ring. Good morning, dear." His mother advanced a rope-soled espadrille and gave him a hug.

"These are yours," he blurted. His knuckles knocked her breastbone as he thrust the three sheets containing Jan and Gerry's suggested program at her. "Sorry." Should he tell her about last night's new wall-length graffiti at the gym? Certainly he'd say nothing about Jan agreeing fifteen minutes ago to dine with him. He had decided to ask her out after all.

Frowning, his mother took the sheets. "And where is Sweet Pea?"

"Wasn't feeling well."

"Oh? But why didn't you phone?"

He glanced past her to see his father facing away from him on the couch. Christopher watched him pick up a tumbler from the bamboo table. He lowered his eyes then to Sissy's, comforted by the perfume he remembered from when she'd fixed him breakfast in bed—what, already a week ago?

"Will she be able to lunch with us?" His mother swept her arm with its new bracelet toward the dining table. "You see? I've prepared for a feast. Summer-squash soup and Kobe beef."

Just outside the kitchen, the dining table displayed four enamel chargers holding roadrunner-enlivened bowls and plates. Paper-doll-like Kokopellis bending toward their flutes rimmed yellow place mats. Each mat held two goblets—one clear and one of cut glass—five-piece silver settings, and white linen napkins folded into triangles. Sprays of Scottish broom flared from a blue-and-yellow vase.

"It's beautiful, Mother."

His father hadn't looked around yet.

"You haven't answered my question, Chrisy." Sissy laid the papers from the gym on a bench beside the door. "Those cuts on your forehead seem to be scabbing nicely—look at me, Christopher!" She reached up to grip his shoulders. "What's the matter at home? I knew there was trouble, I knew it." She withdrew her hand from his shirt and thumped it against a breast. "My heart can't take this."

He saw her green eyes start to glisten. "I've done something unspeakable, Mother."

"To Heather?"

"It will affect her, yes."

"What's the poor sap saying?" Bill growled in a low voice, turning around at last.

"No workmen today?" Christopher called over.

"Your father's in a black mood about those two and he won't leave the whiskey alone."

"Go sit with him, Mother, I need to talk to you both." He grimaced, unable to swallow the lump that had returned to his throat.

He cupped her elbow but she shook it free and preceded him

over the Navajo rug, rejecting the couch where Bill sat for the armchair beside the fireplace. Christopher slumped in the twin chair near his mother and placed his palms on his knees.

But before he could gather words, his father began to talk, as if to himself.

"The rotter phoned that his son came home plastered at three a.m. and announced he's quitting college. Trujillo said family comes first and he can't work today and, yes, I exploded."

Sissy kept her chin low as she muttered, "Your father's language was unspeakable."

"Look, I'll move in here to make sure they finish up," Christopher blurted.

Bill twisted an end of his white mustache as he and Sissy stared at him.

"Heather and I can no longer live together."

Sissy flung a hand to her cheek as if a bullet had just torn through it. Bill drained his tumbler, sloshed the liquid around his mouth, and gulped it down.

"Two days ago I came home early and found her in bed with a man I know from the gym." Christopher grasped his phone holster. "I have the photos here and I'm not feeling very well. It was the man who hurt his back yesterday, Mother."

Sissy opened her lips but said nothing.

"Hold on." Bill lifted a buttock to extract the vial of tranquilizers, teased out a pill, and poured three fingers of whiskey. His Adam's apple bobbed. "Go ahead."

Christopher turned to Sissy. "Most of what I told you yesterday were lies, Mother." He pressed his forehead. "To stay sane I banged my head on a tree after I photographed them through the window making love. This morning Heather left me a note that she'd gone to be with the man. So I killed her pets. I suffocated them—well, drowned one—and left their corpses on our bed. A lovebird escaped, maybe the one she thinks is pregnant. Happy birthday, bird."

Sissy started abrading her left wrist as if to rub off the skin.

Christopher stood and pressed his belly. "It's too hot in here."

"Perhaps," Bill said, shifting his gaze from his wife to his son, "this time you can stay out of court with a trial separation or mediation or collaborative divorce and save yourself a pocketful of change. Having those photos may prove useful."

"How logical. Always the lawyer, aren't you?" Christopher sat down again. "I'm also going to quit my job."

"Also?" Sissy circled fuchsia-glossed lips with the tip of her tongue.

"Besides ending our marriage. Tomorrow I'm giving the Labs two weeks notice. Heather doesn't know the promotion my boss offered me Friday would have meant a thirty percent raise. Hasn't a clue that she could have stopped working and go to all the galleries and poetry readings she wanted to." Tears started welling and he swiped his eyes with his bare forearm.

"And what do you plan to do for income, Chris?" his father asked.

"Go back to teaching. I wish I'd never quit."

At that moment the phone jangled.

Bill jumped up, stooped for another mouthful of whiskey, and strode toward the white cradle side-tabled near the luncheon array.

He set the receiver against his ear, yanked it away, brought it close, and reached to scratch under the back of his collar. His face stayed impassive. "I don't suppose you'd want to drive over here? No. All right, I'll tell him."

The ends of his mustache quivered as he pursed his lips and returned to the couch. "Heather. She's pretty upset. In fact, she's hysterical." He drained his voice of emotion. "Asked me to convey that she won't be home tonight, that she'll be staying with a friend."

"Her lover," Christopher said, returning his father's gaze.

At that moment the doorbell rang.

"Christ on the mountain, now what?"

Sissy closed her eyes. "No doubt Sheila, your rosebush chum."

"It's your contractor," Christopher said. "With son."

Bill stood, clacked across the tiles, and pulled the front door wide.

Armando raised two cans of maple-tinted stain by their handles. He tongued a Lucky Strike to the corner of his mouth. "All is well, Señor Bill. At confession Father forgave Tony for wanting to quit his studies. We picked up many supplies at Home Depot and here we are to work, as you see."

"You're aware that Mrs. Ryan and I leave tomorrow morning at eleven."

Armando dipped his head.

"We can easily complete everything after you're gone," Tony offered, circling his father's shoulder.

"Chris!" Bill shouted, wheeling. "You were serious about camping out here? Then come along for a tour of all that needs doing."

Christopher rose and trudged toward him.

He had reached the couch when he heard his mother's "No!" behind him.

"Christopher is joining me. He had to talk and now I have to talk. You'll see him in a few minutes. And please turn the broiler off, Bill. We'll lunch in a little while. Come along, Chrisy."

He followed her past the hall's bookshelves and entered the master bedroom. A photomontage he'd not seen perched slantwise across her desk. A woman lay in a chaise lounge cellophane-taped to a field of buttercups under a tulip-petaled sky. The scene contained neither house nor roses.

"That's new, isn't it?" Christopher muttered.

"Brand new. Your father and I had a set-to last night. This morning at the market I bought tulips to use their petals."

"What did you argue about?"

"In a minute. Sit there." She pointed to an armchair next to the king-size bed. She moved to the edge of the sliding door that looked out on Bill's garden. Gopher holes gaped in the buffalo grass among the broken lattices and overturned pots of roses. Sissy pulled turquoise-colored drapes across the glass. "Snap on that floor lamp, will you?"

A yellow haze suffused the room.

Christopher leaned forward from the chair. "What's that crap-o smell?"

"Glue, I suppose. Friday morning Tony replaced the window he'd broken." She waggled her feet to free them from her espadrilles, climbed onto the quilt, and scooted back to prop herself against a reading pillow.

Christopher could hear the blurred voices of the men outside the corner window. "So?" he asked.

She stared at him. "You are not my son."

"What?" The near ends of his brows flew together.

"You emerged from my womb but you're Bill's son, you take after him."

"Does he hate himself then?"

"I haven't the faintest idea."

"He can't as much as I do."

"I don't wonder. Where exactly do you hope to find a teaching position, Christopher?"

"Maybe I can get my job back at the university. The desert makes me edgy. Say move into your house here until the work's completed and then live in my old room in Palo Alto until I've landed something. Oh, goddamn it, Mother, I don't know." He grasped the sides of his head and lowered it.

"I don't think I'd feel comfortable any more living in the same house as you, Chrisy. But your father might find it acceptable."

"My father? What's that mean?"

"I have a decision to make."

"Decision?"

"Bill works with a bookkeeper in the Santa Clara office that he sometimes spends a noon hour or the evening with. This isn't the first woman outside our marriage. And now he seems to want to get to know the woman across the street. As she seems to want to get to know him."

"Oh, God, Mother." Christopher pulled out the handkerchief stained with blood and pushed it to his eyes. "I've never been unfaithful to Heather!"

"What I'm thinking is that probably I'll give your father his choice. Perhaps he'll want to stay in Palo Alto and keep on with Silidyne a while. Last night he claimed the company doesn't really want him to retire. In that case I may have my things moved here, especially if Sweet Pea decides to stay in Santa Fe."

"Are you playing with me, Mother? When I went to pick up your program at the gym, that graffiti artist you asked about had scrawled his Fuckin A on both glass doors and across the whole outside wall. This town isn't for you. The altitude makes you dizzy."

"Less than when we arrived." She tucked a stray curl of her permanent behind her ear. "I've always wanted a daughter and Heather's as close as I'll come. Maybe she'd enjoy living with me. This house has lots of room and I rather like this city."

"Heather has a lover, Mother. I've got photos."

"And I'm asking you to destroy them. She and her lover could rent this bedroom and Bill's office. Why not? I'm sure I'd be comfortable in the guest suite. There's a lot to work out, but right now I need to sleep. Please say nothing when you join the men because I haven't made up my mind yet about anything. But if you decide to call this house home for a short while, after dinner I'll explain what kind of sofa I want instead of the one that's here. No bear claws, Chrisy."

She slid down the pillow and curled on her side facing away from him. He gazed at the webs of veins behind her knees as she brought them toward her belly. She lifted her head to rest it on her arm.

"May I lie down a moment with you, Mother? My stomach hurts

and I don't know if I can stand being with Dad."

"Of course you can stand it. You just grew up. Turn off that floor lamp, will you? And shut the door when you go."

NOW WHAT?
MONDAY 23 MAY 2005

Heather sat at Chad's dining table, gazing past the oak-burl bowl to the window beside the fireplace. The room still smelled of sausages and the syrup for blueberry pancakes that Chad had cooked earlier before driving Derek to consult Dan Mickelson, a chiropractor and Chad's best client.

Abigail had stripped the kitchen walls of two giant Kodachromes, the one she'd shot from the porch of D.H. Lawrence's ranch house north of Taos, and the one of sheep grazing along the Chama. She had also taken a couple of ladder-back chairs that had sat outside the master bedroom.

Heather flung her ponytail to the back of her neck. She'd put on her reverse print of ferns to commemorate her first visit here two weeks ago. She reached for the phone brought in from the kitchen, but the receiver slipped from her hand and clunked to the table. She grabbed it, stared at her address book again, and punched the numbers.

"Yes?" The voice was deeper and more energetic than she'd expected.

"This is Heather, Sissy. I called to say goodbye." She pressed a hand to her pounding heart.

"Oh, hello."

"You're driving to the airport soon?"

"In about an hour."

"How complicated everything's become! I'm so sorry. Christopher's told you what's been happening the last few days?"

"I believe so. He left for work this morning after the Trujillos arrived."

"He stayed with you last night?"

"He says he wants to live here until the house is finished, perhaps longer. Yesterday after lunch he went to your place to pick up a few clothes. I have no idea if I can forgive him for what he did to your pets, Heather. But then, can he forgive you for what you did?"

"I doubt it."

"I was able to persuade him to destroy the photos. Though in the end it didn't matter. He said glare from the big window made them blurry."

"It's no longer a home for me, Sissy. I'm staying at a friend's."

"Bill told us what you said on the phone yesterday. Do you think there's any chance of you and Christopher reconciling?"

"Oh, no. I've met someone I'm much more compatible with."

"Christopher did say he plans to try to get back into teaching. He seems to want to leave New Mexico."

"He's always hated it here." Heather wished Chad and Derek would return so she could hang up, afraid she'd start sobbing as the tableau of corpses flared again in her mind. She watched a daddy longlegs pick its way up a spindle of the chair opposite, its thin legs testing the walnut, and wondered if Sissy wished to end the call, too. How sad that soon this woman she'd grown to love would be twelve hundred miles away.

"I suppose you two will need to sell your house," Sissy said.

"Probably."

"Sweet Pea—"

Heather's head jerked. She was Sweet Pea still?

"I want you to consider something."

Pulling the receiver from her ear, Heather waggled her head to clear it so she could concentrate.

"I'll have to talk fast because Bill's outside shouting for me. This could be a shock—perhaps not—but after all these years he and I may go our separate ways."

Heather pushed against the chair's back.

"We've lived with some serious issues I've never shared with you. If my doctor approves, I may want to move to Santa Fe on my own, and if I do, I hope you'll think about coming to live with me, alone or perhaps even with your friend."

"Oh, my gosh, Sissy—oh!" She heard an engine and out the living room window saw Chad's blue Subaru pull up. "The men just returned, I'd better go help. My friend hurt himself at the gym."

"Two days ago. I know."

"How do you—"

"Christopher took me there to visit. I saw the whole thing."

"The co-owner had made a play for Derek and he refused her. Her son told Derek to hunch his shoulders instead of keeping his back arched. The son and his mother set up the injury so my friend would have to quit the gym."

"You're not serious?"

"I am. Oh, sure, Derek said he saw you there. Listen, I'm flying on business to the Bay Area in a couple of days. Let's have dinner in Palo Alto or San Francisco and talk."

"What a happy idea. But I can't believe those people at the gym—"

"Believe it, Sissy. I'll call you tomorrow."

Heather stood, returned the phone to the counter, hurried to the door, and pulled it open. In the blossom-scented air, Chad had his arm around the brace that wrapped Derek's waist. Its white shoulder straps hid some of the mouse heads grinning from his shirt.

Grimacing, Derek listed to the right as Chad helped him past the hyacinths toward the path's gauntlet of yellow roses.

"He's trussed up pretty good, isn't he?" Chad laughed. A weighted bag dangled from Chad's fist. "Watch those thorns, pal!"

As Heather stepped onto the planks of the covered porch, she shifted her gaze to a movement at her left. Across Chavez Lane, the triangular face of a man stared out above the ivy, fingers gripping the edges of lace curtains. When he saw her stare in his direction, he drew the curtains shut.

"Wednesday his nibs goes back for massage," Chad said. "Friday's a bit rougher. Dan needs to readjust the spine, but says our friend's prognosis is excellent. Right now we get him out of this cummerbund and onto ice. And me into the shop." Chad hefted the polyethelene bag he held. "Dan asked me to work this hunk of sycamore into a couple of wine glasses. I'll be glad to leave the world for a little while. The front page of his *Courier* said Sunnis and Shiites are close to civil war. A car bomb's killed another fifty in Baghdad. I read that's six hundred dead in four weeks from roadside and suicide bombings."

"Let's go, Chad," Derek bleated, throwing a palm to the rear of the nylon brace. "Goddamn spasms." He bent and winced.

"Sorry, pal." Chad guided him up the three steps.

Heather pushed her lips to Derek's, then circled his waist. "C'mon, darling."

Chad started unbuttoning his shirt after shutting the door he'd painted scarlet. "I'm happier in frayed cuffs," he said, "and sawdust-spattered cotton."

Heather stopped Derek halfway across the living room, beside the table abutting the couch's rear. "Your phone rang twice, Chad."

"Ab from the road, maybe? She and her buddy and her buddy's dogs lit out yesterday for somewhere in Maine." He laughed. "Misses me so much she's turning back? More likely begging me to FedEx her the old Leica she left. I'll listen later. Heather, will you freeze this?" He moved close, set the bag of sycamore down, and tugged out a see-through pack of blue gel from the slot in the back of Derek's brace. "And fix sandwiches? I'll catch up with you in a couple of hours." He peeled off his short-sleeved plaid, tossed it to the couch, took up the wood, walked into the kitchen, and disappeared down the step to the laundry that opened to his shop.

Heather guided Derek across the planks into the guest bedroom, where he had slept alone for two nights and she with him for one. The closet held clothes Chad had persuaded Natalie to hand over with Derek's toiletries, after Derek had driven directly to Chad's from the gym. Heather had heaped her own clothes near the window that looked out at the redwood towering over the street.

Derek hadn't shaved since he hurt himself. Heather slid her palm down one of his cheeks and across his lips, and helped him sit on the edge of the bed. She unbuckled his straps, ripped the Velcro closures apart, and eased the brace off. She grasped his shoulders and guided him supine onto the quilt printed with photos Abigail had taken years ago at the Bosque del Apache. The soles of Derek's sneakers pushed against the footboard's fretwork.

"Raise your knees, darling, so I can get your shoes off." She untied his laces but left the white socks on. After undoing his belt, she managed to jiggle his cargo shorts past his buttocks and off. "I'll be right back." She grasped the gel pack and left to the screech of Chad's band saw.

The morning before, heading home from here—expecting afterward to drive with Christopher to his parents for Sunday's good-bye lunch—she'd found instead the bodies of her animals. After her rage had ebbed, she'd placed them in the freezer, but had failed at sweet-talking Merciful down to her cage. Heather had returned then, purchasing an ice bag for Derek on the way.

Now she appeared with that and slices of apple. "Smell!" she said, bringing a piece to his nose. She placed the glass bowl holding the rest of the apple beside his pillow and slipped the screw-capped bag, filled with ice and water, under the small of his back.

"It's cold. Oh, balls, Heather, can you believe all that's happened since our picnic? I wish I'd put a month's deposit on that dump on Canyon Road. At least I could have hooked into DSL there. But hearing that raccoon or rat scrabbling under the floorboards, I couldn't make myself write the check."

He frowned up at her. Two brown curls had flopped over his forehead. She stooped to kiss them, pressed his genitals, and lowered herself to the mattress, glad she'd thought to buy lilacs to cheer the room up. The flowers surged from a square vase Chad had fashioned from manzanita. "I'm way behind in my work, too, Derek. But I bring good news."

She pushed the pink thongs of her sandals free from between her toes, then eased the slice of apple into his mouth. "While you were gone, I talked with my mother-in-law. She convinced Christopher to erase the photos of us. It seems he's going to stay at his folks' new home after they've left for the Bay Area. Chad can help me move your computer stuff down to our place and we'll hire a guru to get you online fast."

"Raise my head so I can swallow."

"Tomorrow if you're better, you can help me bury my babies. That shithead!" she exclaimed. "That motherfucking prick."

"Yeah. Hey!"

She'd flung her hand from under his neck, sending the bowl off the quilt to clatter against the wall, scattering its apple cargo across the throw rug.

"I'm sorry, darling, but damn him." She lifted the hem of her dress to blot her eyes. "You know what? Compared to my husband, your wife's an angel."

He lay a moment clasping his right knee above his chest, then let the leg straighten and sucked in a couple of breaths, in an attempt to lessen the pain. "In the car this morning, Chad swore he and Natalie haven't slept together."

"Do you believe him?"

"I want to."

"Do! And listen to this. After I get back from San Francisco, I'm going to start chasing down writing assignments here so we can spend every night together. Did you know that complexity science started in Santa Fe? I've been doing the research. We're a seedbed for new technology, sort of like Silicon Valley thirty years ago. The techno-geeks call us Info Mesa. The Santa Fe Institute's nearby, BioFeed, Informatica, DNAics, a bunch of others. Not traveling will also mean a lot more time for us to work on poetry."

"Maybe," he sighed. "Though it sounds like pie in the sky." He raised his back and resettled it on the blue ice bag and blew out air.

"We can do it!"

"I feel so grungy."

"I'll help you into the shower after lunch. We'll try out the frozen gel after you strap back into that Marquis-de-Sade rig. Maybe Chad can go get your processor and printer and monitor from your wife this afternoon. He's already braved her pit bull for you once. Oh, frig the world, Derek. Chad's right! Let's create the laid-back life he lives, that my folks live. I've got to call them, take you up there—oh, shut up, Heather. Move over, darling, I'm going to lie close to you."

She stiffened as the front chimes tinkled. "Do you suppose Abbie's really come back?"

"You think I'm prescient?"

"I'd better go see."

"The ice is starting to work."

"Of course it is!"

"Ouch!"

"I can't help kissing you." Heather dropped to her knees, threw slices of McIntosh into the bowl, set it next to him, and hurried out.

She glimpsed a woman on the porch wearing sunglasses and a bucket-style hat through the front window. She had clamped a canvas against the side of her purple T-shirt with her elbow. Braless nipples poked the fabric taut.

Uh-oh, Heather thought. She pulled the door open. The stranger smelled of liquor or cologne.

A box showing folded shirts and khakis sat beside her leg. When she saw Heather, she startled. "Who are you? Of course I know who you are. Don't tell me. I left two messages for Chad."

"He was driving your husband to the chiropractor."

"But that's Chad's Subaru in front of my van."

"He's in his shop now."

"I've got another painting to show him." The yellow bags under Natalie's eyes shouted No Sleep.

"Why don't you take it around?"

"Fuck you, lady! I want to see my husband. Is he better?" The bells circling her ankle clinked as she slanted the unframed canvas against the wall and hoisted the carton of clothes. "Where is he?"

"In the guest bedroom, sleeping."

"Out of my way." Natalie tried to push past.

Could this be real? Heather thrust her palms against the advancing cardboard box, squinted up at the clear sky, and back at Natalie's shades. "Look, I feel bad that everything's gotten so out of whack. Your husband's bound forever to stay sorry for what he's put you through. But right now he's exhausted. Let him rest, okay? Yes, he's healing. Give me the clothes and go show Chad your painting. Okay? He'll be glad to see it, I know."

COME TO MAMA
TUESDAY 24 MAY 2005

Such a beautiful day! Natalie told herself in front of her house. So what if cottontails eat these pansies? Or I trade Santa Fe for Schenectady to help out with Mother? "Flowers cheer us up, don't they, Saint Paul?" she called out.

She'd roped the year-old mutt to the trunk of the birch rising from a lawn that, like the pansies, needed too much water. So what? Chad was due in an hour. So to hell with you, Derek, and whatever her name is. And thank You, whatever You are, for this sky's glorious blue.

Having settled on the foam pad placed near the street, she straightened the billed cap she'd found last week to complete the military gear Derek's dead sister used to wear. This morning she'd donned her gardening blouse. The worn cotton hung loose over a dirt-splotched skirt. "We're better off without the son of a bitch, aren't we?" she blurted to a gray-bottomed cloud floating above Mount Baldy.

She dipped her chin. How good the wild barley smelled! How good the mounds of soil already troweled out. Digging another hole, she imagined her possible next painting, a woman festooned in gardenias, eyes bougainvilleas, arms embracing gloxinias as if the bouquets were lovers.

A noise started up. She jerked her head toward the corner where two-story condominiums were rising behind the old stone wall. A couple of carpenters in safety hats had begun securing two-by-eight-inch plates to the tops of the new stem walls. She covered her ears against their drilling, dirt from her rubber gloves' fingertips sticking in her hair.

The year-old Saint Paul continued to snore beside his water dish. An already-massive jaw rested between his paws. How could he do it, Natalie wondered?

She moved her pad into the street to scoop out holes in the planting strip between curb and sidewalk, resolved to keep on gardening despite the din. Ants, their bodies glowing like rubies, zigzagged in and out of their mounds of grit. Like my emotions, she thought.

"Watch it!"

One of her knees knocked the curb. Wincing, she twisted to see a backhoe clattering toward the construction site.

"That was mean!" she cried.

"Could've crushed those pretty ankles," the driver grinned under a toothbrush mustache. He pulled the gearshift into neutral. The engine gurgled as the front bucket shook.

Saint Paul finally had risen from the grass and started to yap.

"I can work wherever I want to. When are you guys going to give our neighborhood back?"

"Meaning this project?" He aimed his finger like the barrel of a pistol toward the corner. "Six months. But the developer has bought four properties to rebuild nearby. Think swank, gorgeous. Soon you won't know the place."

He tilted his hard hat at her. She watched his biceps stretch a torn sleeve as he shifted into drive. The backhoe clattered up the hill.

"Oh, Saint Paul, stop barking!" She jumped up and from a skirt pocket extracted the inhaler she'd bought. She pulled the cap off the mouthpiece, replaced the long arm with the short one, flipped the bottle upside down, and shook it. She closed her lips around the mouthpiece and, plunging it against the bottle's top, breathed a puff of antiasthma mist. She reseated the mouthpiece, buried the contraption in her pocket, and ran to the dog. His drool cooled her forearm as she crouched and hugged him. "I'm so sorry about those fly bites." She stroked the scabs at the tip of an ear. "I'll get you to the vet soon, I promise."

By nine-thirty the roots of all dozen pansies sat snug in their long bed. Natalie was about to lug the hose off the porch when she spotted When Women Vote, Democrats Win heading toward her. She almost wished Chad hadn't come. Her right temple began to throb.

"Shhh," she counseled Saint Paul.

Chad hopped from the car and slapped a sombrero over his bald dome. "Good morning! I'm awfully glad you didn't come round to the shop yesterday."

"I was in a bad mood."

"Understandable. Me, too. Where's the painting?"

"In the living room."

"That pit bull's too close to the path, Natalie." He stood at the end of the drive, scrabbling his fingernails against a sideburn.

"He's a mix, Chad. You two need to learn to get cozy."

"Maybe. But I'd feel better if you put him in your studio or the van." He rotated his left arm to display the scar tissue half-circling his wrist.

She clamped her teeth and turned to free the rope from Saint Paul's collar. She cradled him and straightened, grunting from the weight. His hair prickled her arms as she carried him to the van, managed to slide a door open, plopped him on the back seat, and rolled the window down a few inches.

"Thanks," Chad said. "Still okay for me to cart Derek's computer stuff over to my place?"

"I guess."

"Still too many changes coming too fast, aren't there? Is that some kind of Army cap you're wearing?"

"I'm redoing basic training."

No ankle bells clinked nor feather swung as she approached

the bench. Chad followed her inside. The chandelier over the dining table lit the health catalogs she'd stayed up far into the night flipping through. Her robe draped the chair facing breakfast dishes.

"Sorry about the mess. Derek says I'm a flop at housekeeping. Voilà." She threw her arms at the painting standing aslant the jamb of the kitchen doorway, then turned toward the table to pick up a bottle of osha-root syrup. She unscrewed the cap, squeezed the bulb, and shot a dropperful down her throat.

Chad had approached the two-by-three-foot canvas and stood gazing at it. "Buddy liked the first one and I think he's going to love this."

An open hand, whose wrist bore a square-faced watch, burst from a tangle of passionflowers. The vines' fruits spiraled upward, purple as eggplants but the size of kiwis. Though Natalie had colored the ten-petaled blossoms yellow and pink, she'd rendered the stamens as black as the numbers on the watch.

"Lush," Chad said. "Ominous. That's a woman's arm?"

"I'm calling the painting Woman's Plight." She brushed a wisp of hair from her forehead. The pounding in her temple had lessened.

"Buddy'll probably want three more canvases to make a decision. C'mere a minute, Natalie."

As she went close, her meager eyebrows knit. He gripped her upper arms, inhaling the witch hazel. "What gets me up mornings since Abbie left is pretending that everything that's happening is for the best. It might work for you. I want you to rest easy. All right? Have you got a blanket or something? Let's get this treasure bundled."

She returned with bubble wrap and tape. After he'd cushioned the acrylic, she held the door open for him.

In a few minutes he returned from the car and followed her into Derek's office. "Makes me sad," he said, stopping at the sheet of plywood that Derek had laid across concrete blocks to hold his printer and the big portrait/landscape monitor. A *Websters*, thesaurus, and stack of manuscript pages sat nearby. "I gave him that daybed,"

Chad rasped, "and built those bookshelves for him. You know what? It smells musky in here."

"Yeah, well, he always kept the door closed and the blinds down—and at least wanted a dog." She switched on the ceiling light.

"He mentioned some folders."

She shrugged and pointed to a filing cabinet beside the processor Derek had placed next to the blocks. "They're staying with you?"

"The folders?"

"Not them, silly. Derek and her."

"They're talking about moving to her place." Chad bent to unplug the surge protector.

"I thought you told me she's married."

"They think her husband's moving out. Here, take these."

Her fingers touched his as he lifted half-a-dozen hanging files marked Macmillan and Houghton Mifflin. They gazed at each other until Chad looked away. She took the files from his hands.

Chad followed her out, balancing a small safe that held CDs and flash drives on his forearms.

Four trips later they stood beside the Subaru, its trunk and back seat loaded. The painting rested on the floor behind the passenger seat.

The sun soothing the back of Natalie's neck felt like her heat pad. She watched a painted lady, the tips of its wings polka-dotted white, flutter up from the neighbor's clump of catmint. A black-headed grosbeak sang from a branch of the weeping birch. No sign of Saint Paul peering out the van's window. Hopefully he was sleeping. "Is Meredith going to keep taking carving lessons from you?" she asked Chad, unable to face him.

"Gracias for the reminder. I need to phone her to say we're through. The woman's too explosive."

Drills resumed their chattering up at the corner as the backhoe began to rip out the dead rosebushes that lined the original wall.

"Chad," Natalie asked, attempting to energize her voice and

shifting so that her upper arm grazed his, "will you stay with me tonight? Saint Paul can sleep in Derek's office. You and I could go dancing at La Fonda."

He squeezed her hand, warmer than his. "For me, this is still your and Derek's house. It's too soon."

"May I spend the night at yours? Maybe later I could get out of our lease here and rent your guest room and bath."

"What about the dog?"he asked, miffed to feel desire surging. "And where would you paint?"

"I don't know. All I know is that tonight I want to be with you."

He shook his head. "Everything's too raw. I need time to work without more complications. And anyway, Derek and his friend may not have left. Patience—and paint!"

She walked behind his car and stood near her pansies' bright faces until he drove off.

Her headache started again as she plodded down the drive toward her van. Before sliding the door back, she pulled out her inhaler and pumped out another puff. "I guess it's you and me, kid." The piebald half-breed rose from the seat. His tail became a blur. She gathered him up and kissed his forehead. "At least we like each other's company."

All at once a vision of what she'd paint next spread behind her eyes. She set Saint Paul down. He padded behind her toward the converted garage.

"C'mon, dear heart." She guffawed to realize that she'd just used Meredith's phrase. She twisted the knob, pushed in the side door, and flicked on the full-spectrum fluorescents under a hood that drooped from the central rafter. The tubes tinkled before mercury vapor kicked the phosphor coatings into light. Saint Paul padded to his dish of water.

A couple of fifty-watt halogen bulbs hung from aluminum reflectors clamped to the easel. A pre-gessoed canvas rested against the crossbars. Acrylic smears dappled three card tables arranged around it. On them rested quart-size yogurt containers stuffed with Popsicle sticks and palette knives—brushes, too, and baking pans holding sponges, jars of paint organized by hue, a pile of rags, stay-wet palette paper, and a spray bottle to keep the paint moist.

Tarps covered much of the concrete floor. In the patches left bare sat a couple of heaters, as well as a big fan, which Natalie bent to turn on. The breeze fluttered the cover of the out-of-print journal, *Tropicals*, that topped additional issues. They and flower-identification books lay on a picnic table she'd bought from a neighbor and draped with oilcloth. Canvases painted in her former style—squares and triangles amid long swipes of oranges and green-golds—leaned under the sole window.

Excited, Natalie drew a stick of spearmint from the pack resting near her sketch pads and tray of watercolor pencils. She tore the wrapper off and inserted the gum between her teeth.

"You stay still." Saint Paul's ears perked as a fold of flesh half occluded his left eye.

She grabbed her apron, eased the neck strap over her head, wrapped the strings around her back, and tied a bow. Hair blowing, she pushed her stool aside, switched on the halogens, picked up a pencil, and began to block in her vision. A woman's full breast emerged from the canvas's upper right. Why not add moles like Natalie's? Saint Paul's head and shoulders rose from the lower left corner, his lips surrounding the breast's nipple. A sketched field of orchids—cattleyas, cymbidiums, lady's slippers—began to appear, sanctifying the union.

———————————

Late that afternoon, ten miles to the south, Heather finished digging a mass grave next to the horned-toad Algonquin's slab. A pile of rocks rose beside the mound of soil she'd extracted. Derek, frozen gel pack tucked into the back of his brace, sat watching under a nearby overhang.

Heather leaned her spade on a cholla, removed her straw hat, and fanned her face. Wind fluttered the blossoms of the locust fronting her office. "One more horrible chore, darling." The argyles that rose from her work boots were starting to scratch. "Are you still feeling okay?"

"I need to pee and get back to Chad's to lie down."

"We'll hurry." She pulled a rag from her waistband, mopped her neck, and moved into the shade, resting her palm on Derek's shoulder. "Thanks."

"For what?"

"For helping to carry Christopher's clothes to the sofa. It's better, this new plan. You firing up your computer at Chad's until I get back from San Francisco. Then we'll move your stuff here. I wish I didn't have to leave you! But once Christopher's out of our way, we'll go look over his folks' place. When I called his mother in Palo Alto this morning to make our dinner plans there, she said she's already told his father she definitely wants the Santa Fe house, and for the three of us to consider a living arrangement. It might work."

"Anything's possible. Give me a lift, will you?"

She tugged at his armpit as he pushed down on the deck-chair's arm with his right palm.

He groaned, rising.

She circled his waist but he objected. "I'd rather walk by myself. Dan says I'll heal faster." Listing, Derek followed her into her office. The gingham-lined basket beside her desk still held Trixie's scent.

She pointed out the doorway to the guest bath.

"I remember." He took short steps inside, leaving the door open so she could hear his shout in case he fell.

A loose floor tile shifted as she entered the great room and snatched the lovebirds' black cloth that she'd folded up yesterday from the dining table. She slung it over her shoulder, turned right past the foyer, and right again into the kitchen. She shook out some Cherrios from a cupboard and thrust them into her pocket, then turned to the refrigerator and opened the freezer drawer.

Oh, bat guano! She clutched her throat, then spread the cloth on the tiles, and hauled out the two garbage bags that held Trixie, rigid as a hunk of concrete. Ice silvered the foreleg that thrust through her polyethylene shroud. Ruby and Harold lay obscured by frost in their sandwich bags. Primrose the goldfish showed clearly through the cling-wrap Heather had swaddled her in. But she'd not been able emotionally to do more for the lovebird than to cut his tether to the stone and toss him uncovered on top of the other bodies.

She pulled the four corners of the cloth together and clutched them. Was that Merciful's squeal? She clomped into the great room.

Light slanting through the picture window enflamed the petals of Sissy's sunrise montage. Heather had moved it to the credenza beside the birdcage, hoping its colors might lure Merciful close.

Derek had taken one of the caned chairs at the dining table. He sat with thumbs hooked through the shoulder straps of his brace. "The plaster in your bathroom's curling off the wall," he said.

"That must have started this weekend. Christopher can never reach the contractor." She set her bundle of corpses beside him. "Did you see where Merciful cried from? Yesterday I peeled a banana for her but couldn't coax her down."

As if to tease them, the lovebird let out three rapid-fire squeaks. Derek started to look but arching his back hurt. Heather couldn't spot Merciful in the shadows cast by the ceiling vigas because the little bird had perched out of view on one of the chandelier's blossoms.

Heather displayed a handful of cereal. "Look what I brought you, honey, wherever you are." She stepped to the cage and scattered the tiny donuts among the corncob litter.

"I freshened your water, too," she said and turned to Derek. "Oh, my babies, oh, damn it. I did phone my folks to tell them about you but I keep forgetting Christopher's quitting his job. I've got to warn him not to pick up his junk until we're out of here. What's that noise?"

"It's a car and it's stopping on your driveway and it's probably your husband." Derek pushed himself up in the chair, shut his eyes, and pressed his lips bloodless.

"Shit." Heather moved close to him. They looked toward the foyer and in a moment heard a key turn the lock.

Christopher took a step inside and, glaring, paused on the slate tiles. "What the hell's he doing here?" He whisked his palm back along his crew cut.

Merciful began to squeal above him.

"So there you are!" Heather blurted.

"This isn't your home, asshole," Christopher hissed. "You think you sprained your back Saturday? You haven't felt anything yet."

"Quit hounding us, Christopher!" Heather stretched her tunic's midnight-blue over her hips. "We've put a bunch of your clothes and workbooks on the sofa bed there."

"Meaning his stuff's hanging in my closet? Say your prayers, Heather."

Dropping his head, he started at her. Derek reached into the cloth bundle, grasped the first corpse his fingers touched, and hurled it at him. Pity's frozen body caught Christopher on the cheekbone and, crying out, he stopped short. He shook his head to clear it, stooped, and picked up the lovebird.

Suddenly the red-throated Merciful flapped off her blossom and swooped down, emitting screams like a mother discovering her child drowned.

"Ah, Christ!"

Merciful's beak had struck the back of Christopher's neck. Clapping it, he whirled and grabbed for her but his fingertips slid off her tail. She started to circle the great room's ceiling as the screams became a staccato of screeches.

"Call nine-one-one!" Derek shouted. Heather dashed for the kitchen as he hobbled toward her husband. "Face me, you bastard," Derek snarled.

Christopher dropped the corpse and, clenching his hands,

turned and cocked his right arm. But before he could launch the blow, Derek sent a fist into his belly and, gasping at his own pain, lifted a knee into Christopher's balls.

"Ohhhh," the big man sighed. He collapsed alongside Derek, who had sunk to the rug.

Having punched in two numbers, Heather slammed the receiver down and ran out to see the men huddled together. "Derek, your back!" She crouched beside him as Merciful dive-bombed Christopher again. Heather managed to rap the blue belly with her knuckles and the feathered avenger veered upward to settle on top of her cage.

Heather kissed Derek's shoulder, clutched Pity's icy body, clambered to her feet, and shook the corpse at Merciful. "Look, honey, your mate." She walked over to place the corpse inside the cage next to the water dish. In a moment Merciful flapped down and in. "You're a hero. Do you know that?" she told the bird, then stuck the nail into the catch and tramped back to the rug.

Derek was sitting up.

"You, too," she said.

"Me too what?" He was still breathing hard.

"You're a hero, darling. Can you get up, Christopher?"

"I'm not," he panted, "sure."

"You'd better, because if you don't leave now, I'm going to finish that call to the cops and get a restraining order. Go on, stand up. I'll help you load."

Five minutes later she shut the door after him and eased herself down beside Derek, pressing a breast against his shoulder. She draped her arm over his chest. "We can take Merciful to Chad's. I've got a traveling cage." She kissed Derek's cheek.

They heard the BMW's engine roar, roar again, then fade into silence.

www.ingramcontent.com/pod-product-compliance
Lightning Source LLC
Chambersburg PA
CBHW011342010726
47493CB00009B/2919